Moon Over Madeline Island

MOON OVER MADELINE ISLAND

JAY GILBERTSON

KENSINGTON BOOKS
http://www.kensingtonbooks.com

KENSINGTON BOOKS are published by

Kensington Publishing Corp.
850 Third Avenue
New York, NY 10022

All Kensington titles, imprints and distributed lines are available at special quantity discounts for bulk purchases for sales promotion, premiums, fund-raising, educational or institutional use.

Special book excerpts or customized printings can also be created to fit specific needs. For details, write or phone the office of the Kensington Special Sales Manager: Kensington Publishing Corp., 850 Third Avenue, New York, NY 10022. Attn. Special Sales Department. Phone: 1-800-221-2647.

Kensington and the K logo Reg. U.S. Pat. & TM Off.

ISBN 0-7582-1143-0

First Kensington Trade Paperback Printing: October 2005
10 9 8 7 6 5 4 3

Printed in the United States of America

Dedicated to

K.S.

Why should we be in such
desperate haste to succeed
and in such desperate enterprises?
If a man does not keep pace
with his companions,
perhaps it is because he hears
a different drummer.
Let him step to the music
he hears,
however measured or far away.
—Henry David Thoreau

Acknowledgments

Of course, I'm grateful for my folks, Donna Lou and Eric Gilbertson. Mom was the first person to reassure me that although I hear a different drummer, it's okay. Dad and I spent an entire weekend together when I was in college writing a short story; the pleasure of that memory inspires me still. They're my favorite couple to invite over for supper.

Thanks to my sister, Amy, for bringing me laughter and an endless joy in books. Nina and Reed's mom and dad rock! My brother Kurt's friendship sustains me and besides—we all need someone to remind us of who's younger.

Big thanks to Caroline Hossenlopp for rescuing me from the slush pile and recommending me to my multi-talented agent, Alison Bond. Alison (and her dog, Willie) fine-tuned MOMI and made sure Ruby had the right amount of Brit-Grit. She's the *real* gem.

Little did my wonderful salon clients know that *their* stories would end up in *my* story. Of course, the names have been changed to protect your husbands.

I also am indebted to my first readers: Kate Stout, Ingeborg Sorensen, Sara Nagler, Kate Hearth, Janice Cox, Liz Allen, Laura Westlund, Carrie Maloney, and Mary Flanagan.

Burt Rashbaum first thought MOMI was written by a woman; I considered this a compliment. His e-mails never let me give up and he better not, either.

Thanks to my editor, Audrey LaFehr, for sharing with me where she first read my manuscript. I appreciate her kind advice and inspiring e-mails, but boy do those deadlines come quickly! Thanks also to my copy editor, Margaret Jarpey, and the support of everyone at Kensington. I'm so grateful to you all!

And, as always, thanks to my best friend, Ken Seguine, who from the very start said, "I believe in you—now get writing so you can buy me a tractor!"

Chapter One

Standing in my kitchen, I'm humming along with a favorite old bluesy Pearl Bailey tune, "Easy Street," while making a radish, alfalfa sprout, organic turkey and Swiss cheese sandwich—heavy on the Swiss. I grow my own sprouts, use locally baked breads and recycle everything. I do what I can.

What I *can't* seem to do is quit smoking. What the hell. I like it and since I live alone, who's to complain? I do have smoking rules, though. Upstairs, in this eclectic but tasteful apartment, it's only allowed on the balcony and that goes double for the first floor, which is "Eve's Salon." Believe it or not, I hate the smell!

I'm only wearing a Victoria's Secret leopard-patterned, extra-support-for-larger-gals bra and matching panties; it's August and boy is the air sticky with humidity. My big fluffy gray cat, Rocky, is noisily crunching his breakfast. He eats on the countertop since cats are very clean. Besides, cats on countertops were one of many things Mom *never* allowed, so now I feel as though I'm getting away with something.

Rocky's gotten it into his furry head that it's more fun licking the edges of my sandwich than eating his own food. Sometimes, if I've had enough coffee, this can lead to chasing him around the apartment for several minutes. Not today, though; as I snap the lid onto the plastic sandwich holder, he growls in disappointment, then goes back to his cat food.

Morning sun pours in from the skylight over my kitchen area. There's no way to hide the fact that I only dust seasonally. Dusting—what a waste of time. One of my living room walls is a bookshelf that's packed solid. I usually read several books at the same time. Reading is how I travel. I try to buy used books and limit myself to three when shopping, but that never works. Explains all the piles on the floor, the coffee table, in corners and on top of everything. Looks very urban and studious and besides, I need them all. Love the smell of a new find's binding.

It's hard to part with a good tome, especially if, after reading it, you feel something new. It's as though you've been changed or expanded or that somehow things are going to be different. I have a bookshelf downstairs in my salon. It's there for clients to borrow from or add to. I need to install another one since the darn thing is bursting with titles just waiting for a new home. I've really got to stop hanging on to old junk mail, magazines and to-be-read newspapers. It's just that I'm so afraid I'll miss something important, so that's what's in (as well as spilling out of) the tasteful wood box by my door.

I own this wonderful old two-story brick building on Water Street in Eau Claire, Wisconsin. Have for years. I just turned forty-seven. My period has arrived right on time, so I'm cranky, but I'm booked solid today. My clients are a marvelous group of women mostly around my age. We're all engaged in the battle of fighting back that damn gray hair! I secretly thank the turn-women's-hair-gray hormone as it certainly keeps me busy.

I get such a kick out of the things my clients think of and talk about and fuss over. That's the best part, their lives. Don't get me wrong, I love to do hair, but the true joy lies in what each person leaves with me. Their truths, worries, regrets and hilarious everyday stuff.

While sipping coffee, Q-tipping my ears, putting on deodorant and a dab of "Lusty Redz" lipstick, I riffle through my closet for yet another fashion first. I've twisted my red curls up into a fancy knotted affair held in place with black lacquer chopsticks. I decide on a simple, oversized blouse of pale yellow with big red buttons marching up the front, untucked, over baggy Capri pants. Love Capri pants.

On my way to the door I step into open-toed, two-inch wedgies that always make me feel taller than my five-foot shortness. I've painted my toenails with "Cherries in the Snow," and they glitter up at me. I check my reflection in the wavy hall mirror to make sure everything's in its place.

I'm a little chubby and very busty, but I've always felt more is better and less is so "not me." I can't seem to drop these extra twenty pounds of leftover baby fat, so why torture myself? Besides, the minute I do manage to drop a few pounds, my watch doesn't fit and my bra cups hang empty. What's the point? I heave my non-designer hemp bag over my shoulder and clomp downstairs to my salon.

During the day I don't go upstairs since it makes me crazy to miss out on any of the goings-on. What's more, I love lunching with my other two stylists, Dorothy and Watts. Dorothy is a throwback from the wash-and-set and rat-to-death era. Her hair reaches heights worthy of a second look. Watts, on the other hand, is young, pretty in a severe way, and cutting-edge when it comes to hair trends. The college kids love her and man can she create some wild hair color.

I designed my salon to look and feel like you're in Granny's kitchen. Providing your Granny had some taste, of course. The walls are painted a rich yellow; paint-cracked shelves display oodles of old electric mixers, chrome toasters and zany kitchen clocks. My hair-cutting stations are Art Deco waterfall dressers. I'm crazy about their huge round mirrors. Over the years clients have given me old round mirrors and they're slowly taking over the walls. Today the shop is ablaze with polka dots of sunshine reflecting from one mirror to another to another. I have a drawer of huge, clunky rhinestone cat's-eye sunglasses and sometimes we put them on. Clients, too.

I always come downstairs an hour early to have a mug of coffee and go over my appointment book. Rocky keeps me company, but I know the real reason he follows me is that Dorothy brings him treats. That's why he and I have matching tummies.

Mine is a direct result of Reese's Peanut Butter Cups. I can't get enough. I really should sue them. There's always a hidden, well-stocked supply at hand. I pull out the bottom drawer, flip open the top of an ancient tin money box and check my supply. It's going to be a great day; I have eleven orange-wrapped jewels. I inhale their delicious bouquet, snap the top shut and shove the drawer back in just as Watts comes in the front door.

"Hey, Watts, you're *early.*" I follow her into the break room. "I thought you didn't start until noon today." Watts's usually bright and sparkly blue eyes are red-rimmed and puffy. Even her spiked white hair seems limp. I bet she's broken up with

Mr. Right, again—or rather, Mister Right Away, or more accurately, Mr. Big Huge Loser.

"He took my Juice Master *and* my brand-new purple lipstick!" Watts throws her lunch into the fridge, then slams the door for good measure. "The bastard."

"I have three upstairs," I mention, putting on some Mozart. I fear for her client's tender earlobes. "You can have your pick."

"Three? Juicers or lipstick?"

"Juicers." I've tried a gazillion diets and some of them required the purchase of their "special" blender. The diets didn't work. But the blenders sure as hell do! I pour her some coffee. "You really should try being single . . . for more than a week."

"Hate being alone," she snivels, taking the mug. "Besides, I need help walking all my dogs." She has five and is considering adding a sixth. I pat Rocky, grateful I only have to scoop his box. Dogs need way too much fussing, if you ask me.

I put my arm around her, plop her down at my station and re-mess up her hair. She's proudly tall and skinny as a pole, with the palest blue-white skin. Automatically she slinks down, since I can't reach the top of her head otherwise. The love doctor is in.

This is what I do: listen and counsel. With humor as my camouflage, my real intention is to help my clients (as well as employees), find their way in this crazy thing called life. I do great hair, but this is my true specialty.

I'm not sure when this need to pay attention to people's lives started, but I guess as a teenager. I was much heavier and mostly had my nose in a book and my hand in the cookie jar. But through the years, I've learned how to listen real careful and you know, most people have the answers right there in front of them. I just iron things out a bit and hand their life back a little smoother, is all. I love it.

"Watts, Watts, Watts," I say, tsk-tsking. "I've known you a long time. Looking back, I can't say you've ever been happy with *any* of the men you've dated . . . or lived with or . . ."

"I know, I know," Watts says with a sigh. "I'm in a rut. I should move out of this burg, change my hair color, stop wearing black from head to toe and join a book club." She reaches up, pats my hand, grinning in the mirror. I've got a grin. I need a giggle.

"Moving isn't a bad idea, but changing your hair color—trust me on this—it don't bring you no men!" I proclaim, bursting with attitude, hands on hips. This I know to be true!

"I can't seem to stop looking. Hoping maybe the next—"

"For me, I'm done looking. Through! What's the use, and for heaven's sake, why? I have wonderful friends, a great business and finally a hair color that gives me what I need most: color!" My perfectly arched brow leaps up my forehead in agreement. I pull the chopstick from my hair and swing my curls around for further emphasis.

"Some women *need* men in their lives," Watts says in a knowing way that makes me crazy.

"Need? That's a load of crap," I reply with zest. "Wake up girl. Look around at all the single women happily making it without a man in sight. Oh sure, it would be nice to grow old with someone, but *never* settle for something simply because you *think* you need a man. Me . . . I'd love to find a man who would listen . . . make me laugh . . . teach me something new." Listen to high-and-mighty me. The last three losers I dated are examples of what *not* to settle for. David was more interested in his muscles than anything else. Carl was too nice, too kind, and too damn needy. I could hardly breathe. The last guy cheated on me and not with women, either. He'd find men on the Internet and then invite them over.

"Jesus . . ." Watts breaks me out of my pathetic review. "Those kind of men exist? I mean . . . have you ever met one? Not in novels, Eve—a real live man."

"Oh . . . I knew someone like that . . . once. A *lot* like that, actually." I heave a sigh, remembering. Granted it was a high school love, but, oh Lord, was he wonderful and kind and gentle and sexy as hell. I wonder whatever became of him.

"So you *did* have a love of your life." She grins. "At least you've got that experience to compare to. Geez, even my parents are strangers to me. All they do is watch TV day and night and drink beer by the case. Wish I was from somewhere else . . . raised by different people." A faraway look coats her eyes.

"We all wish that at one time or another. I went through a phase when I was so angry with my folks for having me late in their lives . . . At least they had me, though. That's what my mother would yell back at me when I'd lash out."

"Don't you get lonely? I mean . . . Rocky is cute and all, but I'm sorry, there are things a cat simply cannot provide."

"Ah . . . lonely for *men?* As in *relations* with men?" If she thinks she's going to send me on one more blind date—God, I hate dating. Besides, can't a gal be happily single?

"Well . . . yeah," she agrees. "I mean, men are good for other things too . . . I suppose. Not much that I can see. But sex with a man . . . there's something to be said for that. A lot of things, if you ask me." She watches herself nodding in the mirror.

"Put that way, I couldn't agree with you more. But what about all the time in between the sex?" Rubbing my hands together, I work some molding mud into her do, rubbing a little harder than necessary, hoping to work some sense into her stubborn, hormonally overloaded head.

"Sleep?" Watts asks.

"Watts, my dear. All you need is a nice battery-operated friend. Then there's no making breakfast . . . no waiting by the phone . . . no more stolen kitchen appliances or lipstick. Toss the birth control pills in the trash, and . . . voilá." She's laughing now, and so am I. Time to open, there's the phone, here we go, It's Show Time!

"Morning Ruby," I declare into the phone. I have Caller ID and wonder if I'll ever tire of this game.

"Eve, you smart aleck," Ruby snaps in her crisp English accent. "Can you fit me in for a trim? I've simply *got* to see you. Can't seem to get my hair to fluff up and God Almighty, I need every bloody inch!"

I see her standing in her cozy, spotless kitchen. One hand swinging the curly bright yellow phone cord while she taps her foot to a snappy beat playing on her radio. Whenever Ruby is on the phone she's busy wiping down gleaming countertops, putting this and that away, while placing the finishing touches on a warm pan of her delicious snack bars.

Her well-worn red linoleum has little glitters of silver and yellow. Lace curtains flutter in the open window over the sink, while silly mushrooms with old-fashioned faces dance across walls and over her fridge. Smells of fresh-baked goodies, coffee and, of course, a swirl of cigarette smoke hover in the air like an old friend. I've spent hundreds of hours sitting there, coffee mug in one hand, chewy bar of goo in the other. She was my first client to waltz into this shop the day I opened. The moment we met I knew I'd finally found my best girlfriend. We're like mother and daughter, sisters more like. Without all the hell and high water of growing up together. Damn, can she make me laugh!

She loudly exhales, the smoke from her cigarette surely being released into a perfect ring. I use my pen like a cigarette, swinging it around like she does. She's my best friend and you do those things to make them a part of you.

"*This* is your lucky day," I say as my first client walks through the door and I wave her over. "Come by around six-ish; you can be my final victim. Upon completion of said beauty treatment, you will *graciously* take me out to dinner. Your turn."

"Sounds simply lovely. See you, darling. Ta ta, for now!"

The day swims by and before I was about to say, "Don't you just look sassy?" for what seemed like the hundredth time, in blows Ruby. She stands *maybe* four-ten, weighs little or nothing even wet and is the only size one I know. But trust me, what she doesn't have in height or girth, she makes up for with dazzling energy, a certain English decorum and a dose of pigheadedness that keeps things interesting.

She's blessed with thick, straight hair that's been every color and style at least three, maybe four times. Totally gray underneath, happened years ago, I like to remind her. That's our secret though and to be honest, I'm not far behind her with the gray. Her age is pretty hard to swallow too. Sixty-nine, but she only admits to being fifty-eight. Been lying like a dog for years.

Ed, her husband for a hundred years, was the only one for her and he's been dead for a while now.

She has on dangle earrings and bracelets that clang and chime. Her lipstick is bright pink, complementing her blue-blue eyes. They have a depth that holds you captive. Her accent is wonderful. Originally from a tiny fishing village in the north of England and proud as hell about it too. I've noticed how sometimes her Northern accent becomes more pronounced. Like when she wants something or has had a bit too much wine or if she simply needs to be heard. Wrapped like a glove in an earth-tone skirt and fitted top, she walks jauntily in, her high heels clicking across the hardwood floor to a Martin Denny tune, "Love Dance." I smile and marvel at her amazing presence. She enters a room and the air just kind of opens up to her.

"Jesus Lord our God, what's that *stench?*" Ruby wrinkles up her pointed nose.

"Dorothy is finishing up a perm. Keep your voice down—you'll wake Mrs. Gustafson, who's under the dryer. Now get over here," I say in my take-charge voice.

"I thought perms were totally *out.* Thank God they're back. Sign me up. I miss the height. God I miss the beehive . . . now there was a style with attitude." She checks her reflection in the flap, then clicks her purse closed.

"Ruby . . . I used to give you perms. *Used* to. We do so much color as it is and really, when is the last time you saw anyone on Oprah with a poodle-perm?"

"Relax. Only joking, darling. I'm loving what you're doing now. Texture. Feels like we're discussing the feel of carpet, not hair." She's poured herself a mug of coffee, greeted Dorothy and Watts, as well as their clients, and managed to shove a cookie into her mouth, all while heading to my station.

I guide her over to my chair. "Thought cookies were on the *no* list. Someone skip lunch again?" I ask in my mom-voice.

"Look at these roots of mine!" She points to the part in her hair, "I need a miracle here."

"You look great for being so near death . . . really," I reply, deadpan as hell. "I bet people see you and think, *wow,* she's still alive?"

"I will be fifty-eight . . . again, so you better turn up my color a bit; I will *not* give in to this horrible gray stuff. Never. Stupid gray. Stupid!"

"How many years have you been fifty-eight now?" I ask, both of my brows arched.

"You know, you're right. This year let's shoot for fifty-six. Now get cracking."

I'm drying Ruby's hair and it looks fabulous. She's putting on fresh lipstick, swinging her shapely crossed-over leg while Sarah Vaughn croons, "What Is This Thing Called Love?" The lyrics inspire thoughts of Watts, which are busy crisscrossing in my mind. How different we are . . . yet not really. She's looking. Me, I'm not. Wouldn't mind if someone found *me* for a change. But then again, someone to pick up after, fuss with about the toilet lid being left up, twice as many rumpled clothes to wade through and farting in bed? I'll stick with Rocky.

"Earth to Eve. Hello there. You in there?" Ruby asks, while buffing her nails.

"Sorry ma'am," I say in my most nasally "hair expert" voice. "I was focusing on the completion of your style, as the finish is the most important aspect of the salon experience."

"I bet there's not one woman who can do her hair like you hair professionals." She shakes her head. "It's simply not possible."

"It *is* possible. However, one must stand still more than three minutes, use some goop, and do as I have instructed you to do about nine hundred times! 'Course, if you did it as well as us professionals"—I wave a huge round brush around and arch my right brow only—"it wouldn't be such a treat to come in. You'd miss out on all my worldly wisdom, not to mention the free coffee and cookies."

"You directing or making me look fabulous?" Ruby asks dryly.

"If you'd stand still once in a while and put a little *effort*—"

"You're the one with magic fingers, darling. Entirely worth the outrageous prices you charge, but I wouldn't give you *squat* for the wisdom. I should charge *you!*"

We giggle, clink our chipped cat mugs and toss back final slugs of now cold coffee. I hand her the magic mirror in the shape of a lily pad and give her chair a spin for inspection. I lean against the wall, fold my arms over my chest and bend my tired head this way and that. It snaps and creaks, waking Rocky, who gives me a meow suggesting I quit my noisy creaking.

"Damn. I look good." Ruby steps down and hands me the mirror with a slight bow. "Let's tidy up, then be off for dinner."

I'm touching up my lips for the zillionth time. Nothing stays on these babies very long. Ruby rinses out our mugs, then waters my huge fern. It's bursting out of an old round pink washing machine that sits in a corner by the front window. Rocky jumps onto my throne-of-miracles chair to watch as I try to powder away sneaky wrinkles.

"How long have you been here, darling?" Ruby asks, her head disappearing into the fern. I can hear snaps as she trims and fusses. It's the same upstairs—if I have dirty dishes sitting in the sink, she just pushes up her fancy sleeves and gets on with it.

"Let's see, I opened this place in nineteen eighty-one. . . ." I lipstick my lips and count on my fingers. "So that would make it—gee-suzz—twenty-four years. As long as I've known you, you know?" I kiss the mirror, adding to the collection of lips there. If you look in Ruby's purse, she has balled-up Kleenex covered with different-colored lips. She keeps them until every inch is used up. I love that.

But I *don't* love this feeling that's been nagging at me. Oh, not a big deal, really. Just a worry, I suppose. Another one; I've got a whole slew of them. I don't want to do this forever, I don't. But what the hell *should* I be doing? I glance around and wonder if it's a "where" thing. If not here, though, where? Good grief.

Way inside, inside the secret self I share with no one, there's this void, a hushed sadness I keep locked up. My high school sweetheart and I had a daughter and on my thirtieth birthday, well, I tried to find her—but no luck. I sigh back into the room.

"Have you thought about retiring?"

"I'm forty-seven. Just. People *don't* retire at that age. Do they?" Not my kind of people anyway.

"You're right, darling. I cringe when I hear that word . . . retire. Sounds like you pick out a porch, sit down and rock your life away, filling your pants, drooling. Waiting to take your last breath."

"I'm getting a strong visual here." I shake my head.

"You work so hard, darling. I suppose it's selfish of me even suggesting, but I enjoy our time together—when you're not abusing me."

"I hope I don't have to work this hard right up until I *do* retire. An old-lady hair-burner with tresses piled high, orangey foundation, eyeliner and sagging boobs. Good Lord. Besides, I sunk all my inheritance from my mom into this place. You're *looking* at my retirement," I say, arms open wide.

"I've an idea, Eve. Push your curls around and let's blow this pop stand."

"Pop stand?"

Ever since Ruby danced into my shop all those years ago, well, my life has never been the same. Thank God. We fluff Rocky's fur and give him noisy air kisses since we mustn't smear our lips. I flip the metal sign hanging on a hook by the door to CLOSED, and off we stroll down the sidewalk to our favorite watering hole, Mona Lisa's.

"Hey ladies! Right this way," the owner, Zed, says, leading us to a nice table by the window. "I'll bring you wine."

Zed is a fifty-something, sexy little Italian number with bulging biceps and the thickest mustache you've ever seen. This restaurant is his pride and joy and it shows in the way he claps customers on the shoulder and greets everyone walking in the front door.

"Did you see who Darcy Laming was all cozy with? The little tramp." Ruby spits "tramp" out while rooting around in her designer purse for a smoke.

"Her husband has been dead for over a year now. I'm happy to see her out and about and yes, I *did* see, and he's quite a hunk." We laugh a bit too loud, as usual. The gray-haired, tanned-to-leather golf-clutch of women nearby glance our way over their highballs.

"Here you are, ladies. Sure do love your hair, Ruby. Going over to Minneapolis to have it done?" He grins, plunks our goblets down and before I can say something smart back, is gone.

"Little bastard," I mutter. "If he didn't fill those jeans so well . . ."

"I hadn't noticed," Ruby says, noticing. "Besides, no one pours a glass of wine like Zed. Let's make a toast, darling: to a couple of classy broads with naturally beautiful hair." She shoots a look toward the ladies. We clink, take a nice long sip and settle in.

We've been coming here for so long, it feels like an extension of my living room. The smells of garlic, fresh breads, cigarettes and Zed's energy all swirl in concert. There's a roar of laughter mixed with talking that always gives me pause as it rolls over us in waves, then recedes.

"Now Eve . . . I've been thinking . . ."

Whenever it starts like that I know something's brewing. Last time Ruby started out with one of her "I've been thinking" segues, I ended up with a new set of fall-pattern mixing bowls, a complicated programmable electric mixer, a blender stick with all the attachments and a Crock-Pot covered with geese. I don't need any more kitchen items.

"You know . . ." Ruby fiddles with her expensive necklace. "I still own the cottage on Madeline Island, but I don't get up there since it's such a drive. Frankly, I've had so many memories of Ed and I together there I simply couldn't. Hell, he's been dead since two thousand—I do need to do *something* with it, don't you think?"

"He *has* been dead for a while now, but I didn't think you really liked the cottage. Damp and old, I believe are the words you've used to describe it."

"It *is* damp and the old part is true too, but you know . . . it's also lovely. I think I needed to let go of Ed first."

"You've invited me up there so many times and I always meant to . . . I work too much," I say, realizing that's about all I do.

"You do, darling, you do. I could have gone alone over the years, but I've realized I was keeping it to myself until I felt ready to let Ed be . . . well . . . dead," Ruby replies. She blows a huge smoke ring as if to circle the word "dead." It slowly fades and then disappears altogether.

"I totally understand. Until my mom died, I hadn't ever really felt that kind of loss. And you and Ed . . . all the pictures you have around your house . . . you two together."

Ruby pats my arm, her tiny hand warm and soft. "We always spent our summers up there." She has a distant look in her eyes. "Up until Ed got too sick, that is. One good thing about being a professor, we had summers off. . . ."

I feel softness for this woman, knowing how much they loved each other. Sadness too since he's gone. There's a black-and-white picture of them sitting on the end of a dock, holding hands, water glistening all around. A younger Ruby is looking into Ed's eyes with such tenderness. Looking at the picture you feel as though you should look away quick, it's so personal. But you don't.

Ruby says, "How long have you stood behind a chair, listening to the likes of me, women wanting to look younger, prettier, sexier? Certainly it must drain the zip out of you, darling."

"I was seventeen when I got out of high school. Tried becoming a professional waitress, then spotted an ad for a new beauty school opening in what used to be a funeral parlor. It was called Carol Greckner's Professional Cosmetology School of Beauty. Oh Jesus, was that a trip. Been behind a chair ever since."

"You *are* an expert. Professional, I mean. You are. But all you do is *give*—all day long. You need to take better care of *you,*" Ruby lectures, leaning way in when she says "you."

"You're right. I am tired, doing hair day in and day out. Who wouldn't be after twenty-nine years? Love my clients, the stories and the laughs. That's what keeps me going. But—and I haven't wanted to admit this—I've been feeling restless . . . bored maybe."

"With the salon or . . . ?"

"Business is fabulous. I'm booked *weeks* in advance, months during the holidays. It's my own fault, but I've not taken a vacation in years. I'm going through the forties thing. There, I said it out loud." I take a nice long slug of wine. "Tell me more about the cottage," I add, wanting to change the subject. I'm terrible when it comes to talking too much about me. But really, should I be more concerned here? Great, something else to worry about.

"Well it's on a point, the very tip of Madeline Island— which is located off the very top of Northern Wisconsin. This tip is called Steamboat Point and the cottage faces Lake Superior, a lake that seems the size of an ocean."

"I'm embarrassed to admit this, but I've never been that far north. I honestly had no idea Wisconsin even had an island *large* enough for a cottage."

"It sits up on a hill overlooking the lake. An exquisitely charming, two-story log cottage with a lovely barn out back. There's also a boathouse with a flat on the second floor and a little creek, too."

"Good Lord, Ruby, I had no idea. How the hell could you let it just *sit* there is beyond me. You said a barn? Was it a farm or . . . ?"

"No, it's more for storage; it's big and airy with a loft upstairs. The cottage is super—a rock fireplace, wraparound porch and so much sunshine in the summer."

"Sounds dreamy. Like the cottage in *On Golden Pond,* and on an island." I marvel at the idea of an island and see myself in a straw hat, making sandcastles next to a long wooden dock.

"Just talking about it brings back so many memories. It sits there, all closed up, waiting."

"Waiting. I wonder if that's what *I'm* doing." I absently twist and untwist a curl around my finger. "Sitting around waiting for my life to begin. I told you about Watts and all. At least she has her foot in the water—you know? At least the girl has something she *thinks* she wants."

"Maybe all you need is a push."

"You know, you're right . . . I *did* open my salon. Yet for all these years . . . that's all I've done." I feel like humming a few bars of "Is That All There Is?" Smart-ass Ruby beats me to it.

She hums a bit, then says, "Opening your salon, employees that adore you, money in the bank, you've done amazing things. Now, drink up love, I've changed my mind. Let's go back to your flat. I hope to high heaven you have something we can eat in that fridge of yours."

We leave some cash on the table, grab our purses, dash out the door, down the alley behind my building and up the rickety stairs to my second-floor apartment.

"I thought you were taking me *out* to dinner," I say, switching on lights, patting Rocky's head as I pass him stretching on the sofa. "But it *was* getting busy in there."

"*Too* busy, could hardly hear myself think. Besides, I love it up here." She kicks off her heels on her way to root around in my fridge. "You have all sorts of leftovers in here. I'll get busy and whip something together. Here . . . put the kettle on, darling." She hands me my battered teapot.

"I'm stuffed." Ruby blows smoke into the air. We survey the kitchen table, now covered with assorted containers and bowls of reheated Chinese take-out, which Rocky is checking out.

"Me too." I start clearing things away. "Wash or dry?"

"Wash. You get everything so damn hot I nearly burn my fingers off!" She reaches for the rag I use to plug up the sink.

"What did you mean when you said that maybe something should be done with your cottage?" I take a dripping-wet platter from her.

"A thought. Does seem silly not to make use of it. There's a quaint town on the mainland called Bayfield and—"

"Ruby! I smell a rat. What's going on here? I've got that you have a cottage most of us only dream of, it's all closed up and . . ."

She holds her sudsy hands up. "I am so horrible at this kind of thing . . . I . . . Here, dry this bowl. Hey, this is mine. Let's have some coffee. I have something to give you." Ruby hands me her bowl. Turning it over, sure enough, I see that it says, "property of Ruby Prévost" on faded masking tape. I dry it and put it back in my cupboard.

Since we're done tidying up in the kitchen, I fire up the coffeemaker. We sit down on my huge, over-plumped sofa to wait for the sputtering and spewing to stop. Rocky joins us, so we both pet him. He purrs and purrs, spoiled rotten.

"Eve, you're my dearest friend. There's *nothing* I wouldn't do for you. You could go on doing what you're doing and that would be that. There's not a thing wrong with it either . . . not a thing, darling." She straightens her blouse. " I've been racking my brains trying to come up with a good idea. I want to give you something special for your birthday. So . . . here it is and happy, *happy* birthday, my dear wonderful friend." Ruby hands me an envelope, then sits back, folding her arms, watching.

"What's this?" I tear open an official-looking envelope. "What in the . . . It says, 'I, Ruby Prévost, a resident of the state of Wisconsin and city of Eau Claire, and being of . . .' " I read on, the color rising in my face, my heart racing as it all sinks into my brain. "Your cottage? You're willing *me* your cottage? For my birthday? You're not . . . Are you *sick?*" My voice reaches an all-time high and my hands instantly are damp and clammy. I think I'm going to pee my panties. I start to cry.

"Oh for heaven's sake, darling, of course I'm not ill and please don't cry, darling, I'll never forgive myself. Besides, I haven't any children and let's face it, *you're* my family and, well . . . happy birthday and it's too late. The place will be yours and you *know* how stubborn I am." We're hugging and I'm crying, even laughing a bit.

"I don't know what to . . ." I sniffle, feeling very loved. "I've never even *seen* it and you're going to hand it over to me? Just like that?" This is so Ruby.

"Not until I croak, of course! You need to have some security, dear, for the future. Besides, it feels right giving it to you. I've been going through a lot of Ed's papers lately and thinking about life and death and all." She wipes her eyes and then digs out some tissues, handing a few to me. Opening one up, I show her the lipstick prints all over it and we both chuckle.

"Ruby . . . I'm lost for words. It's so . . . generous, so amazingly, insanely generous."

"The thing is, you created this flourishing salon here." She stands up, moves around the living room. "If we put our heads together, think of something we *both* could do . . . together. A bed-and-breakfast . . . a retreat center . . . a home for spinsters?"

"Hmm," I say, thinking. "There's the cottage and the boathouse and . . ." I reread some of the fine print. "Ten acres. That's a lot of land."

"Eve, darling, that cottage meant so much to Ed and me. We were something else there, I can't explain it."

"I've always known how much Ed meant to you." I rub her forearm. "A person would have to be blind not to notice how you light up when you just mention his name."

"Yes, I loved that man something dreadful," Ruby says, remembering. She snaps back to the present, shrugging her shoulders. "But it's time I went back there. Ed's long gone, but I'm not. And by *God,* I feel like seeing it again."

"I think I understand why you let it sit there empty for all these years now. I waited three years before selling my folks' place. Even kept Mom's plants going. Heated the whole, rambling house for those damn plants. I *do* know about hanging on and then, all of sudden, it's time . . ."

"To let go," Ruby finishes for me softly. We nod and something changes. The room shifts a little. We sigh and know that something new has begun.

Grabbing blankets, I lead the way out onto my balcony and up the little stairs to the roof. Up here it's very private, a secret world above the noise of Water Street below. Over the years I've hauled up several patio tables, huge wooden barrel pots, now bursting with geraniums, and assorted chaise lounges. I shove several together and spread blankets out so we can both plop down. The stars are hanging up in the sky and seem to be winking just at us.

"I'm so grateful, Ruby. I really am. I mean . . . I guess now I'll have to plan your murder, but . . . details," I say to the stars. Ruby chuckles while smacking my arm; hard too!

"Remember when Ed was doing so poorly. I couldn't *imagine* leaving his side at the hospital. I wanted to be there should he wake up. I was so exhausted and lost, too. Overwhelmed, knowing the end was near. Then you show up . . . with that daft shopping cart."

"Oh Jesus," I say, remembering. "I knew you wouldn't leave. So I stole—borrowed—it from Kmart. I shoved it into my van and headed over to Woo's Pagoda and filled it."

"I have never laughed so bloody hard." We giggle. "I was so hungry too, since all I'd eaten were measly bites of dry sandwiches I bought from that ghastly machine down the hall. Couldn't have what Ed was consuming, being tube-fed and all.

He wasn't much company either, seeing as he was in a coma. Poor love."

"There's nothing like Woo's Chinese food to get your mind off . . . well . . . things," I reply tenderly.

"You brought a tablecloth, dishes, everything. The point is, Eve, you did it. I felt so . . . loved. And the laughing . . . the kind that stays with you for a lifetime . . . and then some." We sigh, remembering.

"Can't believe I tipped over his IV bag, though. My foot got caught in one of the wheels and before I knew it . . . What a mess, tubes every which way. I can be such a klutz."

"Oh heavens." She waves away my words. "His brainwaves were long gone. Then the day came when we had to shut him down." Ruby folds into herself, but only for a moment. Then she shrugs her shoulders in a movement I know so well.

"There were so many switches, it seemed as though it took them forever. He had more wires and tubes coming out of every hole and . . . sorry." I shake my head.

"I loathed that ominous sound when his heart monitor made its final bleep. He slipped right out with his last breath. I'm sure he's grateful to have been set free of that tired old body. It was all used up."

"I sure as hell hope so." I imagine Ed, tubes and electrodes flying, running at me with a shopping cart. "For both our sakes."

"Of course he is, darling; he's probably fishing somewhere right now."

"An island cottage," I say to the sky. "I can't imagine many people live there, not year-round anyways."

"No, mostly a summer getaway spot."

"So if we did do something, it would have to be something other than a service thing. I mean a salon wouldn't work. Have to be a separate thing. An item, a tangible."

"Good Lord—I've got it!" Ruby sits up, twirling her glowing cigarette. "A psychic hotline. My classy accent and your . . . your . . . We'd have to re-create one for you, darling. Sorry, but a Midwestern twang would just get us hang-ups."

"You bitch."

"Snob, darling. *Please,*" Ruby huffs and lies back down. "Maybe a cottage-themed Martha Stewartish show. All shot live with Oprah boating over for a tasteful lunch every month."

"Good grief, give it a rest. I still think we'd have to make something that would then be sent out into the world."

"I could dictate my life story—it's terribly fascinating—and we could do it all from the cottage and invite photographers to record the event. Me, sharing my life while you jot it all down, surrounded by trees and water and—"

"I have an idea." I sit up. "I can't remember the last time I took a road trip. How about throwing some stuff in my van and *you* showing me the cottage this weekend?"

"That sounds lovely, darling."

We look up as a falling star lights the sky. It leaves a trail of stardust that slowly fades to night. There really is such a thing as magic and possibilities, hope and being filled to the brim. No half-cups for these two gals; we're beginning again.

CHAPTER TWO

It's a great day for a road trip. Golden sunshine peeks out from behind puffy white clouds. The air is that nice early-morning, cool stuff, before the humidity sets in. We've packed my rusted yellow and red VW van with all sorts of goodies. She rattles and squeaks, but she runs and doesn't guzzle *too* much gas. This was one of those "custom" jobs, complete with orange fringe around the windshield and, *no,* I don't have an eight-track tape player. Anymore. We're listening to "Soft Winds" by Dinah Washington while sipping iced coffee.

We'll be tooling through small towns all the way up to Madeline Island, making it a nice sight-seeing excursion. North up Highway 53 we go. I'm surprised at how giddy I'm feeling seeing Eau Claire fade away in my fur-covered rearview mirror. I've not been on an adventure for a long, long time. It's so weird that I haven't explored Wisconsin more. Mom never cared for the "road-trip" concept and I guess I've not stepped out of that, what? Role? Something so simple as getting in the van and heading north, leaving all that daily routine behind and not knowing what's ahead. I like this.

"Good God, Eve. What in the *world* is the rush? How fast are we flying?" Ruby asks, waving me off, but letting me know her anxiety all the same. "No . . . don't tell me . . . I don't need one more gray hair. Anyway, I'm insured up the—"

"Relax. Enjoy the scenery," I reply calmly, but slowing the van down to a reasonable seventy just the same. "I forgot how beautiful Wisconsin is. So many rolling hills and . . . I can't get over all the dead deer rotting along the highway—pretty."

"I'm glad we brought Rocky." She gives him a pat. "He'll *love* all the nice fat mice we'll need escorted out of the cottage."

Rocky likes to stand up every so often and look out the windshield. I brought his favorite wicker basket, the bottom made cozy with a beloved blanket. His makeshift home is wedged in front of Ruby's tiny feet. His fur is flying since he's forever shedding. The windows are rolled down and we're being forced to bear witness to the bug splats on the windshield, which are slowly connecting and growing into shapes. I can't stand it and turn on the wipers. That's worse! Yuck.

"Well . . . I don't know if Rocky will *chase* the mice out or if they'll suddenly have little micelike heart attacks. Either way, he never lets me down and I never ask questions. Don't be too freaked out if he brings you a victim, placing it ever so lovingly on your foot. Just say, 'Thanks, keep up the great work,' and act as cool as possible. Sensitive." I whisper the last word.

"Oh, this is so exciting," Ruby says. "I've not been up here for such a long time." She reaches up just in time to snatch a map about to sail out the window.

"Good catch," I remark. She wrestles it back into its proper folds.

I've got my hair down and it's blowing all to holy hell. I'm wearing baggy shorts and a huge, loose-fitting T-shirt, deep red with big green cat eyes on both sides. My feet are a bit chilly because I washed my favorite Keds slip-ons, and they're still a little damp.

Ruby's in a faded jeans outfit I'm sure she paid a fortune for. Her hair is tucked into a yellow scarf I gave her on one of her countless fifty-eighth birthdays. Both of us have our dark "movie star" sunglasses on, but mine keep sliding down my oily nose.

We're heavily doused in perfume; I read in Martha Stewart that certain aromas keep mosquitoes away. I'm lavender oil. Ruby is Chanel No. 5. Or did Martha say *not* to wear perfume? We could be in serious trouble.

"Did you have to move a lot of clients today?" Ruby asks. "Always thought Saturdays were your busiest day."

"Well, actually, I had Watts re-schedule all my clients and since it's so rare I shift people around, everyone was fine with moving. *Except* Mrs. McCallister . . . gave Watts hell on the phone."

"Didn't she demand a house call to fix her bangs a while back?"

"The old hag. I tell *all* my clients they get one free bang trim in between haircuts. So, what does she do? Cuts them herself. What a mess."

"Isn't she blind?"

"Yes."

"Well?"

"Well . . . I rushed right over, she sounded so pitiful on the phone—a real hair emergency if I ever . . . Too late. She'd cut them so short they went clear up into her hairline on one side. All I could do not to laugh out loud. Wasn't a damn thing to do with what was left, so I snipped some hair off one of her countless wigs . . . glued them right to her scalp."

"Very resourceful."

"Love a challenge."

Ruby pauses a beat or two, rearranging her seat belt. She seems to be searching for the right words. "Last evening I had this dream," she says thoughtfully. "I wanted to think about it for a while until I told you. Before you *analyze* it to death."

"I promise I'll keep an open mind . . . really."

"Good. Ed and I were sitting on the end of our dock up at the cottage. Like that picture I catch you staring at in my hallway." We look at each other, smiling. "I don't recall the exact words, he said something having to do with spirits and passageways. Isn't that odd?"

"Hmm." I wrinkle my nose and then unwrinkle it quick since I don't need any more damn lines. "Maybe you're on a spiritual passage."

"I imagine, yes, that's quite possible," Ruby replies, checking her lips in the visor mirror, again. "Spirits. Ed never was much for church, but that man *loved* his scotch."

"Sounds like Ed was giving you some hints about something. Maybe there's an evil spirit in a tunnel and he's—"

"You really can be a smart—"

"Ass," I say, and she swats me on the arm.

"Think what you wish, darling," Ruby huffs. "There might be *something* to it. I just don't know what it could be. Perhaps he meant message instead of passage. Like how life is full of messages, you know?"

"I guess that could work. I think next time Ed pops into your dream, you need to ask more questions."

"Speaking of questions, darling, would you consider turning off at the next exit? Since it's only you and me, I'll put it in plain English. I have *got* to *pee!*" On "pee," Rocky leaps over Ruby's shoulder, heading to a quieter spot in the backseat and I floor it.

I pull off the highway at every wayside in order to read all the Wisconsin Historical Markers. So while making our way north, we learn about lumber barons clear-cutting every white pine as far as the eye can see and who fought what Indian war and when. It's also a necessity, since neither of us has much "cargo space" in our small, dainty bladders. Coffee goes in one end and oh, man, does it whiz right on out the other!

Actually, it's not a long drive at all, four hours, give or take. The time zips by, seeing as we're presented with vista after vista of Norman Rockwell farms and meandering creeks with the occasional well-placed cluster of cows lazily chewing cud. They look up as we pass. Sometimes I moo back and Ruby occasionally joins in. Rocky's flying fur sticks to our lipsticked lips, so we're constantly pulling it off. Eventually I say screw it and wipe mine off. Ruby follows suit, but I know she'll have it reapplied in no time.

A road sign made of long logs sawed in half, charmingly informs us we're five miles from Bayfield, "Best Little Town in the Midwest," written in white sloppy letters. Last night I did some research and learned that Bayfield is a port town; moreover, it's a tourist favorite, teetering over the edge of Wisconsin and sloping dramatically into Lake Superior. Ruby informs me we'll be catching a ferry from there in order to cross the lake over to Madeline Island.

My favorite sign so far is a huge green and white trout leaping out of a rowboat. In big, snappy, dancing-red letters you're informed that in three short miles one can have the pleasure of visiting the world's largest live bait and tackle shop, cheese house *and* a taxidermist to boot. Who needs Target?

"What a gorgeous town Bayfield is, right out of a movie set," I dreamily reply, slowing down in order to let a huge rust-colored dog lazily strut across the lane in front of us. "You hungry? Must be around lunchtime."

"No thank you, darling. Honestly, my stomach is a little knotted." She pats a stretching Rocky. "All the excitement of seeing the old place."

"Mine too."

"Besides, we brought enough food to double our sizes in one weekend!"

"Oh boy, just what I need—to grow a size. What'll that make *you*? Size *one and a half*?"

"Smart aleck. Keep your eyes on the road now," Ruby orders. "Follow on down to the pier. Pull up to that little drive-through booth. Get a ticket and we'll catch the next ferry."

"Isn't it weird? An island up here in the great Northwoods?" I question into Rocky's ear while he leans over to look out my window. "According to the sign hanging on the side of the booth, Lake Superior is the greatest of the Great Lakes. A genuine inland sea."

"Someone's honking. We're next, darling."

We buy our ticket and drive onto the ferry. A huge metal gate clunks into place behind us, some orders are yelled, and then the entire boat lurches from the pier and we head out onto the lake. I give Ruby a wink. The anticipation of actually seeing this special, hidden-on-an-island cottage is setting in. I can just barely see an outline in the distance and it's *something.* I take a puff from Ruby's cigarette.

We're watching an unbelievably overweight kid, clad in a stretched-to-busting striped T-shirt, ram a gigantic corn dog into his ketchup-splotched face. His mom sits primly next to him, dabbing at his bloody-looking lips with a flowered napkin. She's skinny as a rail; a breeze could knock her over. I don't get it. How could she let him eat that junk?

"My goodness, children are plump these days, aren't they?" Ruby asks, tsk-tsking.

"Well, not *all* kids." A puff of smoke wafts from my lips. "Just every one we've *seen* so far."

"Ed and I used to bring Adeline, his mother, up to summer with us," Ruby says as we watch mother and child. "Poor dear, she could hardly make it up the stairs. Thank goodness for the general store—Lori's, I believe it was called. She was constantly running low on suppositories—*hemorrhoids,*" she whispers. "How she could use so many—"

"Thanks for the fascinating information." I squirm in my seat a bit.

"You know, I found an old casserole left over from Ed's funeral—way in the back of my freezer." She clucks her tongue. "Can you imagine?"

"You dumped it. Right? That sucker's over five years old. Talk about a *left over.*"

"It's in the cooler. *Guess* whose name is masking-taped to the bottom."

"I will *not* eat a five-year-old casserole."

"It says, 'Created by Eve Moss, return this dish or suffer the consequences.' In bold letters, I might add. Now how in the world could I throw *that* out?"

"Girl . . . there comes a time when letting go can go *beyond* one's memories."

I'm amazed at what she hangs onto. Peek into any of Ruby's kitchen drawers and you'll find hundreds of assorted plastic bags, refolded tinfoil, a choice of twist-ties in every color, rubber bands and pencils in different stages of use, banded together according to color. Every corner's tucked with several mini–tissue packets. The kind you have several of in the bottom of your well-stocked purse. I do.

"Perhaps some of them . . . darling," Ruby retorts with an "air." "Except *this* is your scrumptious Tater Tot Surprise casserole. What's more, food frozen in *my* freezer stays frozen!" Her chin held high. She's very proud of her appliances.

"Well . . . what the hell. We'll heat it up and I'll watch *you* eat it." I do make a great Tater Tot number, you must admit. The secret is in how you add the water to the prepackaged mix. It was a happy day when Mom discovered Hamburger Helper at our local market. The addition of Tater Tots was *my* idea.

Nearing the island I can see hills rising up in the background with stately white pines hanging over a cluster of shops on the approaching shore. There's one main street, only a couple of blocks long. Clusters of people are coming and going while clouds of seagulls squawk in the sky above. A marvelous breeze sends woodsy-pine smells into our snoots. So this is Madeline Island. I think I'm in love.

The kid is now shoving in orange potato chips by the fistful. His mom discreetly sips diet soda from a long, thin straw, making painful mouth shapes so as not to spoil her perfectly applied glossy pink lipstick. Ruby watches me watch them.

Shaking my head, I say, "He's going to have a tough time dropping weight the older he gets. *She'll* splurge on boob jobs, face-lifts and keeping the pantry stocked. He's going to end up the last one to be picked for kick ball, called nasty names and . . . keep right on eating."

"Oh he may not, darling; he may have a growth spurt."

"Maybe," I reply doubtfully. "But those early habits—take it from me—they're with you forever . . . no matter *what* color you dye your hair." I can still hear the horrible fat-names I was called. Never being picked by *either* team in gym class and never *ever* having a prom date.

"Eve, you know what you need, darling?"

"A sixpack of Reese's Peanut Butter Cups, my feet in warm slippers and a big huge hardback . . . book."

Sighing contentedly, Ruby agrees.

Our ferry slips alongside the pier and the vehicles on board rev to life. We watch The Kid waddle and Lipstick sidle down the pier along with the other people on foot. This time, the front end of the ferry opens up in order to let us drive off. We follow the procession up a short cement pier, veering right; we're smack-dab on Main Street. The entire downtown and surrounding neighborhood is called La Pointe, Ruby explains to Rocky and me.

"LaPointe is *really* . . . charming. Small, but charming." I move the van along at a speed of ten. "La Pointe Post Office, The Beach Club, Grandpa Tony's, Lotta's Cafe . . ."

"What? You think I can't read the signs?" Ruby asks with a sarcastic chuckle. "Now how about making a left here onto Middle Road, then left onto—"

"Rice Street," I reply, letting the steering wheel fly. "These bungalows must be worth a fortune."

"Right . . . here, darling," Ruby pronounces, pointing with one of Rocky's paws. "Follow this for a bit."

"You know, one advantage to being on an island is the fact that it will be much *harder* for me to get lost. Especially since the entire island is only fourteen miles by three." I'm famous for getting lost.

"Keep an eye peeled for North Shore Drive," Ruby informs me, settling back into her seat.

"I'll be a son of a . . . Guess who's passing by," I say. "In a limo, no less. The Kid and Lipstick."

"You best get used to seeing familiar faces," Ruby cautions, giving them a royal wave.

Either side of the van is a view into dense pinewoods. Every so often we spy an enchanting rutted drive curving down into darkness, then disappearing altogether. I've always thought of islands as small little circles of sand, a lone palm tree and a bearded man sipping a drink with a miniature umbrella sticking out. Here, we're engulfed in a forested beauty that makes you whisper.

"Since I've been studying up," I boast, "would you care for a little Wisconsin field-guide naming of some of the trees and plants here? I have a great memory for this kind of thing."

"That would be lovely, darling," Ruby replies. I slow the van to a crawl.

"The trees are a mixture of white pine, spruce and oak, as well as white and yellow birch," I say and look at Ruby to see if she's bored. She's not. "The wildflowers are amazing and look, there's a cardinal!" I point to a bright red bird watching us from a low-hanging branch.

Rocky's tail twitches, so Ruby pulls him closer. "That lovely bird is welcoming us to the island and isn't lunch!" she tells Rocky. He growls.

"Let's see . . ." I resume sharing my newly acquired knowledge of our surroundings. "Over by that stream, forget-me-nots, and I think the red one is cardinal flower. Along the road you've got your black-eyed susans, purple coneflower, and I bet those tall orange babies are turk's-cap. Just to name a few of the local beauties showing off their colors today."

"I am very impressed, darling, and from now on I will come to *you* for clarification of all trees, flowers and whatnot in the wild. Now—would you care for a bit of *island history* while we suffer on through this *horrid* drive?" Ruby asks with a big grin.

"Yes please."

"Well . . ." she begins, lifting her cigarette to director-mode, "the island was named after Madeline Cadotte, daughter of Chief White Crane, *wife* of fur trader Michael Cadotte. I've heard she was a real looker. The Ojibwe Indians lived here hundreds of years before the Europeans gave them the heave-ho. It was a main outpost for fur traders, back when women had the good sense to *wear* fur. Nothing does a gal's wardrobe better than to have a fur or two hanging around. During Prohibition, the island's popularity soared. A lot of cottages had stills, bottling houses, and some were rather famous jazz bars. All in the name of a good . . . stiff—"

"Drink!" I declare.

The road has begun curving to the right and on our left, surrounded by several tall milkweeds and a clump of golden prairie grass, stands a faded yellow sign in the shape of a sun.

"We've arrived," Ruby announces. "To the entrance any-way. We're still a ways from the cottage."

I pull up to a sagging iron gate, held together in the middle by a huge paddle-lock. Next to it stands the sun sign. In faded pink letters it proclaims PRÉVOST PLACE. We get out and walk over to the gate. Beyond is a tree-canopied tunnel with parallel dark ruts worn into the grass leading off into the woods. I shake the gate for the hell of it. The noise causes a big cloud of white butterflies to stir to life around us. We watch, mesmer-ized, as they soar up and away.

"Now let's see here—too many keys. I'm sure I'll remember which . . . Ah *ha!*" Ruby declares, holding up a long skeleton key on a ring with about twenty others. " It's *this* one, I'm sure of it. Here, you do the honors."

The lock is a little persnickety, but with some fussing, it clicks and falls open. We each take a half of the gate, pushing it out of the way and into the long grass. I drive the van through, hop back out and pull the gate closed behind us.

I carefully creep forward. The narrow drive veers right. Bright afternoon sunshine quickly fades to a dark, eerie green. Looking up through the bug-smeared windshield, I marvel at how the trees lean over the driveway on either side, weaving together to form a cavern of green leaves and branches. The air has turned cool. Suddenly one of the tires slams hard, dropping into a pothole that somehow snuck up on me.

"Shit!" I yell loud enough to send Rocky leaping over the stick shift and into Ruby's lap. "You forgot to tell me about the *booby* traps!"

"If you would watch where you're driving," Ruby calmly replies. "This is the north, *way* north, and roads are tricky. Now take this next left slow—please."

"Not like I have much *choice*."

We come to a major bend in the road, which abruptly dips almost straight down. I shift into low, hoping like hell the brakes hold. At the bottom of the gully we come to a rickety wooden bridge. I slow, then stop. A creek as wide as the van snakes through the dense woods, under the bridge and off to our left. I look over at Ruby as we both "oooh" and "ahh." Rocky's tail twitches. He licks his lips while intently watching sparrows chase one another.

"Get this buggy up the next hill and we're home free," Ruby instructs.

"You got it lady." I shift, hit the gas, and laugh out loud.

VW vans do not speed *up* anything, let alone a hill as steep as this one. After the van's initial shuddering, up we inch. As we curve to the right, sunshine gradually breaks through the canopy of leaves and we're suddenly in a clearing that goes on and on all the way to the water. Straight ahead is the lake, endless lake, reflecting sun and sky of the deepest blue. I let out a soft whistle.

To our left stands a two-story log cabin; behind it is a red barn, its front corner consumed by leafy hanging vines swaying in the breeze. The cottage sits on a ridge overlooking the lake, with stately old pine trees all around it. They stand sentry while giving off a feeling of history and quiet. Mystery too.

"Oh man, it's way more than a little cabin in the woods. God, It's so—"

". . . good to be back." Ruby sniffs, dabbing at her eyes with a tissue. "To think the last time I was here was . . . Oh hell, time to move on. Time to get a move on!" Ruby announces, her voice getting back to its snappy self. So I do—move the van, that is.

"Pull up to the back porch there. First we need to say hello to the lake," Ruby informs me while hopping out and setting Rocky on the seat. She then plops a huge straw hat on her head with the air of a woman with resolve.

"You *greet* the lake? I mean, it sounds entirely normal to me, I guess, considering who . . ." I have to trot in order to keep up with her as we pass along the side of the cottage.

"Oh look at this, isn't this the most beautiful sight in the entire world?" Ruby asks with arms open wide as we fly down wooden stairs and end up on the end of the wooden dock.

"God, it's *gorgeous,*" I say, catching my breath.

"You always need to say hello to the lake first; it's tradition," Ruby says, and I totally agree.

I silently promise Ed I'll do my best to watch over this amazing woman while at the same time I have this other feeling too. Like I've been here before. It usually happens when the world and I are *right* or something happens and it feels as though it was supposed to turn out that way all along.

Rocky has caught up with us, meowing through a clump of reeds on the shore. Slowly he steals his way out to the end of the dock and purrs around our ankles. I put an arm around Ruby. We stand there and just—are.

"Over there"—Ruby's cigarette points—"you can just make out the outline of Hermit Island and that one over a bit is Stockton Island. It's rather large. Then we've Michigan Island and hiding behind that is Gull Island. To the right of that and on and on is water all the way until you smack into Canada."

"I can just barely see the mainland." I squint in that direction. "Or is that another island?"

"Since we sit on this tip that juts out into the lake, sometimes you can spot a tiny bit of Bayfield."

After several more minutes of taking in the lake I break the silence. "How about you and I taking a look around inside?" Scooping up Rocky, we head back up the stairs, around the side of the cottage to the back.

An enclosed porch wraps around the entire first floor, its big square windows reflecting the afternoon sunlight. Beyond are reed curtains pulled down tight. Wooden red shutters with stars carved into the tops are latched shut over all the second-floor windows. White window boxes, weeds shooting out of them, hang beneath. An impressive river-rock chimney peeks out of the gable roof.

Ruby shows me which key will most likely open the porch door. It unlocks easily, swinging silently open. The porch is decorated with wicker, the real stuff. Chairs, love seats, tables and lamps, all in shades of faded green and white. Hanging on the wall next to the door leading into the cottage itself is an enormous fish. A dusty, spider-webbed tie is wrapped around its garish head. It's turned from the wall, looking about ready to slap its tail.

"*I* caught that mother!" Ruby boasts, scratching Rocky's head. "Nearly pulled me in the drink, too. I'll teach you how to fish. I love to wet a line now and again."

"Okay, but there's no way in hell I'm cleaning the slimy things. Yuck." Picking out a frozen, tastefully packaged fillet from the freezer section at the market makes so much more sense.

"You catch 'em, you clean 'em. Rules of the lake," Ruby states as if reading my mind.

"Great."

We step up the stoop leading to the back door. It's an unusually beautiful door, arched at the top and covered with carvings of trees and birds. A round, lace-covered window looks down at us.

"Ruby,"—I hand her back the keys—"you open this one," I speak softly, taking Rocky from her. He meows in agreement.

She fits the key in. The lock clicks, allowing the door to open. A breeze of cool, musty air rushes out, surrounding us, then melts away. Rocky leaps from my arms, disappearing inside. Ruby and I stand on the threshold, shoulder to shoulder, breathing silently. I give the door a push and it glides open, squeaking all the way. I smile with satisfaction.

Stepping over the threshold, we're in the kitchen, which opens into a big main living area. Beyond you can see out a wall of French doors to the front of the cottage. A hulking yellow and chrome gas stove stands proud, surrounded by knotty pine cupboards with dark green countertops.

In the center is a huge varnished tree stump with four wicker barstools around it. It's the most amazing waist-high island table I've ever seen. Stepping closer, after wiping away a layer of dust, I count hundreds of age rings, dark against the amber-colored wood. A well-worn brass footrest winds around the bottom. Above it, suspended by chains, hangs a circular well-stocked pan holder.

"Cooked up some lovely feasts with this sucker." Ruby pats the gas stove with affection. "I rang ahead to make sure the electricity was turned on. I'm so glad the boys next door put the dock in. Such a nice surprise. Now be careful opening drawers, cupboards, everything really. Hard to say what'll leap out."

"Oh?"

"You'll get used to it . . . *them,* I should say."

"Them?"

"Besides . . . we have Rocky," Ruby reminds me. Who, on cue, leaps into my arms, dust stuck to his whiskers.

"What a stove, must weigh a *ton.* And does this work?" I ask, standing next to a matching yellow fridge, its rounded corners and circular door handle making it look more like a muscle car than an icebox. Icebox? Where'd that come from?

Ruby reaches around me, plugging it in. A subtle but gratifying whir fills the air.

"Smart aleck, 'course it works. It's not *that* old," Ruby says, leading us out of the kitchen and into the living room. "This is my favorite spot. A crackling fire warms it up in no time flat." Ruby yanks several sheets, revealing furniture.

A whimsical assortment of Art Deco, sixties kitsch and some interesting tables and chairs made from wooden sticks. Everything is turned toward the fireplace. A big overstuffed faded red sofa is flanked by several chairs in varying states of slump with a marvelous sparkly green coffee table in the middle. Underneath, in stacks and rows, are board games—Monopoly, Scrabble, Shoots and Ladders, Yatzee, an Ouija board. Hmmm.

The walls are smooth logs, stacked horizontally, varnished to a similar amber as the stump table. A cathedral ceiling arches up beyond the second floor, exposing rafters that crisscross over to a balcony. A suspended staircase made of logs sliced in half curves up around the left wall, ending at the open balcony.

"It's my favorite room too—well, so far anyway. What a place." I'm itching to get a look at the rest. I notice a collection of framed pictures along the walls and make a mental note to peer into them later.

Piling the sheets from the living room on the kitchen counter, we set off past the fireplace, down a hallway illuminated by a floor-to-ceiling stained-glass window. As we get closer I realize it's a human-size toad. A golden crown tilts over one of his bright yellow eyes; his lips are puckered, ready for a kiss.

"Ruby?"

"Long story . . . Ed's grandfather, Gustave, had it made years ago. He loved *The Wind in the Willows* and come spring, down by the creek, there are toads by the pail-full. You can hear them croak all night long. He looks just like Ed, if you ask me."

"This place must be really old." I gaze into the toad's eyes.

"Gustave and Adeline built it around nineteen twenty-one," Ruby says reflectively and I have to whistle in awe. "This is a room I think you'll really enjoy." She pushes open a door on the far side of the toad-window.

"You have a library? For God's sake . . . a library," I stammer as though I'd seen a ghost.

"Ed's family loved books," Ruby explains as we enter the cozy room. "Just like you do, darling."

She pulls a sheet off one of the two high-backed chairs facing a potbellied stove. Rocky sails into the room, onto one of the chairs, then leaps through the air, landing with a karate-chop meow on the other. A dust cloud puffs up around him. He sneezes.

"Bless you, darling. My Lord, what I wouldn't give to have that kind of energy." Ruby scratches him between his ears. "This was Ed's room." She clicks on a Tiffany-style lamp. "We used to sit in here when the sun was elsewhere. Read . . . and talk . . . enjoy the coziness."

"Truman Capote, Dante, Dickens, Emerson, Mary Stewart . . . a little of everything." I read aloud a few of the hundreds of book spines, my palms getting sweaty at the thought of all these worlds to explore.

"Ed had quite a collection. Come along." Ruby leads us back down the hall, into the living room.

"You know, we *really* should have something to celebrate with." I feel a tad naughty and love it. "Just a tiny sip of something to commemorate the moment."

"Oh there are all sorts of that in the basement. Shall we?"

"There's a basement?"

Back we go into the kitchen and sure enough, there, smack-dab behind the door we came in: another door. This one is covered with wooden pegs holding hats, coats and umbrellas in every color and design. It groans and creaks as Ruby pulls it open. Rocky leads the way down the stairs; damp musty air wafts up to greet us.

"These stairs have always been squeaky," Ruby cautions. "But they're strong." We slowly descend, squeaking all the way. We laugh.

"Since the cottage sits on a ridge, the basement has never flooded and well, as you can see, we used it to store all sorts of junk. Over there, through that metal door, is the wine cellar." Ruby points to an ominous metal door.

The basement is a labyrinth of rooms. Bare light bulbs dangle from wires coated with dust, and furniture, boxes, crates and appliances of every shape and color fill the place. Over in a corner stands an old round pink washer like one at my salon. Its rollers clutch an old sock, making it look as though it's sticking its tongue out at us. The furnace is huge, like an octopus, pipes and gizmos going this way and that.

"Wow, look at all this wine in here!" I pull open a door and stare at several racks of dust-covered bottles lying on their sides. "No wine-in-a-box in here!"

"We made our own, too. Some is from the patch of Seyval grapevines that grow alongside the barn out back. There's even a few batches of hard cider made from our very own apple trees. It has *quite* a kick."

"Very impressive. I had no idea grapes would even *consider* growing this far north." I select several bottles. With a foot I close the metal door and we squeak our way back upstairs.

"Be a dear and take down a couple of goblets." Ruby heads toward the French doors facing the lake. "Can't stand another second without letting some sun and fresh air in here. Try the cupboard to the left of the sink, darling."

Walking around the stump table, I reach up and open the cupboard. I was expecting a couple of nice stems and cottage-y dishes, but not this. Plates, platters, bowls and cups in every pattern and color; not a thing matches. The top shelf is filled with goblets. Rows of them. A mishmash collection that beats mine dead. I choose a deep red goblet with a slender stem and a plain crystal one covered with etchings of birds.

After the water runs from deep rust to clear, I give them a careful rinse. Pipes clang and rattle in the walls; a sound like a pump clunks in rhythm underneath my feet. Seems like a lot of work to get water to the faucet.

"Lovely, darling." Ruby wipes the stump table off with one of the sheets from the living room. "I have stacks of different place settings and mismatched stemware, as you probably noticed. I do use matching silverware, though. I have my eccentric limits."

"Corkscrew?"

"One of the drawers next to the stove. But maybe, you know . . . you need to be careful of . . ."

I'm opening, then closing, the top drawer, the next, the third and then, "HOLY-LORD-GOD-MOTHER-MARY-SIS-TER-ESMERELDA!" I yell really, *really* loud, yet—with control. Mice. Hate the little fuckers.

They've taken up residence in the damn *third drawer down*. And with all the drawer opening, I scare the hairy rabid creatures from hell. Several leap straight up, miraculously landing on all fours, then scurry across the countertop. The entire time I'm imploring my list of saints, Ruby is laughing so hard she can barely breathe. I eventually join in.

"Oh Rocky, darling," Ruby singsongs into the living room, "Auntie Ruby has a job for you."

CHAPTER THREE

Ruby and I head up the log stairs to the second floor carrying our well-earned wine. I'm damn grateful to be out of the kitchen. The hall is completely open on one side. I can look down into the living room and on out to the lake; it's beautiful. Only a single log banister prevents one from falling overboard. The opposite wall is paneled with gleaming knotty pine and more "tastefully" framed pictures.

"Here's to the second floor." I raise my glass to hers. "I sure as hell am glad Rocky chased those bastards away."

"Cheers, darling," Ruby returns. We clink our goblets and the sound is as delicious as the wine and the day and this moment.

Ruby informs me that we should start at the far end, then work our way back to the top of the stairs. We pass several arched doors before coming to the end of the hall. I figure we're directly above the frog-window. To our left, French doors open onto a small porch over the library. Opposite this is a beautifully carved door. Ruby turns the glass knob and we step inside.

"This is . . . amazing," I say in a hushed tone. "A bed made out of willow switches and logs—you must miss waking up here." I run my hand over the heavy quilt covering the bed. I walk over to one of the corner window seats and lift a book lying there on top of a pillow. "Thoreau's *On Man and Nature.* One of Ed's favorites, I bet."

Ruby takes it from me in a gentle, careful way. "Yes . . ." She holds it to her heart. "He was reading this the last time we were here." She puts it back in the exact spot. In a brighter voice, "I am so thankful nothing has been broken into and not a window blown out from a storm, which we get now and again up here. Really, the old place simply needs a good fluffing." She sets her empty wineglass down and goes about opening windows and shutters.

Oh boy, what have I got myself into here? This is all her . . . memories. Their furniture and dishes . . . her's and Ed's life was here. A *shrine!* All that's missing is the velvet rope.

I busy myself snooping in the armoire, look into her enormous bathroom and then take a peek in a wooden chest sitting at the end of the bed. It holds colorful quilts and a cedar smell that's wonderfully old. Rich with the past. The rag rug covering the floor beside the bed is in the shape of a big green grinning toad.

"You made this, didn't you?" I tap the tip of my Keds shoe on the toad's rear.

"I did indeed. *We* did actually. Ed helped me cut the rags and when it was finished I wrapped it around my naked self and . . . It was for his birthday. I was very young," Ruby explains a bit hurriedly. She looks radiant telling me, though.

"You bad girl," I admonish her with a shake of my head. I glance over at the window seat, the book. Ruby will move it when she's good and ready and that's just fine.

Thank God we stocked the cooler full of my special cold sandwiches, pasta salad, some fruit and a pan of Ruby's bars. We're gathered in the south corner of the porch; before us is our lunch feast wobbling precariously on a wicker table. The windows have been opened wide. A marvelous breeze washes around us while the lake's waves slap in rhythm against the shore.

"I say . . . after lunch and fresh mugs of coffee," Ruby informs me with a mouth full of pickle and sprouts, "let's do a bit of cleaning, more airing and make up the beds. Whip the lot into shape."

"Okay. I don't think I'll be so freaked out when my next mouse encounter happens. I had no *idea* they could jump so damn high. I *hate* crawling, creeping things." I shiver at the memory.

"Oh, you'll get used to them, mark my words, darling. . . . It's so lovely to be back. What in the *world* was I thinking, staying away so long." Ruby sits back, looking pleased as punch. "But it feels as though I never left. For some reason I thought—in the back of my mind, mind you—that it would seem too sad or lonesome or something ridiculous like that without Ed here. But . . . it doesn't. Not one bit."

"I'm glad to hear that. But *do* let me know if you see Ed's ghost or if you dream him again."

"I think he *could* be here. . . . Oh, not a ghost—wipe that look off your face. More of a feeling, an impression. Like when you know someone's in a room but you've just not spotted them yet. It's a *nice* feeling, actually."

"Hmm, you know, I've felt that about my mom. It's so strong sometimes. I swear I see her out of the corner of my eye, just for an instant. Several times, when I've been really down in the dumps and I want her there so bad, I *smell* her."

"Yes," Ruby agrees, nodding her head slowly, thinking her own thoughts.

"I love the room at the top of the stairs, by the way. That narrow passage to the watchtower is a riot. What in the world was it used for?"

"We watched storms roll in and sunsets are nice up there too." Ruby gives Rocky a pat. "I think it suits you dear, I know how you like to be on roofs."

"I love it."

"There are a few more surprises left, but first let's open and air out the place, shall we?" she asks while stacking plates and gathering up lunch. "Then we need to sit out on the dock and soak up some of the quiet."

"Sign me up."

In a corner of the living room I find the most amazing collection of old jazz records. First of all, I haven't seen an actual *record* in ages. Then there's the stereo itself—the thing has *tubes!* After it warms up, literally, I pile on Jackie Gleason, Artie Shaw, Frank Sinatra and, thank God, she has Pearl Bailey.

We spend the better part of the afternoon sweeping, shaking, wiping, washing, and vacuuming. The vacuum cleaner, a canister affair that slides on narrow metal sleighs, belongs in a museum. I, of course, so inform Ruby, who responds by adding that *she* belongs in one as well. I agree and she smacks me on my arm. Surprised?

"I think we can call it spick-and-span, folks!" I announce into the living room from the kitchen. A cottage should never be too clean anyway; it's just not right.

The old Maytag rumbling in the basement has been at it all day. Sheets, blankets and drapes flap wildly in the wind on the clothesline outside the back porch. You can glimpse Rocky's shadow leaping and pawing at the possessed laundry dancing in the sun.

I'm covered in spider webs and grime and who knows what all. Ruby reaches up to swipe a web from my hair. We both have wrapped our hair up into big, brightly flowered scarves. My makeup is long gone; clothes are a shade or two darker, too. Ruby, on the other hand, looks ready for a photo shoot. I could hate this woman if I thought she really took herself seriously.

"It looks so . . . tidy," I say as I take a big ol' drag of my cigarette, chased with cold coffee.

"My God, we cleaned the whole joint; I *am* impressed," Ruby says as she pulls my hand with the cigarette up to her mouth and takes a long puff.

"I say, hot showers, fresh clothes and then to the dock."

"You're on," Ruby replies.

Rocky meows in agreement.

I take a nice long shower in the bathroom off my bedroom. It's actually a miniature claw-foot tub with a plastic curtain covered in huge bright red ladybugs that I've pulled around me. Not much room in here, but the water is warm and wonderful and it's relaxing me into a state of nice clean peacefulness.

I'm softly humming. Rocky sits on the toilet watching. I towel off and head over to my suitcase to root around for some clean, cozy clothes. Looking up, I realize we had left the door leading up to the watchtower open a crack.

Wrapping up in my furry pink robe, Rocky and I climb up the narrow staircase. I push open the short little door at the top and we're in a curious, square room of windows facing every direction. On the floor is painted an elaborate four-pointed star indicating north, south, east and west.

Peering out, I can just barely see the mainland to the south-west (which I gauge by looking at my handy floor guide) with Bayfield perched, storybook-like, on a hill. To the northeast and on and on is Lake Superior.

After a few moments of gazing at all that water, we scurry back down into my room. I button up a crisp white shirt (no bra; I'm at the cottage, for heaven's sake) over faded jeans and head to the dock for my meeting with Ruby. It's our official lake-welcoming ceremony and one should never be late for that. I have to admit the end of the dock is fast becoming a fa-vorite hang.

"Why Eve, you're simply beaming," Ruby exclaims, looking up at me. "It's the iron in the water, I've always felt it makes your hair shine too."

"Thanks. From the looks of the tub upstairs I'll never have to color my hair again. I've seen *rust* stains before, but geez." I plop next to her at the end of the dock and join in her bare-feet-lake-soak. After the initial shock, it's okay. If you're into having numb feet, that is. "How was *your* shower? You look pretty darn beamy yourself there, missy."

"Why thank you, darling. I feel rejuvenated. Being here is

getting my blood moving again. I forgot how beautiful the water is."

"The lake is so vast. No shore in sight. It just goes on and on."

"Funny how I recalled the cottage in my head," Ruby says thoughtfully. "I forgot to add all the colors; there's so much *color* here."

"I know what you mean." I swish the water around with my toes. They're frozen solid.

"It's like when someone dies." Ruby looks up to the sky. "If you shared memories with that someone, they kind of lose their color after time. The memories fade like a picture that goes from sharp to blurry."

"Reminds me of when my mom passed away." I sit back on my elbows. "About a month after the funeral, I freaked out because for the life of me I couldn't remember her face. Can you imagine?"

"Yes, I can, darling. It's scary at first, but after a time, you add those that have passed on from your memory to your heart." In a stronger voice she continues, "Now . . . I need to welcome you *officially* to the lake." From a string tied to one of the support posts of the dock, Ruby pulls out of the lake a bottle of champagne!

"I'll be! Now that's what I call a *good* catch. Say, can you pull up some crab dip and crackers while you're at it there?"

"Smart aleck, really. Make yourself useful and open this. "Ruby hands me a rag for my hands along with the dripping bottle of bubbly. "I purposefully forgot glasses to commemorate—"

"That's *right*. Oh my God. We were sitting on my roof in

the rain after my first anniversary at the shop. We got *so* toasted." We laugh.

"*I* was toasted, darling; *you* were shit-faced. You were sooooooo shit-faced."

I was so shit-faced. "Damn, this thing is really in here!" I pull with all that's left of my might. Then, POP! The cork is out, flying through the air and into the lake, landing with a soft plop.

"Well done," Ruby declares, taking the bottle from me and tipping it back for a nice slug. She passes it back to me and I take a long swallow. It's sweet and cold and bubbly as hell. My eyes tear.

"Here's to you my darling. Welcome to Madeline Island, where anything—*everything*—is possible." She raises the bottle high.

We both have a slug for good measure, then lean back. Looking up, we marvel at the colors the sun is throwing into the clouds as it slowly kisses the horizon. Crossing my arms behind my head, I sigh all the way to my roots, which are in need of a touch-up, by the way.

"I'd love it if the two of us lived here . . . moved here . . . now, while we can both still enjoy it," I say, thinking out loud and full of the moment, when all things *do* seem possible. And yet, what in the hell am I saying? Could I fit in here—with Ed?

"It's the end of the *world* up here and the winters *must* be lonely," Ruby says. "I've heard that less than two hundred people live out here full time. Ed and I just spent the summers, then headed back to Eau Claire to suffer winters there."

"You said yourself you'd love to live here year-around. The

cottage seems like it would keep us very cozy. Besides, there's that mega heater in the basement, *and* I have a plan, sort of a plan." This is how I do things. I jump into something new and you know, it usually pans out. Usually.

"You *always* have a plan, darling," Ruby replies. "Trouble is, it's typically a lot of work, costs tons of money and I'm never quite the same. But . . . I'm listening."

"Well, I know my way around the Internet pretty well and what I don't know, I'll figure out. Now, if we were to create some kind of web site . . . You have to show me the barn, by the way, and what's in that building over there?" I point to the left of us. I have a terrible habit of skipping all over the place when I'm brainstorming. Thank God Ruby's used to this.

"The boathouse. The second floor is a cozy little guest house. Ed used to do some of his writing there, and whenever we had too many visitors for the cottage, they slept there. It's lovely . . . really."

"So much to this place."

"What do we need the Internet for?" Ruby asks, sitting up and swatting a bug off her shoulder.

"I was thinking . . . if the barn or maybe that boathouse had some workable space, and electricity, and we hired a few of the ladies with nothing to do out here in the winter . . . we could make toad rag rugs and sell them on the Internet." Where did that come from?

"Well, I'll be . . . Set up a sweatshop right here on Madeline Island." Ruby thinks it over. "I don't know if they're that un-usual—rag rugs, I mean—and wouldn't we have to make heaps of them?"

"You wouldn't *believe* the stuff women are buying on the Internet. It's amazing. You can even order a man." Ruby raises both of her perfectly arched brows.

"Did you bring your laptop, darling?" she asks, absently patting her perfect hair.

I sigh. "I'm serious, I think we could do this. I saw the shops and galleries and all the fancy cars when we got off the ferry."

"There *is* a rather wealthy bunch up here in the summer, but the natives are much more earthy; they hide from them." She gets up and smacks her rear back to life. "How about you and I get into cozies, throw some pasta in a pot, put a log on the fire and figure out our next move, or moves, for that matter,"

"Deal." I stand up and do the same thing to my hind end. Feels like ginger ale has taken over my rear.

All hands are busy stirring things in the kitchen over the big, hulking stove. It gleams in the golden light reflecting off the pine walls. Steamy smells of fresh basil, garlic and pasta fill the air. Everything is bubbling away in blue-speckled enamelware pots.

Rocky is on the stump table crunching out of a beautiful crystal bowl Ruby found for him. There have been *five* mouse heart attacks so far, but hey—tomorrow's another day.

"This smells wonderful." I take a whiff from a spoon Ruby has put under my nose. "Why is it that food you make with someone always tastes better?"

"Oh I think it's just the making of it that matters. You can cook good feelings right into a thing. *Especially* the way you stir." Ruby grabs the spoon I was stirring with from me. "Good heavens, Eve, you're going to end up with mush if you don't let those noodles be."

"Sorry, I do my best thinking when I'm stirring."

"Here then . . . *think* this sauce." She points to the pot of yummy sauce loaded with secret ingredients. She has a cache of canned tomatoes in her pantry back in Eau Claire that could feed armies.

"I *love* the idea of living on an island and being somewhat unplugged from the masses, yet *way* plugged in, thanks to the Internet." I stir this way and that, thinking.

My hair has become tight curls thanks to the steam. I'm all cozy in a sweatshirt, favorite jeans and Winnie-the-Pooh slippers. Ruby has one of her fussy walking outfits on, blue with white piping. The kind that has matching top and bottom. The front is covered in garish stones, a starburst design. On her . . . it's cute.

"If I were to sell my house, it could bring in a nice bit of cash." Ruby grabs the spoon out of my hand. "It's always been too much house for me. I bet it would be ideal for a young couple to redo."

"I honestly think I'm ready to do something else, not as . . . safe, *and* different. To live here, on this wonderful *jewel* of an island . . . Well, knock me over!" I smack the top of the stump table for emphasis.

"You know . . . I think if we really are sure about this, if we go about it with as clear a plan as possible, well *hell's bells,* the sky's the limit and what's to stop us?" Ruby asks, opening and closing cupboards, handing me brightly colored plates, miss-matched glasses, napkins, silverware. She points to the stump table. I set the table, marveling at its rings and caramel colors.

"Let's eat and keep thinking." I turn a plate just so.

The pasta sauce is divine, and since it's challenging to shove tasty food in your mouth and talk *and* think—we eat. After-ward, we go and sink down into the sofa in the living room, put our toes up and warm them in front of a very decent fire. Girl Scouts taught me a *few* things.

"I've not been this beat for a long time. Feels great," I mur-mur in a sleepy voice. " We're going to sleep like logs. If logs sleep, that is."

"We did so much today," Ruby adds. "The place has not been opened up and full of life for such a long time. I love the way I feel when I'm here."

I sit up to get a better look at all the stuffed deer heads, an entire owl frozen in midflight and animal skins hanging way up high from the rafters. The firelight throws dancing yellows and golds all over the walls. The snappy crackling of pine logs is a music that makes you very sleepy.

"This is sheer heaven." I slouch back into the cushy sofa.

"Mmm hmm," Ruby mumbles while petting Rocky, who's snuggling in her lap.

We sigh, watching the flames flicker and whisper. Just as my eyes are sliding blissfully shut . . . BOOM! A thunderclap echoes over our heads and the entire cottage shakes. We leap to our feet, instantly wide awake. Rocky lands on all fours on the coffee table. Then it starts to rain, the drops clattering on the roof.

" Good God!" It takes me a second to find my voice.

"I love the pitter-patter of rain on the roof, marvelous way to fall asleep. Let's turn in, darling."

"Okay."

I'm lying under sun-fresh sheets and a heavy quilt decorated with little squares of pastel colors. A cool, rainy breeze carrying the soft scent of pine hovers around me while raindrops tap softly above. Rocky gently purrs, snuggled by my side; in a second or two he's asleep. I can see out my window to the sky. Every so often it flashes as lightning cracks, illuminating the night.

Being here, I feel lighter somehow. Like the cloud of guilt— heaps of it, thanks to my Catholic parents—seems less now. The rain-soaked air smells so . . . delicious, too. I did nothing wrong—well, okay, we did the deed and all, but the baby . . . I didn't plan on *that,* and at seventeen . . . I shake my head.

Am I going to be in this in-between place forever? *No.* I shift to my side and give the pillow a good punch. Just because one detective couldn't find her doesn't mean I give up. 'Course, he did suggest that maybe she doesn't want to be found, either. Who the *hell* wouldn't want to meet me?

Chapter Four

The next day I wake at dawn to total and complete quiet. The kind of sleepy quiet that's reassuring, like a spell has fallen over everything around you. In order not to break the spell you do everything carefully, trying your hardest not to make a sound. I've always loved waking up slowly, with strong, sugary-sweet coffee and a smoke. I'm going to quit smoking, I am, but honestly, isn't everyone entitled to at least *one* really bad habit? Okay, maybe two.

I braid my curls up into a fancy French twist and secure it with a scarf, pull on gray warmups and slip down to the kitchen. Assuming Ruby's cupboard system up here is similar to the one in Eau Claire, I open the door to the left of the stove and violà! I take down instant coffee, a bowl of sugar and a mug. After zapping the filled mug in the microwave, I have a sip and sigh as I feel my head begin to clear.

On the way through the living room, I grab a fringed blanket. Careful not to let the porch door bang shut, I head down the path to the dock. Sparkling dewdrops are chilly, splattering onto my toes. My wet feet make my flip-flops end each step with a squeaky-slap that's very satisfying. I thump down onto the dock and snuggle into the old blanket.

A crisp, clear morning awaits. I take another sip of coffee; the warmth fills my empty stomach and I let out a little laugh. Who would've thought this is where I would be at forty-seven. I was beginning to think that maybe I'd missed out, not having a family of my own. But I'm realizing that I *do* have a family right here.

I'm learning that who you end up with doesn't have to be a husband and two-point-five children. Sometimes you're lucky enough to have a "someone" that makes you feel whole. I know a lot of people feel that way about their partners, but I know *just* as many that don't. I put my toes into the ice cold water and shiver so badly I spill hot coffee on my thigh.

"Shit!" I yell across the lake; my voice echoes back. I imagine some housewife hearing me. She looks up from her dishwater, plate in one hand and scrubber in the other, in some cozy little kitchen over in Bayfield. I wonder if she feels this satisfied, this complete. I wonder.

Since I thought to bring the keys, I figure now is a good time to explore the barn. Besides, my toes need to thaw out a bit and turn back into more of a flesh color instead of this blue. I pull the blanket around my shoulders and head up the path around the cottage. Halfway up, I stoop to pick a few daisies, which I weave into my hair.

Walking around the side of the cottage, I run my hand along the logs, admiring how well the building is put together. At each corner, the ends of huge pine logs are notched into one another like Lincoln Logs.

The barn has a big accordion door, half covered with vines that are heavy with grapes. Beside this is a regular-sized door. One of those charming divided-in-half Dutch doors. It's locked with a big paddle lock similar to the one on the gate at the entrance. With the fifth key I try, it clicks open.

Smells of electric machines, oil and damp all escape the barn in a huff of cool air. On the wall is a battery of switches. I figure what the hell, and in no time flat, the entire place is lit up.

"Huge," I say to the vast, yawning space. My words bounce off the walls and high crossbeams. The barn is much larger than it looks from the outside. Straight ahead, built underneath the staircase, is what looks to be a workbench. It consists of a long, waist-high counter with shelves above. They're filled with jars of every size and shape holding screws, nuts, bolts— you name it. Around the corner, on the other side of the staircase, is a jumble of chairs, lamps, boat paddles, a huge stuffed moose head and a wooden canoe hanging from the rafters.

In the middle, covered with a green tarp, is a boat. Reaching up, I yank the tarp off, making dust fly every which way. The boat is painted a bright white. It's around twenty feet or so in length and as wide as my van is long. A red-and-white striped canvas awning stretches over five rows of seats with an aisle down the middle. The weird thing about it is the fact that it has wheels.

What the hell? Is it a boat or a bus? Then it comes to me. Has to be one of those boat-tour contraptions called a duck. Similar to one I'd ridden years ago when my folks took me to the Wisconsin Dells. As I recall, they were originally used in World War II.

Hmmm, we could give Madeline Island tours, weave rugs, maybe do some wine-making on the side. It's a shame I'm not a fan of bed-and-breakfasts, what with all the room here. But I'd go nuts if I had to eat breakfast with strangers. I'm deep in thought, moneymaking wheels cranking away. So when I turn, apparently having gone momentarily deaf as well, I bump head-on into Ruby.

"Good Lord woman. Where the hell did you come from? You just aged me about a hundred years!"

"Good morning, darling." Ruby grins, ignoring my outburst. "I didn't mean to scare the *bejeezus* out of you like that, though I must say it was most satisfying."

"Good morning to you. I was deep in thought about *this*." I pat the duck. "Does it work?"

"Oh of course it does, love. Ed's been caring—used to care for it ever since he hauled it here. Ran like a charm. We would take it out to one of the Apostle Islands, pull up on a nice sandy spot and have a picnic."

"How romantic," I mock. Ruby sticks her tongue out at me. "I'm jealous." I climb up the ladder on the side. "Looks easy enough to drive." For kicks I turn the key that's hanging in the ignition; nothing.

"*Do* be careful, darling."

"The battery probably needs charging and a bath in the lake wouldn't be a bad idea, either. Things always seem to work better if they're cleaned up."

"Spoken like a true hairstylist/boat mechanic." Ruby absently smoothes the apron she's wearing over her lavender outfit.

"I would love to get this puppy going."

"There's a workbench," Ruby offers, pointing to it. "I'm sure there's a charger over there . . . somewhere."

"How about you make breakfast and I'll see if I can get this started?" I pull the key out and climb down the ladder. "We could have our very own lake tour this morning, if it works, that is."

"Sounds lovely, darling. Don't go blowing anything up, for heaven's sake." She turns back toward the cottage.

I head over to the workbench. On the way, I pass a stack of dusty steamer trunks, several pairs of wooden snowshoes, a deer head and an enormous stuffed bear on wheels wearing a lampshade. Beyond this, nearer to the workbench, are winches, pulleys, coffee cans overflowing with nails, and blowtorches. After rooting around and sneezing myself silly, I find it.

I've had to hook my van up to many clients' cars over the years to give them a jump, so I consider myself an expert. After attaching the charger, I realize I left the keys on the workbench.

"Damn." Heading *back* over, I notice a painted wooden sign in the shape of an enormous key. It has about twenty little hooks running along the bottom holding every shape and length of key, most of them with a string attached to a handwritten label. Hats off to Ed for being so organized. After swiping away spider webs, I read the labels. "Lawn mower, boathouse, guest cottage, porch door, front door, back door, duck keys. *Duck keys*."

I grab them and then of course, I find the key I left on the bench, too. I take both sets, just in case. Since I'm really *not* into inhaling fumes, and since I half expect the boat to run, I need one large barn door to open.

I can see a motor way up there at the top of the door and by following the wires down, I walk over to a round green button the size of a saucer. I press it and am impressed by the small concert of squeaks and groans that echo all the way down from the ceiling. The massive door smoothly folds to either side of the opening, leaving a veil of grapevines to sway in the wind. Morning sunshine floats on dust clouds into the barn. I stand next to the duck, looking out toward the cottage and the lake beyond.

I decide not to try turning it over until *after* we have breakfast so it will get a good dose of juice. On the way back to the cottage, a meowing Rocky greets me. I scoop him up in my arms and give him a big fat kiss, right on the lips, and he purrs. Then I remember his lips have clamped around mice necks and I spit into the grass. Rocky gives me one of his looks.

"*There* you are, darling. Did it start?"

"Needs to charge for a bit." I plunk down on a wicker stool and spin.

"Good thinking." Ruby pulls two bowls from the fridge and plops them down on the stump table.

"This looks great!" We dig spoons into yogurt with bananas and granola. Rocky meows, wanting some. "He really shouldn't be eating anything other than his special-diet food. 'Course, I wonder if mouse would be considered *special diet. I* should talk about diet!"

"Eve, you've been fussing about your bloody weight ever

since I met you. I think you should face the fact that you're . . . well, you're a fine figure of a woman. Who the *hell* wants to be as skinny as I am, anyway?" Ruby asks through crunching granola.

"I appreciate that—I do. I've fought with my weight forever! Diets . . . food plans, rice-only, protein-only, liquid diets . . . you name it. The only thing that ever *really* worked was Weight Watchers. But I cheated every chance I could."

"We need to back off women nowadays. There's nothing wrong with just being the best and healthiest you can be . . . without killing yourself." She scoops up Rocky under one arm and carries her bowl with the other. "Let's finish eating out on the porch. Seems a shame to waste all this nice morning sunshine."

"I love the porch." I follow her and sit on a cushy love seat.

"I enjoy eating out here when the sun is just beginning to come full force." Ruby pulls up a wooden stool. "Where were we? Oh yes . . . women and weight."

"It's all a part of fitting in and not being different and *God,* I used to hate taking showers in gym class. I had breasts *way* before the other girls did. I could feel their curious eyes on me. Made me feel so . . . busty." I absently pull my sweatshirt out a bit.

"In my day," Ruby says with a sigh, "it was pretty much the same . . . the 'fitting in' part. Everyone trying to look like everyone else. I was short and skinny."

"I *know* the short part—"

"In high school it was more important to have your hair rolled just so, your blouse pressed right and a wool skirt with shiny shoes."

"For some reason I thought Ed was a high school romance. Were you doing all that fussing for him or . . . ?"

"I met Ed my second year of college. I saw him coming out of the library and just *knew* he was the one for me. That and the fact that he was the most handsome man I ever laid eyes on. Had the most stubborn head of wild black hair, always falling into his eyes. Green—the greenest eyes." She looks out to the lake.

"A college romance. Details, I want details!"

"Well, it's really very simple: we started dating and before you could say 'Prince Charles has big ears' we fell madly and completely in love. After he graduated—*I* still had two years left—we married. I dropped out; the natural thing in that day was to get busy making a family." Ruby fidgets with her fork.

"The kid thing . . . right?"

"We tried and tried, they didn't have the fertility drugs that make you have litters back then. No matter what, we couldn't get me pregnant." Ruby shakes her head. "Though I have no regrets of all the effort put into it, mind you." She winks.

"Did you ever stop to think that maybe it was him?"

"I have never told a soul this." She leans way in. Like someone's going to hear us out here in the middle of nowhere. "It *was* him; he was so embarrassed."

"Ah ha!"

"And you know, I wasn't as fired up about having children as Ed was anyway. I think a part of me was so relieved I wouldn't have to face some possible dread or resentment I may have had towards anything that took time from Ed and me."

"You would've made a *fabulous* mother, but I'm glad you couldn't either. I would've been out to lunch as far as you and

I . . . the cottage. Things would have all been different. Makes you realize how everything we are is connected to everything else."

"Who's to say? Life does seem to turn out exactly how it's supposed to," Ruby says. "Have you given some thought to looking for your daughter—for Amy—again? That was simply *years* ago, and maybe there's a new . . . Why, that laptop of yours could do the trick."

"No, not really. And, yes—shit, all the time, Ruby." I'm grateful she never pushes the issue, but mentioning it I appreciate. She knows it's a tender place. The sound of her name spoken out loud—something way inside me shifts, opens somehow.

I don't know if I have the right to open up that wound for *her.* The excuse I've told myself all these years is that it wasn't my decision, I was only seventeen and my parents just sent me away. Besides, *she's* never tried to find *me.* That's partly what keeps me from looking. That and the fact that I am scared to death of what could come after that.

"Well . . . if you change your mind, I'll be right here with you, darling," Ruby assures me and the matter is put away. "Now, let's give that contraption a go. I would love to ride in it again and *you* will love the island even more from the water!"

"Let's," I reply, grateful to step away from all these feelings I have crowding the porch. But do I think of looking for her? Has she tried to find me? Oh, great, now I'll be thinking about it all over again. Actually, maybe it's time to do more than that. Maybe.

Standing beside the duck, we say a little prayer. After un-plugging the charger, I climb up and sit down behind the huge steering wheel. A cloud of dust puffs up around me and I sneeze and sneeze.

"Bless you, bless you, and bless you! You have exceeded your sneeze limit for the day. Good heavens, it's filthy." Ruby shows me her black fingertip.

"We're going to need a bath. Well, here goes nothing." I turn the key. It sputters and coughs and then a big puff of smoke bangs out the back. "She lives! It works! The damn thing turned right over!"

"Sounds like it used to; purrs, doesn't it. Well, let's undo all these wires and take it into the sunshine," Ruby says with obvious pride.

I shift into drive and with Ruby standing up behind me, edge slowly out of the barn into the glorious sun. Suddenly feeling brave, since it *was* meant to go in the water, *and* since we happen to have this huge lake right here in front of us, I zoom down the lawn and straight for the lake.

Ruby and I are screeching and laughing as we fly down the grass, across the sandy little beach and splash into the lake. We float out and then head west toward Bayfield. By studying the gadgets on the dash and flipping a few switches, I move the duck forward. Ruby sits down beside me. I turn a few more dials, tuning the radio, and soon some nice jazz is shaking the dust from the speakers.

I grab the microphone hanging from the rearview mirror, click it on and say in my monotone announcer's voice, "Good morning campers. Welcome to Ruby's Roving Duck Tours. Please notice the captain has turned off the no smoking sign."

I light up, take a nice big drag, give the duck some gas and we're off. From this new vantage point, I can see the island is long and very narrow.

Tall, elegant white pines tower over the shoreline. They look ready to waltz right off into the lake at any moment. There are hills and inlets, creeks cascading over rocks and high stonewalls diving into sandy strips of land. Long wooden docks lead up to cottages of every shape and size; on some of the docks people stop loading their fishing tackle to look up. Some wave, trying to figure out what in the hell we're riding in.

"It's a beautiful day in Wisconsin!" I sing over the mike as Ruby waves.

CHAPTER FIVE

After tooling all around the island, we end up back at our cottage. Shifting into neutral, we glide up to the right side of the dock as snug as can be. Okay, so I smack into it a tad— but Ruby would *not* have fallen flat on her butt if she'd been sitting down and of course I told her this afterwards.

"I figure we can give it a bath right here in the lake." I hop out, looking for some rope and a clue as to how to secure it to the dock.

"Let me do that darling—here." She takes the rope and knots it to the dock in seconds.

We end up untying Ruby's complicated knots and pulling the duck as far onto the sand as we can since neither one of us has any desire to get soaked. We do anyway since the damn thing weighs a ton and we can only pull its tip out of the water. Oh hell. After giving it a nice scrubbing, we're on the sandy shoreline, all slathered in sun block, wearing straw hats and making sand castles. Mine is your typical mansion-by-the-lake complete with spires, moats, servants' quarters and a place for torturing guests that stay on too long or have bad hair.

Ruby's is a miniature of our cottage, using seaweed, stones and twigs, no less. She's made a lovely herb garden, complete with a pond and a little falls that she can make work by pouring lake water out of one of my Keds. I'm impressed. We're very intent on our work and don't notice that someone has walked up until the all-important throat clearing.

"Ahem. Ah—good morning ladies. Ruby . . . is that *you?*"

"Good heavens. Howard Tillingsworth, how *are* you?" Ruby stands up to hug this tall, rugged man.

He must be somewhere around Ruby's age, with faded blue eyes and gorgeous thick silver-white hair above a proud nose. He's wearing chinos, a denim shirt with the arms cut off and beat-up work boots. His muscled arms lift Ruby clear off her feet, giving her a nice bear hug. Her hat slides off, landing right on top of my castle. I'll have to rebuild the entire west wing. Great.

After Ruby is back on firm ground, she says, "Howard, this is Eve Moss." I reach up and watch as my hand gets lost in his enormous one. It's rough, but warm and inviting.

"Hello Eve, nice to meet you." Howard's voice is deep and smooth, like thick syrup.

"My pleasure, Howard." I pull back my hand in slow motion. "Where'd you come from? You about scared us half to death."

Ruby invites him up to the cottage. On the way, she explains that Howard was one of Ed's dearest lake buddies. They did cottage things together. Fishing, repairing, exchanging tools and of course, cracking a beer now and again. I'm relishing the kind way he speaks to Ruby. The word *"nice"* comes to mind.

Not to mention he's darn good-looking. If you like the rugged, macho type, that is. Who doesn't? And oh my, does he look good from behind!

We're sitting in the living room and I can't help but notice Ruby has on a fresh coat of lipstick and somehow managed to shake some sense into her lake-damp hair. While straightening myself and settling into the cushy sofa, I look down at my blouse. In a controlled panic, I slowly pull a throw pillow to my chest, excuse myself and float upstairs. I'm not wearing a bra and would have much preferred slipping *under* the sofa . . . *hanging jugs of Madeline Island.* Being well-endowed does not translate into having a pert and perky chest.

Safe in my room, I close the door and let out a little embarrassed chuckle. Rocky helps me pick out a nice support system, as I refer to my collection of bras. There's nothing more marvelous than a fresh, clean bra. One that's white, still somewhat new and full of long-lasting support. Checking my face in the full-length mirror, I let my damp hair down and head back downstairs, Rocky at my heels.

The walls and ceiling of the living room are alive with dancing sunlit-water reflections that leap and jump everywhere. Howard and Ruby are seated next to one another, her hand resting lightly on his shoulder. She whispers something into his ear and they giggle.

"There you are, darling. The color in your cheeks makes you look lovely," Ruby remarks as she takes a long drag on her cigarette. "You've managed to tan through all the gunk I demanded we put on."

"Your hair color is such a *rich* red, I hope you don't mind me asking," Howard asks meekly, "but . . . is it natural?"

"Not any longer. I was a *real* redhead—once. But thanks to hormones, aging, stress and hanging around Ruby, I'm this color—this week." He and Ruby smile. "Now *your* hair—I could *never* color that. It's a true silver." I attempt to run my fingers through my hat-mashed curls.

Howard blushes and clears his throat. "The colors you've been using on Ruby's hair, I would bet they're made by Wella. I'm only guessing, but I can tell by the integrity of the blue undertones. She looks beautiful."

Ruby is watching my face as I'm trying to figure out who the hell this guy is. He's right about Ruby's color. I work my tail off to make sure her ash tones are truly ash and not gray. That's a color no one wants, especially after turning fifty-eight . . . again and again.

"Are you in the beauty business? By any chance?" I ask, oddly self-conscious all of a sudden.

"Eve, darling," Ruby says in a knowing voice, "Howard and his partner, Johnny, owned the largest beauty-products company in the Midwest. They *also* own the cottage next to ours. You can just barely see it through the grove of birch trees that divide our properties."

"You and . . . Johnny? Not *the* Johnny, as in Johnny Peterson?" I ask, then feel stupid.

"The one and only. As you probably recall, he was a very well-known hairstylist—still is, if you ask him. He did a lot of platform shows, some print work—and had a waiting list a mile long. We met, well . . . years ago now, and we've been together ever since. He had this idea for using herbs in shampoo and one thing led to another and before we knew it, we were in the beauty-products business." He says this with a wave of his platter-sized hand.

"Then they sold it, retired—sort of—and live like kings and *still* talk to us of lesser means," Ruby explains.

"I'm really glad to meet you Eve and I'm also grateful to you for bringing Ruby back up to the lake." Howard puts his arm lightly around her tiny shoulders.

"I just couldn't come up here for a while. Too much of Ed . . . sounds silly, really." Ruby smoothes her smooth shorts. Then she quickly brightens. "Hey! How about a dinner party, the four of us," she asks with sparkly eyes.

"That sounds fantastic. Let's see . . . it's almost one now." Howard rises. "If we reconvene at, say, around sixish, that would give Johnny time to try on all his clothes, twice."

"We'll find something to put on the grill, if we can *find* the grill . . . and for a salad . . . Have you anything to make a salad with, Howard? And oh, I have this special casserole I can heat up too." She shoots me a conspiratorial wink.

"Oh I'm sure we can find something green. Well, I'm off. Welcome to the lake Eve and welcome back, Ruby." He pecks her on the cheek, then does the same to me.

"I forgot all about these dresses. They *have* seen better days. But oh my, this one has your name written all over it," Ruby says, holding up the most fabulous deep-blue satin party gown a girl has ever dreamed of swishing around in.

"If this fits *you,* I don't know that . . ." I say with not *too* much hope. She can be so kind and *blind,* too.

"Some of these were *far* too big for me, but in the old days you had everything fitted anyway, so I'm sure this will work. We're both *about* the same height, when I wear my heels, that is. And have my hair real high and . . ." Ruby says with determination in her eyes.

"Hmm, it *might* fit if I push things up and don't breathe . . . ever." I hold the dress up and sway slowly around the room. "What is it about a long dress that makes us women feel so . . . glamorous?" We laugh. It's true, though. Throw a Ginger-Loves-Gilligan gown on and you become . . . who? "How fun. I'm going to go and make sure everything gets lifted and separated. Meet you on your deck in a minute." I sail out of her bedroom. "You won't recognize me—*I* won't."

Holding the dress up, I saunter down the hallway to my room. I wave to the clump of gray fur watching me from downstairs atop a newly polished cabana bar. Rocky looks up from licking his front paw, shakes his head and resumes his cleaning.

We're backlit, the sun is beginning to slowly set and we look smashing. I've put my hair up in a soft, loose curly do. Feeling inspired, I've woven a piece of purple ribbon through it. My low-cut gown is proudly displaying my girls; they've *never* been so perky. The waist *is* very fitted, and fit it does. The best part is the huge, billowing skirt. Bare feet are a must as we *are* at the cottage. A gold chain with a single ruby is snug between my breasts, compliments of Ruby on my fortieth birthday.

Then there's Ruby herself, a dazzling dish in a red taffeta and satin gown tailored to her upper body perfectly. The skirt puffs and swirls around, swishing with her every move.

We both have cigarettes burning from the ends of long, elegant holders I found in Ruby's endless collection of accessories. We're sipping wine; lipstick colors the rims of our tall goblets. The faint mothball scent fades into the evening air—thank God.

"I can't remember when I felt so damn expensive." I take a sip. "We sure clean up good."

I salute the lake with my glass held high and Ruby joins me. We clink and turn to the dashing gentlemen walking through the birch tree grove and wave them over.

"Hello loves!" Ruby proclaims in her bright English accent while waving.

We both say together, waving in harmony, "Arm-elbow-arm-arm, repeat. Arm-elbow-arm-arm." This is an old movement left over from my involvement in parades as a child. My mom had me practice my waves in the bathroom mirror until I had it down pat.

The boys laugh and return the favor in synchronized wave-harmony as well. Howard has changed into a snappy outfit. Johnny has on moss-colored slacks and a brilliantly white shirt. He's strikingly handsome in a sharp, angled way. He's a good foot shorter than Howard and has a goatee shaped around his mouth in the form of an O.

"My God Ruby—they are *so* gorgeous." We turn to walk down and greet them. "I would be nervous if they weren't a couple . . . you know?"

"This is such bloody fun!" Ruby loops her arm through mine and we head down the stairs.

At the French doors opening onto the porch, we each take a doorknob, exchange a quick wink and in unison, pull open the double doors. With eyebrows raised up and noses held high, we curtsy to the boys, who are just stepping up the stairs to cross the veranda.

"Ladies. Lovely to see women in gowns again." Howard gives us each a peck on the cheek.

"I imagine in your lot it's the boys wearing them," Ruby says with disdain, then laughs. "How about a drink, darlings."

Howard introduces Johnny, who gallantly kisses my hand. Suddenly, catching wind of his rather powerful cologne, I feel a tingle in my nose, not a good sign. How in the world does one accomplish a full-fledged tickle-in-the-nose *sneeze* in a dress that's cut so low?

"Ah choooo!" explodes from between my lipsticked lips. The force of it creates a huge surge of gown-bursting power that causes both of my girls to leap forth into the room. Completely uninvited! Thank *god* I just had turned away from the boys as the tickle was festering, but they sense that I now have a few things in need of covering. If ever I wanted to evaporate, seep into the floor and disappear forever, it's now. Talk about making a memorable first impression!

"Let's take a walk to the dock while Eve gets straightened out, shall we?" Ruby suggests smoothly, not loosing a beat. She turns the men away, heading down the stairs and toward the lake. As they walk arm in arm, Ruby in the middle, I escape upstairs to repair the situation.

Now I know why no one wears these damn things anymore. Standing in front of my mirror, I take one look and burst out laughing. Trying to catch my breath, I can still see Johnny's eyes bug out. Howard's mouth simply dropped to the floor. Rocky comes in to see what's so darn funny. He leaps onto the bed to look me over. Putting my girls back into submission, I give Rocky a scratch before heading out to join the laughing trio on the dock.

It's after dinner. I've made it through without another *falling* out, thank God. We had melt-in-your-mouth grilled lake trout (caught by Howard), tossed salad and that casserole. Which really was very good. We're stuffed. A crackling fire blazes in the fireplace.

Everyone's feet are up on the coffee table or tucked under yards of satin, like mine. We've reached that nice warm place after eating, laughing and, *of course,* dessert. Now it's the calming sound of fire snapping in the background. An owl hoots outside; Rocky looks up from Johnny's lap and then goes back to being scratched between the ears, his favorite place.

"What a lovely, lovely dinner." Ruby fluffs her dress, then scoots her feet underneath. "I am stuffed to the gills. It was marvelous of you two to have brought . . . well . . . just about everything."

"We're glad you've returned. It's been deathly quiet out here, what with your cottage empty," Howard breaks off as Johnny punches him after the "deathly quiet" part. "I mean, not *deathly*, just—sorry."

Ruby dismisses Howard's apology with a wave of her hand. "Before I forget, just for the record, and since you're our neighbors, you'll be happy to know . . . I've willed this place to Eve." The boys exchange a glance. "Not that I'm planning on dropping dead or anything."

"You're not . . . ill or . . . ?" Howard asks carefully, leaning forward, alarm in his voice.

"Lord no, knock on wood. Eve here thought the very same thing." Ruby knocks on my head. "It's something I've been thinking about for some time now. You know, Ed and I had no children, I'm not getting *much* younger and *what the hell!*"

Everyone laughs with relief and the tension disappears. When Ruby swears it just sounds so right.

"We're considering the idea—*just* an idea, mind you—of *living* here . . . maybe," I say as I sit up while carefully holding my front—in case. "If for no other reason than to get out of the city. I've lived in Eau Claire all my life and the thought of living on an island has an exotic appeal."

"We're trying to come up with some ideas for making an income up here too, and then there's the winters to consider," Ruby adds.

"What *kind* of ideas?" Johnny asks.

"Well . . ." I sit up straight, then stand up, thinking of my top and swish over to stand in front of the fireplace. "I've had a business of my own for years and though I love Eau Claire, I'm feeling there's opportunity here." Suddenly I realize it's more than that. "Seeing the lake, the dock with sunsets like I've never seen, I'm starting to feel like the minute we *do* leave for Eau Claire, we're going to *miss* something."

For the first time in a long while I feel just great about something other than my salon. There's more to me than what I do. I look around and wonder if I could make this place *Eve and Ruby's* instead of Ed and Ruby's.

"Eve's salon is a lovely little shack," Ruby chides. "And she's the queen of color and God knows I've paved her way to success, handing over *buckets* of money to ensure my beauty is . . . maintained."

"Thanks buckets," I chide right back, then feel as though my rear is starting to blister from the fireplace. I quickly move away and sit back down, my skirt puffing around me. "You know . . . I've been doing hair forever. I've seen the same hairstyles come and go and come and go and maybe it's time for me to go too—*way* time, actually."

"I know the feeling," Johnny says. "Like any job you do for too long. Especially being responsible for someone's look. It takes a lot out of you, and clients can be incredibly demanding *and* unforgiving."

"No kidding," I say, agreeing somewhat. I must admit I've never had a client leave mad, but there's been a few I would have loved to . . . Never mind. "I have concerns for all the chemicals I inhale too, but more than that, maybe it's simply time."

"One of our ideas is to give tours while dodging about the island in the duck," Ruby says. "I could chat it up over the mike. Maybe we pop over to Bayfield, hit some of the local restaurants for coffee, then on to an orchard or two."

"Or . . . we could turn the barn or the boathouse into some kind of sewing or weaving or rug-hooking place . . . maybe," I say, pondering while gazing at the flames as they snap and sputter.

"I think you're onto something and both of us"—Johnny gestures toward Howard—"admire you. Hell, we did pretty much the same thing."

"You know . . . dear one," Howard says through a big yawn, "it's time we head home."

"Well, it *is* getting late," Ruby says, getting up. "Eve and I have to go back in the morning as she has to be in the salon

Tuesday. My goodness, have we really been here just the week-end?"

"Seems as though we've lived a lifetime up here." I rise up carefully, smoothing my dress. "Has nothing to do with the fact that slave driver here worked me to death to clean this joint!" I jerk my head in Ruby's direction.

"Builds character, darling." Ruby winks at me.

We pack up the leftover casserole for the boys. It *has* to leave our fridge. Hug and kiss them like the friends they've so quickly become to me and wave them out the door. We stand on the veranda, dressed in gowns from another era and breathe the crispy night air. I'm thinking that all of life leads us to just the right place at the most perfect moment.

We wander back into the living room and sit down on the sofa. In a sleepy daze we watch the last of the fire burn down to glowing red embers. It pulses as though breathing; the whis-pering sounds slowly disappear.

"Such a weekend! So many things to consider!" Ruby says. "And you know, love? We are only building up steam for . . . well . . . something."

"Something," I reply, agreeing with her. I haven't strayed from my salon life *ever,* yet thoughts of letting it go are feeling more and more right.

"I remember the day we met. You didn't have a single client on your books. I stole a peek," Ruby admits and I smile. "So . . . after you made me look so heavenly, I went and got us some lunch from Mona Lisa's. You were quite surprised. It was worth it just to see your expression." She sighs.

"You've been so good to me. I wish you could've met my folks, they would have gotten such a kick out of you," I say for the hundredth time. Some things you need to say over and over.

"Let's go out and bid goodnight to the moon. Shall we?"

"I have a better idea. Grab a couple of coats off the back door and meet me out front."

"What the hell?"

"Ruby darling . . . do as you're told!"

I blow around the corner of the cottage in the duck, stop to pick up Ruby, who's standing on the stoop in the glare of the headlights with her thumb up for a ride, and down into the moonlit lake we splash. The stereo is blasting Billie Holiday singing "God Bless the Child" and we're singing along. I couldn't imagine it getting any better.

CHAPTER SIX

The next morning I wake early, throw on my robe and head downstairs for a coffee fix. For some reason I'm rushing, so I catch myself halfway down the stairs and slow my movements, trying to notice everything for future reference.

"Hello Rocky. I wondered where you ran off to last night," I say as I walk into the kitchen. I pet his purring head and give him fresh water. Filling my mug full of java, a cat mug of course, I head to the dock. The day is beginning to take shape and it's leaning toward the cloudy side. When the sun peeks out, it's like a burst of color that quickly slinks behind bruised-looking lavender clouds.

Sitting down at the end of the dock, I slip out of my furry slippers and dip my feet into the cold water, which sends a wake-up shock from my painted toes straight to my heart. Nice way to get it pumping and my mind thinking and freezing my ass off all at the same time!

So much has happened. I'm feeling odd inside. This morning the cracked, chipped mirror in my bathroom upstairs reflected a different me. I look, well I can't seem to put my finger on it, but there's a change somewhere.

I've read, in one of my many read-this-and-be-a-better-person books, that when you grow or try new things, *that* in turn can lead you to *think* new things. Which in turn allows you to *do* new things. Maybe "allows," is a silly word; it's more like you just have to or you'll burst.

I'm changing and it's so *nice.* I'd actually like to seriously consider a life on Madeline Island. How's that for being steadfast and true? Like saying, *I'd love to do this or that, maybe, possibly, I'll let you know.* I'm ready to move, not really away *from,* though; it feels more like *to.*

This new ritual of putting my feet in the water seems to clarify my thoughts. Sometimes I can get to thinking and doing about a zillion things all at once. Makes even *me* crazy. Something as simple as being connected to the water brings my internal rhythm down a notch or two.

I hear the familiar clatter of dishes inside the cottage and realize it's time to say good-bye to the lake. I'll settle for "see you later." Rising slowly, stretching up toward the sky, I slip my wet feet into my Pooh slippers. I dash up the dock and through the screened porch door, which slaps behind me. Stopping on the veranda, I turn and give the door a swing to hear that wonderful porch-door-slam noise again.

We close up the cottage, roll all the shades down around the porch and then give every door and window a final check. After all the window-latching and door-pulling, we light up and sit down on the back-porch stoop for a good smoke.

My Levi's are turned up, showing off my flower-covered

sandals. My hair is a mass of curls, knotted in back. I push up my nose, raising the Jackie O sunglasses that eventually slide back down. Ruby is in a long summer dress, her wrists loaded with bracelets. She reaches up to adjust leopard sunglasses, her green earrings glittering in the sunshine.

We both took our sweet time getting ready, neither one of us wanting to go. So here we sit with the van all packed. Rocky's asleep in the front seat surrounded by coffee-stained maps, lipsticks, an empty cooler and my music. Even the toenails are done. I look down and wiggle a few.

"I guess we should hit the road—huh?" I make a smoke ring that catches in the wind, then disappears.

"The sooner we do, the sooner we'll be back, I should think," Ruby adds with the gusto I need.

"Do you feel anything weird? Or is it just me?"

"I feel wonderful, actually," Ruby says as smoke puffs out her nose. "Just wonderful."

"Me too, I guess. The weird feeling is actually the newness of finding all this here," I say, opening my arms wide. "But I think we smoke too much *and* if we intend to live this cottage-by-the-lake life of God only knows what, well . . . maybe we should *try* to quit."

"I've smoked on and off for the last hundred years and I honestly can't *imagine* quitting," Ruby stammers uncertainly. "It *is* rather expensive though."

"Not to mention the smell. How about we quit?" I stand up, fling my cigarette butt to the ground and grind it out with my chunk heel. Hands on hips. Knowing full well Ruby loves a challenge.

"I have so few bad habits left, darling, I just don't know."

Ruby looks her burning cigarette over skeptically. "I think I need *one* horrid, icky habit—just one."

"If *I'm* quitting, you are too and that's that." My painted fingernails drumming on hips now.

"Well . . . I could find some *other* terrible habit. I mean, if you're going to put it *that* way." Ruby drops her cigarette and stamps it out with the dainty point of her designer sandal.

We hop in the van, pull the doors shut and off we chug. The van slips through the trees, down and around and back through the way we came, all to the sounds of Connie Evingson singing "Fever." Snapping along to the beat, we ease through the gate, lock it behind us and head off to the ferry-boat landing. Not looking back once.

In line ahead of us, waiting in designer fashions, are Fat Kid and Lipstick. This time he's munching his way through a bag of potato chips while sipping soda out of a huge straw. She's delicately worrying an apple, taking small, feeble nibbles so as to maintain her perfectly applied lips. I look over at Ruby and we bust out laughing.

We've been driving for about an hour, smooth and easy. Rocky is still asleep in his basket. I'm sure he's dreaming of all the creatures he munched, crunched, chased and then dragged into the kitchen to present as gifts.

Right outside the city limits of Rice Lake, I turn to Ruby. "About this smoking thing . . . the quitting part, I mean."

"Let's start stopping smoking . . ."

"Next week!" We both say in a burst of energy that makes us laugh.

Before you can say "Eau Claire, Wisconsin," both of us are

taking deep cancerous puffs while rolling down the windows. Chris Isaak croons over the speakers, "Baby Did a Bad Bad Thing." I know that smoking is bad, but hell—it's not *that* bad. Is it?

"So . . . what's the plan?" Ruby asks, smoke slipping out her nose.

"Feels weird huh?" I say and Ruby nods. "Like we've been gone for *weeks.*"

"You know, I haven't felt this sure in the longest time. It's really very simple. Moving . . . starting over, but at my age it's usually to a nice assisted-living apartment."

"For God's sake, you're not *that* old."

"So true, so very true." She hands me a Reese's Peanut Butter Cup all unwrapped, then pops one in her mouth too. With goo sticking to her gums, she admits, "These are really very tasty. I've never been partial to chocolate with peanut butter, but I see the appeal."

I nod and smile. "Are you *really* going to sell your house? I mean, you could *rent* or—"

"Oh I suppose I could." She opens another Reese's. "But really, I'm not the landlady type."

"Me either. It's really the best time to move on, while the iron's hot, so to speak. My business is great, clients are wonderful but I click into autopilot and drift through the days. Must explain why so often lately I haven't the foggiest idea what day it *is*. I hadn't realized it until I got away from it. You know what I mean?"

"*Do* I," Ruby says with vigor. "When you've mastered a thing, eventually it becomes second nature and you stop being there. I certainly know what *that* feels like. I felt that daze when Ed died. I knew how to be 'Ed and Ruby' so well, I forgot who *I* was."

"I would love to *not* be in a business that has my varicose veins under pressure, not to mention those chemicals."

"Let's unhook," Ruby says slowly. "Sell out and pack up as soon as possible. Why not?"

"I don't know. . . . I haven't any loose ends, I guess," I say, thinking. "Maybe Watts would consider managing the salon. Or Dorothy. No, she's not the salon-manager type. Then again, neither is Watts, but I'd love to help her out. Dorothy's got a husband and all those kids to feed and fuss over, but Watts—I know she could use the extra money, but more importantly, this will give her some responsibility, the boost into being independent. I'd really like her to have that."

"How that Watts dresses, all those torn clothes, but I must say, she's a feisty one—and you need that to run a salon."

"I *love* how she dresses; it's her style. Besides, I've been saving since junior high school. I *do* have an IRA and a little money invested, thanks to that handsome man at Bank One. Damn, it's sick how much it takes to live. How much is enough?"

"Money. You know, it seems to mean more to people all the time. "More" certainly is the word of the hour, week . . . whatever. But as far as *my* money goes"—Ruby pats my arm—"I have a little savings, the house and cottage both paid for, but— I'm not actually dripping with cash; I only dress that way. Having all this class is such a burden at times."

"You smell something? Really though, what better motivation for finding some sort of income source than food, cigarettes and property taxes? We'll simply have to . . . rob a bank."

"Even though Ed's grandfather ran a successful trucking company and left his only son—Ed's father—well taken care of, he was a big spender. Very showy, lots of fancy parties and such. So by the time it got to Ed, there wasn't a whole lot left."

"Oh man—I want this to work, but we'd have to make some dough, ya know?"

"Enough to cover the basics. Besides, I can't imagine a little thing like money stopping the likes of us."

"You know, we're just crazy enough . . ."

"Certifiable . . . I hear you chatting it up with your clients. Chucking about all those encouraging adjectives like candy. Isn't it about time you did some *just-do-it, sisters?* Hmmm?"

I smile and nod—busted by the Brit. Again.

I've dropped off Ruby at her place and am back upstairs sitting in my apartment, sipping a mug of Sleepy Time tea and thinking, while Rocky purrs in my lap. Looking around, I wonder if I'll miss it here. I will. I won't.

Odd how small it feels. Closed in, and there's not much of a view from any of my windows either. Unless you call looking at an alley or on to a busy street a view. Funny, I used to love these views. Now I'm wondering where the hell the trees are.

It's weird how quickly I fell into the magic of the cottage, the oldness of it, the lake, and of course, the dock. The sky up north seems so much bigger too—more vast and endless. Even in Eau Claire you can't see nearly that many stars at night.

I can't imagine slipping back into the person I was just last Friday. I try to see myself *not* moving up to Madeline Island and there's nothing. Besides, I'd always wonder what my life would have been like there. Here, I'm pretty sure it would meander on—nothing *wrong* with that. Oh hell, it sounds awful. "My life meandered on and so did I." End of story. Yuck.

I've missed out on not being closer to nature, too. I'd rather hear the call of a loon or be able to knock around in the woods. Take a moonlit boat ride or ice-skate right out the front door. Share wine and thoughts with the familiar glow of a smoke on the end of that wonderful dock.

I put Rocky on my shoulder and go downstairs to my salon. It's dark and the air is heavy with smells of hair spray and coffee. My old home. I put on Irene Kral. She softly sings, "It's a Wonderful World." I sit down at my station and ponder my reflection. I smile back and really *see* myself. I *am* pretty. Oh not your normal pretty, but I have a certain beauty. I do.

I spin around and look at all the memories, hear the insanity of a typical hectic day here. I picture myself helping clients relax, laugh, share their lives—dare to *change* their lives—and now it's my turn.

I feel complete with my decision and sure now of how to proceed. I'm done with this; I no longer fit here. I'm ready. Besides, if I don't make this change, Eau Claire will always haunt me in a way that I hadn't wanted to realize. I think I've always held it in the back of my mind that Amy would come looking for me and so I couldn't move—in case. But she never did. I take one more glance around, looking through different eyes. With Rocky at my heels, I head back upstairs to make a few phone calls, take a nice hot shower, a nibble, a book and head to my comfy bed.

Chapter Seven

"Good morning, Watts," I practically sing. "I hope Dorothy's not far behind you, I'm wanting to have a little chat with both of you. 'Course, Dorothy is *always* late, so—"

"What did you and Ruby *do* up there, anyway?" Watts asks while tossing her bags into the break room. "You look . . . different. You change your hair color? No . . . it's not that. Lost weight?"

I wave off that one. "Thank you, for noticing *something,* anyway. To be honest, I *do* feel different. I've so much going on in my head right now, and I—"

"Whatever it is, I sure would like some." Watts moves her eyebrows up and down.

"Let's grab some coffee and go sit out back for a minute."

We fill our favorite mugs and head through the back door to sit on the patio furniture in the alley. I feel like a visitor here now and that seems okay.

Rocky jumps into my lap, right on cue, to give me moral support. This *is* a major event for me and hopefully for Watts, too. I'm more excited than anything. I light up and blow a nice big smoke ring, Watts follows suit. She smokes those horrible clove things. As if my smoke smells nice.

I study Watts, envying her in a way that catches me for a moment. What would it be like to be so young again. 'Course, I wasn't ever *that* young. I've always taken things so seriously. Will I come back here in two weeks begging her to hand me back the salon? Have I lost my mind?

"I've never learned how to do that." Watts pulls me back as a clove cloud sweeps over me. "You getting married or something, Eve? I know! You did that artificial sperm thing." She grins.

I take a deep breath, then plunge in. "I'd like you to manage the salon; tell that landlord of yours to take a leap—move into my apartment upstairs." I pull out a simple contract I drew up last night instead of cashing in on some much needed beauty sleep. Watts reads the salary I'm proposing and looks up with enormous, bulging eyes.

"You're going to pay me *what?* Is this some kind of a joke or something? It's too early for this shit, Eve." She plants both feet on the ground, about to bolt from crazy me.

"I'm done doing hair and *yes* . . . I want you to manage for me. And since I own the place and if you hire another person . . ." I'm enjoying this. It is the right thing to do (I think).

"What will *you* do? My God Eve, half of Eau Claire comes to you and the other half would die to get in and you're just handing it over to me?" Watts asks, a bit confused but slowly catching on. "I don't get it and I think it's time you started on the medication thing, 'cause honey, you have *lost* your mind."

"Look, Ruby and I are—"

"You know, if you ask me"—she straightens in her chair—
"I think it's really kind of weird, you hanging around with a
woman old enough to be your mother and . . . well, I worry
about you. When is the last time you were *laid,* for crying out
loud? You and her—you're not *girlfriend*-girlfriends, are you?
Not that there's anything wrong with that, but—"

"Oh Jesus, Watts, for heaven's sake. Ruby is my best friend,
you know that . . . I mean, she's cute, but I only have eyes for
Rocky." I sing the last part. "As far as the last time I was laid . . .
hell, must have been . . . Never mind." It's been that long.

I wonder if other people wonder about Ruby and me. Who
the hell cares? The thought of that scrawny woman naked
makes me want to hand her a robe and show her to the
kitchen!

"My God, if I go more than a week . . . weekend . . . I can't
imagine. You poor thing, I had no idea. No wonder. Oh, Eve, if
you just got out more. You know . . . I have this friend of mine.
He's not all that much to look at, but I hear he's a real tiger in
the hay and—"

"Watts . . . *hello,* I'm trying to tell you I'm leaving and all
you can think of is getting laid?" I have to laugh. Just then
Dorothy's enormously tall and swirled-up hairdo peeks
through the back door. Over her rhinestone bifocals she says,
"Good morning all. You got laid, Eve? Oh my, I would *love* to
hear the details, but I have to run my husband over to the Y
and then take little Billy to practice; see you all in a couple of
hours. You *do* look peppy, Eve; you're glowing, you little sex
kitten. Bye now," Dorothy singsongs, waves, and disappears.
We hear the front door open and close. I glance at Watts, shaking my head and we burst out laughing.

"How could you leave *that?*" Watts asks. "Have you been smoking weed, Eve? Is there someone I can call?"

"I'm serious, Watts. You've worked with me for over eight years. I've watched you struggle with so much and it would give me a hell of a thrill to help you. Consider it payback for all those years of putting up with me." I feel old, wise and motherly all wrapped together.

"I don't know what to say," Watts replies quietly. She gets teary-eyed; so am I. It's all coming to be. I'm really doing this. I haven't lost my mind after all. Besides, I could come crawling back if—no, I'm far too stubborn for that.

Through snivels she asks, "You *are* going to fix those roots before you move, aren't you ?"

"How the hell can I afford to at the rates they charge here?" I reach out to give her a hug. What a wonderful feeling to be able to pass along a part of something that's been very dear to me. So this is what it feels like to let go of something that all at once I realize was holding me back. Now Watts can grow it into her own and maybe, if things work out, Watts could buy me out someday.

"What're you going to do? This is your home," Watts asks in between honking her nose.

"Ruby and I are moving to Madeline Island and we're going into business for ourselves. Doing what, you ask? Well . . . we haven't figured out the details yet, but hey, what's the rush?"

"You *have* flipped. That's the end of the world up there. What will you do in the winter? I've been there, though . . . It's beautiful. I bet they could use an upscale hair salon, but in the winter, Eve—you'll go crazy."

"I can't wait."

* * *

It's around lunchtime. I've asked Watts to begin the process of moving my clients to hers and Dorothy's already packed schedules. Now that I've made my mind up, I can't seem to get things done fast enough. That's how I've always been, though; I make up my mind and then I can hardly stand still until I'm doing what I made up my mind to do.

Watts and Dorothy have been crying on and off and it's driving me crazy. Maybe I have come a bit unscrewed, but if it feels this good, I have nothing to worry about. I've invited them up for dinner tonight so we can spend some time together *and* I want to show them I'm not falling apart or joining a cult or any of the other things I overheard Dorothy whispering about. Ruby is taking me to Woo's Pagoda for lunch. I can't wait; I need to get out of here.

"Eve's salon," I say into the phone.

"It's all over town and it's just noon!" I hear the familiar blowing sound as Ruby exhales a big cloud of smoke and I wait a beat for her to take a breath. "I called my Realtor and he thinks it's a quick sell, so let's pick a date and—"

"They think we're lesbians, you know," I whisper into the phone so that no one in the salon will hear.

I'm giggling though, and after Ruby is done cackling in my ear, she says, "Oh I will miss this town, but it's not like we're moving that far away or anything. Lesbians eh?"

"Get over here and take me to lunch," I demand, a bit louder than I mean to.

"I'll be there as soon as I've located a fresh, clean bra and matching panties. Can't seem to find my Tuesday set and seeing as it's now . . . Oh, never mind . . . ta ta, darling . . . see you soon," Ruby clicks off.

I scoot upstairs, shuck off my jeans and whip over my head a favorite cotton dress covered with white daisies. I twist my still damp hair up into a French roll and rush around trying to find my other sandal. I'm hopping by one of my bookshelves in the living room and notice how the sunlight is slanting in from the skylight and hitting a picture.

It's of my mom and me. We're sitting on the front stoop of my folk's house; I must be around thirteen. I wipe the dust off with the hem of my dress and can't help but notice that my mom is wearing this very dress.

How could I have forgotten? This was *her* dress, and today is the date she died. It hits me in the heart and I slink down on my sofa, clutching the picture to my chest. I close my eyes. Remembering, I see her in the hospital bed. She suffered a se-ries of strokes and was not doing well toward the end.

"You mustn't worry about me, Eve," my mom had said in a faint whisper. "I saw your grandfather last night in a dream . . . he looked so happy. He told me not to be afraid, that he'll take care of me. So now you can take care of you, dear."

"Oh Mom," I murmur out loud now—as I did back then, too. Fresh tears slide down my cheeks.

"Follow your heart Eve. I'll not be too far away, not too far, dear." She slipped away, was in a coma for a while and then left altogether.

Sighing, I swear I can smell her perfume in a breeze that whispers across my neck. I know in my soul I'm doing the right thing and that Mom is with me, always.

My thoughts drift over to Amy—again. Ruby's right; it *was* years ago and now there's the Internet and maybe, just maybe

I'll find her. Rocky jumps into my lap, scaring me to death, or rather—to life.

"I'm starved." Ruby pulls out a red vinyl chair and sits down across from me.

"I told the girls at the shop," I say. "Watts will be taking over and all they can do is cry and look at me as though my arms fell off or something."

"Oh, I'm sure it's a shock," Ruby replies, checking her face in a tiny mirror. "You've been their strength for so long, as well as their fearless leader. You'll be very missed."

"Thank you, that's sweet. . . . I know that, I guess. I just don't want everyone to be so *sad*. Dorothy had to have me blow out one of her clients' hair this morning 'cause she couldn't stop wailing." I sip my green tea.

"Things will all settle down, you'll see." Ruby touches my arm lightly. "Hey, I listed my place right after we hung up. How about you and I throwing together a garage sale?"

"I think we should donate whatever we don't want." I know that if I sold my old junk I'd have too much time to think it over and most likely end up pulling everything out the last minute and then buying some of Ruby's stuff too!

The waitress zooms by, takes our order and in minutes our food arrives, so we eat, sip our tea and enjoy the hustle and bustle around us.

"Have you any regrets or change of heart, darling?" Ruby asks with a slurping sound as a noodle snakes into her dark red mouth.

"Yes, but only fleeting."

Fleeting, more like *freeing*. I honestly wasn't one hundred percent sure, but once I made the offer to Watts to take over my salon, well, then I knew this whole change is real. Amazing how one action puts into motion so many others. Why in the world didn't I do this sooner if it feels this right?

"I've lived in my house on Rust Street for over thirty years," Ruby says. "I can't wait to sort through the lot Ed and I collected and let go of some of it . . . lighten up a bit."

"If you help me, I'll help you. God, I have so many books, I don't know if I can get rid of them either. A few . . . maybe."

"Oh heavens, we have that huge old barn to store things in and anything we can't part with—good Lord—bring it!" Ruby smacks her teacup down for good measure. A table of blue-hairs next to us looks over; I smile politely. Ruby can be a little heavy in the drama department.

"Ruby, I don't have *that* much stuff, but you're right, we should try to get rid of the extras."

"Actually, the cottage *does* have about everything we could need. I can't *wait* to take some of those dead animals down from the rafters—creepy glass eyes, following you every-where."

"There *are* a lot of stuffed things hanging around." I won-der if grizzly bears ever stuff their human victims. "Thinning out that collection would be a very cool idea." I wonder if she'll let me move around the furniture.

"Yes—very cool: Eve and Ruby hit the road and head to the islands and it's so *cool,*" Ruby replies. "Cool" just doesn't seem to work for her. "I wonder if the *Leader-Telegram* will run pho-tos of us waving from the van?"

"I'm off the books and officially done at Eve's Salon," I say. "It feels weird. What are you looking at?"

"I am thinking how fortunate I am to have you as my confidant," Ruby simply states. "I had no *idea* this would be how things would turn out. You know . . . doing *this,* making all these changes together. A girl my age doesn't usually think that all of a sudden the sun is going to be shining again . . . and so *bright,* too. I'm so grateful, darling." She brushes my arm like she does, to let me know she feels more but can't say more.

"Me too; me too. Let's blow this joint. I have to get dinner going for Dorothy and Watts. I think I'll lay in some extra wine, I'd really like to have a big ol' girls' night. You want to join us? I could use some help and I'm sure it's going to be a hoot."

"Sounds lovely, darling. I need to do some errands this afternoon. Then I can swing by around, say . . . five, so we can get things cooking."

"You're a gem."

"I know; I know."

I'm walking through the park and along the river that flows quietly underneath the Water Street bridge. Thinking back, I can remember as a child how I used to try to keep up with my mom and dad as they went from one shop to another up and down Barstow Street. Now it's a ghost street. The old J.C. Penney building is office space and Kresge's Department Store, where I bought my first box of tampons, stands empty. Some changes I don't get.

I *will* miss all the beautiful homes in what we locals call

Third Ward, the neighborhood across the river. It's an area where the lumber barons built their enormous, lavish mansions. They stand three and four stories high, with turrets and dormers galore. The woodwork, stained-glass windows and crystal chandeliers can all be spied by simply "happening to be out for a stroll" when it's dark. I figure, if the drapes are open and the lights are on, I'm peeking.

It's like a favorite rock, like the one on my windowsill upstairs. It's from out of this very river and I know exactly where I'll put it in the cottage. It's funny how something as simple as a rock can connect you to a place. I'll still be me; I'll still have all this with me and that makes me happy, complete. Taking a deep breath, I turn and walk back to my shop, up the back stairs to my apartment. Reaching into my pocket, I put a new rock beside the old one, right there on my windowsill.

CHAPTER EIGHT

"Found some *gorgeous* red-leaf lettuce I thought we could use with whatever we find in your fridge," Ruby says, unloading her grocery bags. "That Kerm's Market across the street has everything. Whose garden did you nick these lovely daisies from?"

"For once, I didn't pinch them; they're from Avalon's flower shop and aren't they huge?" I arrange them in a favorite old milk bottle. "What *is* it about a vase full of daisies? 'Course, I would have gotten more, but they cost a fortune."

"You must have done some *getting rid of* already," Ruby remarks. "Feels more roomy in the living room here. Oh, I know what it is: no more books piled on the floor!"

"They're gone from the floor, the tables, and most of the stacks I had in corners have been sorted through, too. I gathered them up and unloaded them into the very happy hands of the guy at the Wax Paper bookstore." I'm pulling a volume of poetry out from under my sofa. No wonder it felt hard there.

"The ones I couldn't part with are packed up in boxes and piled along the wall in my bedroom."

"I'll get some water to boil and start some wild rice. When are the girls due?" Ruby asks while opening cupboards and slamming down a big pot onto the stove. She is the noisiest cook.

"Dorothy is finishing up a perm, in case you hadn't smelled it, and Watts ran home to get something."

"When I had the House of China all those years ago, I should have had the crew over to the house more. I simply did-n't have the energy or the time, I suppose." Ruby fills the pot with water.

"I forget about your shop. You sold china and what else?" I ask, watching her make a mess in no time flat.

"China, stoneware, giftware, glassware and silverware, too. We had an enormous bridal registry. It was wonderful fun for a time, then the highway in front was moved, the malls came and . . ." Ruby sighs. "Ed and I decided to finally shut it down. So I have far too many sets of dishes and glasses *and* silver-ware, not to mention an entire closet full of crystal bowls. Never can tell when you may need a last-minute gift," she says in defense.

"How can one have too many sets of anything like that? I have such a mixture of mismatched everything, I bet I don't even have a matching table setting for one!"

"You don't, darling."

"Knock knock, is this a good time?" Dorothy asks, standing in the stairway leading up from the salon.

She's wearing peach-frost lipstick and is dressed in slacks and a long beige top bulging slightly around her middle, but all you notice is the hair. Glow-in-the-dark carrot red, piled high and swirled, like it's about to leap off into the air. I am not a big fan of backcombing, not the entire *head* at least; Dorothy does it all day long. She grins over her bifocals.

"Get in here, girl," I command while absently shoving the poetry book back under the cushion and letting it plop down. "Let's pour you some wine. Pull up a sofa and take a load off."

I offer a glass and she sits down next to a sleeping Rocky, putting her feet up on my newly cleared coffee table. I love it when people feel so cozy they do that.

"Oh this is so nice of you, Eve. Hello Ruby—my goodness you're the sight. Is that a new color or have I not seen this one yet?" Dorothy asks, adjusting her glasses.

"Lovely to see you, Dorothy. No . . . this is—well, it could be new. We brightened it up a bit, too," Ruby replies. She wipes her hands on her apron, then slips a wooden spoon into one of the front pockets and pats her hair.

"My goodness . . . had such a busy day, what with fitting in Eve's clients *and* my own. All the gossip about what's going on and all . . . well, I'm so grateful to sit." Dorothy blathers on and on. I shoot an eye-rolling face to Ruby. " 'Course it's nice to be here and not at *home,* where if it's not a kid pulling on my leg, it's that man of mine; oh he's such a—"

"I am *sure* your family can handle one night of you being away, at least for a little while." Ruby gives the rice a stir and pushes me out of the kitchen area. "Besides, maybe you'll be appreciated more when you *are* home."

"Oh Eve"—Dorothy pats my arm as I sit next to her—"I'm so proud of you . . . jealous too. I mean, picking up and moving like this." She takes my hand in hers, holding it for a moment.

She reaches up to push her shellacked bangs around, pulling this and moving that. Her hair doesn't move one iota, but this is what she does when she doesn't know what to do with her nervous hands. I'm wondering what stupid habit I have that must drive people nuts!

"Boy, would I love to retire," Dorothy laments. "But with three kids, college looming in the future, lordy. Just to put food on the table and beer in the fridge, well I don't have to tell *you* how much it costs to live." She sighs, fiddling with her charm bracelet.

"No, but then you do have a family and for heaven's sake Dorothy, loosen up and tell that husband of yours to get a better job or something." He irritates the hell out of me. "Besides, we have no intention of *retiring*."

"I wish I had the guts. He is such a lazybones, can't seem to find the *right* job. His back gives him grief, too, and now he has to watch his blood pressure, not to mention his terrible allergies."

"Listen to you. For pity's sake, Dorothy . . ." I can feel myself getting testy. Why is it we all consider ourselves victims? As if on cue, Watts appears at the balcony door.

"Right on time." I slide open the screen door. "Come in and join us; we're busy solving Dorothy's problems. I was telling her to get a small handgun, something with a silencer, and say to the cops she was cleaning it when all by itself it went *BANG!*"

"Hey everyone!" Watts breezes in. "I've been here a full minute; drink please." Ruby smiles and waves her into the kitchen.

Watts is dressed in torn-to-shreds jeans and some of the

highest-heeled chunk sandals I've seen on her yet. She tosses her "road warrior" leather coat on the floor and pushes up the sleeves of her skin-tight mint green top.

"You're such a kidder, Eve—really." Dorothy chuckles. "You wouldn't have a gun I could borrow though, would you?"

"What would you like to sip, darling? Wine? I bet I could find a beer in the fridge if I look hard enough. What the *hell* is this?" Ruby holds up a mold-covered something she found in my crisper drawer. I take it and dump the whole works into the garbage. It thuds to the bottom and we giggle.

"Wine of course!" Watts sits down on a chair in the kitchen, then pops up again. "Make it a double. Whatever you have brewing on that stove sure smells amazing," she says, lifting lids and taking big sniffs.

Ruby is all about her cooking. Garlic bread browns in the oven, a huge salad is being tossed into bowls—mixing bowls, mind you—and the nutty-smelling wild rice with raisins and vegetables is cooling in the sink. A Ruby original. Nothing can drive a hungry person crazier than yummy food smells.

We end up sitting around my coffee table, eating on our laps. I've lumped a bunch of throw pillows together and am sitting on those.

"I don't know really *where* to start," I say around a mouthful of crispy bread. "I mostly want you two to know how much I've appreciated working with you. I *refuse* to make this a good-bye, but I wanted to spend some time together and—"

"Eve . . . I think it's *us* that should be thanking *you*," Watts interrupts. "All the times you've spent trying to put my life on track. Giving out all that wisdom and advice . . . and bullshit too, of course. Then there's me repeating the same stupid things with the same stupid men."

"That's so darn true. Why, all those times you slipped me extra cash to cover the rent!" Dorothy slugs back a big gulp of wine. "Lordy . . . I'll never forget when you grabbed me and we went rushing over to Luther Hospital, nearly running into some old woman on a bike, then you parked on the lawn and *hurried* me into the emergency room.

"That was the time my little Billy had swallowed a bottle of allergy pills and had to have his stomach pumped. He's always been far too clever at opening things. I remember I was putting in a perm and . . . Whatever happened to her?"

"I've never had the heart to tell you," Watts says, "but Irma's hair got fried all to hell! We had to cut most of it off." Everyone looks at Dorothy. She bursts out laughing, practically throwing her wine in the air.

"Her hair was fuzz to begin with! Oh my, all this time and I could never figure why she'd always bring her own timer out when I put her under the heat!" A tear runs down Dorothy's red face. We all laugh some more.

"What a team you three have been," Ruby states. We look at each other. All four of us raise our glasses to meet in the middle of the now dish-laden coffee table.

"To the best group of hair-miracle-workers Eau Claire has ever seen *and* to three very dear friends," I cheer. "To the future!"

"To four really fucking fantastic babes." We all look at Dorothy, who never says the F-word, then laugh and laugh. Cackle is more like it.

Ruby pours more wine around. Later, everyone gets up to

help tidy. Ruby is the washer, handing off clean, piping-hot, dripping dishes to Watts and Dorothy, who in turn give them to me to put away. We're done in no time at all. The group re-assembles in the living room, where all feet are up on the now spotless coffee table.

"What a wonderful time I've had. I'm stuffed clear to my brain and am *I* going to have a whopper of a headache in the morning." Dorothy straightens her straight bangs. "Hey, hold on—Madeline Island! I have a cousin who lives in Bayfield. We talk all the time. The gossip is thick up there, seeing as it's rather isolated, especially in the winters."

"What *kind* of gossip?" I ask. "I mean Eau Claire's pretty darn chatty, if you ask me."

"Well, Lilly, that's my cousin's name, has been telling me about some creep—Al, I think is his name—who owns the Liquor Lounge on the island. It's a bar," she spits out "bar" like it's a dirty word. "*Apparently* he's his own best customer *and* Bonnie, the poor wife, has been in and out of the hospital with suspicious injuries. Word has it"—Dorothy leans way in and half-whispers—"he's been in jail a few times, even." She leans back with a "Top that one" look.

I'm thinking what gossips we are, but—that being said—I pull closer and ask, "Just how do you know all this?"

"Lilly has a lady friend that works in the gift shop at the medical center."

"God, what is it with some women?" Watts offers. "I would never let a guy hit me; he'd be on his butt in seconds flat *and* I guarantee he'd never have children either!"

"Oh shoot, let's get back to my up-and-coming headache," Dorothy says. "Maybe one more little sip."

"Leave it to Ruby," I reply. "I don't think there's anything left. Hey! What the *hell* was *that?*" I say, hearing a loud pinging sound.

"Sounds like someone threw a rock at your balcony door," Watts says.

"What the . . . ?" I open the glass door so I can look down and yell at the jerk for pinging something at my door, but I'm met by a resounding . . .

"SURPRISE!!!"

There must be close to a hundred people crammed into my back alley, all looking up at me. I about pee my panties. The other three girls gather around me, and we all look down. Watts lifts her glass and leads the whole group in a "Hip-hip-hooray!" Over and over. Then there's a huge wave of voices as everyone starts talking and yelling for me to come down. Music from somewhere blends into the fray.

Ruby puts her arm around me and yells into my ear, "I'm so proud of you, Eve Moss. Now get down there and enjoy yourself!" She gives me a squeeze.

Watts grabs my hand and down into the crazy crowd we go. I look up to see Ruby and Dorothy looking back with tears in their eyes, as are in mine, too. In this moment, I feel so darn lucky.

It was way into the early dawn before the bash-of-my-life broke up. I think I talked to every client I ever had in my chair. Had a bottomless glass of wine and *far* too many smokes. But the hugs, well wishes, promise of visits and all that love was amazing.

This morning, wrapped up tight in my furry yellow robe with several pairs of warm socks on my feet, I'm nursing my second mug of coffee. The sunshine is *way* too bright today. But any second now I'm going to fly into high-packing gear, as it's time to box up my life and get things going.

"Did you have a nice time, Rocky?" I have him all snuggled in my lap. He's purring like crazy. Looking around me, I realize how I'm not going to miss it as much as I thought after all. I slug down the rest of my java, root around for the phone and start down my list.

It's almost three in the afternoon and Ruby and I have been at it here in my apartment for hours. We delivered tons of stuff to Goodwill, but I'm shocked by all the stuff I *still* have. We decided to hire a group of college kids to come over to Ruby's place and haul away the heavy things. We want to have her house ready to put on the market by the end of the week.

"It's hilarious—all the treasures we collect." I shake my head. "We keep this crap, identify ourselves by it and on top of it, pay *more* money to have it insured—yikes!" I fold over the top of yet another box of stuff I could live without, maybe. "It seems a *little* lighter. Yet there's still this mountain of boxes of all the stuff I *can't* part with." I follow the cord back to the phone and call Sammy's. I order a large pizza with shrimp, pineapple and tons of cheese; it's a favorite of ours—we've earned the fat grams.

"I want to donate as much as they'll take of my lot, too." Ruby pulls the coffee table closer and puts her feet up. "Good heavens, who *knows* what we'll find in my attic, not to mention the basement. I only want a few treasures; the rest goes. Speaking of . . . I've got more clothes than a woman ought to, but parting with them, that's going to be nearly impossible."

"I really want to feel as though we're starting fresh. Just think, no Target or Details to shop at, no Kerm's Foods or—"

"What will we do? Oh my God, have we lost our minds?" Ruby sits up, then stands, tossing her head back, laughing her deep, huge laugh. I stare at her, waiting for her head to spin around. "Free! Oh my God, we'll be free of all that crazy spending. Think of all the money we'll save, all the time we'll have to do *other* things. Like, take a walk along the lake or do some canning or plant a garden and really for once, smell the goddamned coffee." She sits back down and I shake my head.

"So . . . you've finally come to your senses and lost your mind on the way, great. There's the pizza . . . Clear a place— some place—and let's chow." I go to pay the kid standing outside my door.

"Hey Eve, heard you were moving north," the handsome teenager says through braces. "Put your money away; this one's on the house. Man—all the times you *way* overtipped me." He hands me the biggest pizza box I've ever seen, leans over it and gives me a kiss on the cheek, turns and takes the stairs two at a time.

He can't be more than seventeen. Tall and as skinny as a bean with the most beautiful brown eyes. Why do men get the lashes that hang clear down to their cheeks? I stand there in the door for a beat or two before turning back to my box-filled living room.

"We haven't any glasses . . . you gave away your dishes and where in *heaven's* name are the forks?" Ruby asks.

"Ruby . . . pour some water into that vase and bring it over here, the hell with etiquette. Anyway, I refuse to eat pizza with a fork." I plunk the box down on the coffee table. Opening it, I take a big, glorious whiff. Sammy's Pizza, this I'll miss.

There are a lot of things I'll miss. I glance over at Ruby and sigh. She plops some ice cubes into the vase, inserts two straws and plunks it down. This is just a place and I'm the one that's filled it with all the memories. To be honest, it's so full of them there's little room for *me* anymore. I reach under the cushion, pull out the book that's been poking me in the rear and toss it into a box. *That* comes with.

We lunge at the pizza, slurp big gulps out of the vase and end up stuffed, happy and pooped. Slumping back into my big old sofa, feet up, tummies full, both of us fall deliciously asleep.

We're down in Ruby's cramped basement. I have a mink stole wrapped around my neck and a huge broad-brimmed purple hat on my head. Looks great with my bib overalls and red Keds. We've been trying on ancient clothes, coats, gloves, hats, you name it and she's got one in every color. All morning we've been lugging boxes upstairs and stacking them in the garage to be hauled somewhere.

Ruby's wearing a pillbox hat with a long ostrich feather curving from the side, the netting pulled down over her face. We "yea" or "nay" to this frock or that scarf; a lot of these gems of yester-fashion we've decided to take with. You never know when you may need a snakeskin bag, rhinestone heels, or full-length vinyl coat—in bright orange, no less.

"We have to keep *some* of these dresses and the hats, not to mention all these great old jazz records you have. My God woman, have you never had a garage sale?" I ask, pulling on long, silky gloves.

"Oh, I'd lug a few things over to the neighbors when they had a sale, but no . . . never had one myself," Ruby says. "I think some of this should go to the Chippewa Valley Museum. I'd say we're about done here . . . then to the attic. When do we pick up the moving truck?"

"Three. The college kids said they'd help us load it. We need to make sure that Howard and Johnny can help us on the other end, though. We're pretty much done down here. Let's hit the attic!"

We take off our hats and gloves, tossing them into a boxy old suitcase. The top falls with a heavy clunk. We go up to the attic.

"There's really not too much up here. That's a relief." I part a sheet of spider webs. We head over to a dark corner where a huge steamer trunk stands. I try to open the damn thing, but it's stuck.

"Here, let me help you with that." Ruby comes over to my side. "I think it's latched in the middle. Of course—there." She unsnaps a rusty hasp. We each take a side and pull. It opens like a book sitting on its spine.

"How cool is this." I riffle around inside. "All these funny narrow drawers. One half is crammed full of clothes, looks mostly like suits. What's that smell?"

"Mothballs, mildew, mustiness . . . take your pick," Ruby replies. "This was Ed's grandfather's, I believe. He had a trucking business and traveled all over the states when he was a young man."

"One of the drawers is locked, or stuck, or—oh, there, got it. That's odd, this looks kind of new. Here, you open it." I hand Ruby a leather notebook that's zippered shut.

I keep on with my searching; I'm very nosy. Opening drawers and snooping is something I've always loved. Ruby goes and stands next to one of the attic windows, unzipping.

"Well, I'll be damned." She turns pages and tsk-tsks as some loose papers flutter to the floor followed by the clatter of a key.

"What is it?" I ask, bending down to pick up the papers as well as the key. I peer over her shoulder.

"It's a journal of Ed's when he was stationed over in Germany during the war. My my . . . I wonder if he put it here for me to find. How peculiar. He could have tucked it into a drawer downstairs or something. Oh look—some pictures of *me* in here, oh for . . ." Ruby's voice fades away in thought.

"You look beautiful. Was that here in Eau Claire?" I ask, looking at the pictures as she hands them to me.

"Yes . . . my engagement party. I still have that dress somewhere. Here . . . this is our wedding picture that was in the *Leader-Telegram.*"

"Ed was so dashing, my God. I forgot how tall he was and how *short* you are," I say.

"He filled this whole book up." Ruby pages through the notebook. "Look . . . it goes all the way to when he retired from the university. That little devil; I had no idea. You just never know someone all the way through."

"I kind of like that. I think everyone has things and thoughts that are just theirs."

"I don't think I would ever want to know *all* of Ed's

thoughts. He was very deep, you know, yet so . . . tender, a darling."

"These look like old receipts or something." I try to read one of the loose papers. "The pencil writing is so faded, but the year is nineteen twenty-one . . . June thirteenth, and it's about an order being sent out . . . thirty-two somethings. Signed G.P."

"G.P. Hmm . . ." Ruby takes the paper from me and ponders it. "Of course. Gustave Prévost, Ed's grandfather."

"What a curious key and look at the design." I hand it to Ruby.

"That's peculiar—a toad." Ruby rubs away some gunk and shows me. I'll have to give this all a good going-over." She zips the notebook slowly shut, then holds it close to her heart.

The house is full of college kids who are sorting, packing and hauling like crazy. The air crackles with good energy. Madonna is blasting "Holiday" on the stereo, keeping everyone moving. I'm rustling up some edibles for the crew to munch while Ruby chats up a storm on the phone.

Since she has one with the curly cord, it's trailed over the kitchen counter and right on out the back door. I have to lift the damn thing every time I walk across the floor in search of this or that. I'm putting together a platter of cream cheese, lox, sliced onions and lettuce to put on your own bagel, while singing with Madonna. All the windows are open and a marvelous breeze is zipping around.

"Well, that's that," Ruby says, unwinding the cord from around my waist and hanging up the phone while adjusting her hair and closing the fridge door for me.

"Hmmm?" I ask.

"The house . . . it's sold." She admires my platter of tasteful eats.

"You have got to be kidding, it's not even been *shown* yet, has it?"

"My amazing Realtor, Mister Gorgeous, at the Donnellan Agency. He knows a university professor who will take anything in this neighborhood. Didn't even flinch at the price."

"Hot damn woman, give me five." We high five, then stand back, looking dazed. All four of our artfully shaped eyebrows are standing in "shocked mode." "My God. This has been so . . . easy."

"No kidding," Ruby says.

A desperately skinny college dude with spiked blue hair and wearing the tightest T-shirt I've ever *seen* walks into the kitchen. He's holding a stuffed deer head with an old necktie around its severed neck. "You want to donate this or—"

"Donate!" we say, then laugh.

CHAPTER NINE

Once again on the road, we're headed north for the last time as residents of Eau Claire. We opted to pull my VW van behind the moving truck so we can sit together. Ruby's house closing will be done through her attorney and Watts has started repainting what just a few days ago was my apartment. I made her promise not to paint anything black.

I've got on comfy clothes, imitation Ray Bans and, yes—a smoke between my lips. Rocky's tucked into his basket all snuggled with a mink stole. Ruby's clad in leopard stretch pants. Her red shades match her lipstick. Of course.

"What are you staring at?" Ruby asks.

"I was just admiring your skin." Ruby checks her lips in the visor mirror. Oh she's got wrinkles, but when she smiles her face beams, defying time. I pull the visor down and look at *my* face. Bloodshot eyes peer back and I snap it back up.

"Thank you, darling," Ruby replies. "I used to fuss more, then I saw a close-up of Katherine Hepburn and she was lovely. So I said—"

"What the hell!" I feel the same way. "You want to say a little something to properly send us off?"

She thinks for a second. "May the sun always shine, may the creek not rise *too* high, may the Lord protect us, may the furnace run, may the roof not leak, may the plumbing hold, may—"

"Jesus, Ruby," I cut in. "How about 'MADELINE ISLAND, HERE WE COME!' "

We raise our mugs of chocolate-laced coffee and tap them together over Rocky, who lifts his head. He looks at me—at Ruby—and then lets out the strangest meow. We laugh.

Why in the world we've left Eau Claire in such a flurry, I really don't know. Maybe because we know in our hearts that life really, honestly does march by and by *God,* we have things to do!

We sail past the towns of Bloomer, New Auburn, Chetek, Cameron, and then, outside Rice Lake, it's decided a little lunch is in order. I hang a right off 53 and head east to Pioneer Street in search of Norske Nook. Famous for their lefse, which they roll around *anything,* from cheeses to meats.

Lefse, by the way, are flat griddlecakes Norwegians are known for making, mostly around the Christmas season. Then there's the pie. Blackberry cream cheese, cranberry apple, raspberry cheese and sour cream apple blueberry, just to name a few. Topped with half a pound of real whipped cream! Heaven.

We settle on two cups of the soup-of-the-day (vegetable noodle with chicken) and a slice of blueberry pie with two forks. Should do the trick.

"Would you look at the size of this slice of pie?" I ask, knowing full well every bite will be consumed. Weight Watchers would deduct big time for this.

"Poor darling," Ruby whispers between chews. "Our waitress mustn't have a good stylist. You see those roots?"

"I did . . . I can't get over how some women, like Dorothy, *still* spray their hair into a big poof ball. So many women get stuck in a hair time warp," I say, wondering about myself.

"Oh, we are such cats."

"Meow."

"Maybe time warps *do* exist," Ruby suggests. "Could be . . . what you get used to and find the easiest to do. Then you only do *that* for the rest of your life."

"Interesting concept. But I don't know one woman that wouldn't look better if she would *not* backcomb her *do* into a mass of cotton candy. She's attractive—and look at her skin." We both turn and look at her, then back at each other and I know damn well Ruby's thinking we—

"Do you ladies need anything?" I look up into the waitress's blue eyes.

Her name is Marsha Kleven. She's lived in Rice Lake all her life, raised an only daughter by waiting tables and baking wedding cakes. She's just finished helping put that daughter through nursing school. Husband left them high and dry when Alice Anne was just a baby.

Marsha's never remarried, nor even dated. Apparently, there are not a lot of choices in Rice Lake. We're sitting in her spotless pink and white kitchen enjoying some French vanilla coffee. I'm putting the finishing touches on her new hairstyle.

"Well I'll be." Marsha admires her new look. "I wonder if Charlotte of Nila's Cut and Curl Beauty and Tan will be able to copy this."

She's peering into a silver hand mirror. I'm beaming, because, well, not to brag or anything, but Marsha looks one hundred percent better. Softer, more like a woman and not so much like a *character*. Ruby is petting her cat, Putty, shaking her head, grinning.

"I've been slinging hash over at Norske Nook for years, had some pretty interesting offers, mind you, but when you said you *needed* to do my hair. That you had this *vision,* I figured— why not." We laugh.

"Who in the world hasn't wanted a makeover?" I ask, stubbing out my cigarette. "To be honest, I stole the idea from Oprah. I've been *itching* to try it and for some reason I had the feeling *you* were the one."

"I'm so grateful . . . really. It's reassuring to know there are people in the world willing to put their neck out in the name of beauty." Marsha smiles. "What I wouldn't do to take my new look right on out of this town." Ruby and I catch eyes and I'm thinking of humming a few bars of "We're off to see the wizard . . ."

"This seems like a *lovely* town, darling." Ruby looks out a window to the backyard. "You're lucky to have a quaint downtown *plus* a shopping center and all these lovely old homes."

"I guess so, but thanks to the mall, the downtown is dying. Its *nothing* like Eau Claire." Marsha rinses out our coffee cups. "There's so much more to do there and *their* mall is huge, and—"

"Um, we've just left there and . . ." I catch Ruby's raised eyebrow. "It *is* growing and growing and—"

"We're moving north," Ruby adds. "Eau Claire—Rice Lake—all lovely places, but sometimes you need to move in order to know you're changing. A place is just a place, after all."

"I suppose you're right," Marsha says, arms folded, leaning against her gleaming sink. "I'm getting antsy to be somewhere else, though. A different set of people, you know?"

"We *do,* darling." Ruby gets up and pushes in her chair.

"Um, which way to the ladies room?" I'm ready to burst on her shiny floor. "My Keds can hold only so many cups of coffee." Marsha points down the hallway.

"That's Eve, always the lady," Ruby says as I slam the bathroom door.

"It's been hours since inhaling all those fat grams at Norske Nook and I'm still ready to explode!" Ruby adjusts her belt two notches for good measure. "If you plan on rescuing every time-warped hair disaster from here to the cottage . . ."

"Hey . . . so I lost my mind," I say. "I just *had* to do it."

"It was typical of you, darling," Ruby says as we slam the truck doors. "I felt as though I was looking at myself for a moment. Me, twenty years ago—I went out in public with my hair *that* high! Good God." She pats her hair.

I shift into drive and we shimmy up the entrance ramp, easing back onto Highway 53.

"Hey . . . we've all had some amazing 'hair moments.' I'll show you my high school graduation picture. Now there was a style to be afraid of."

"You didn't perm your curly hair, did you?" Ruby asks, knowing the answer.

"I did."

"Oh my."

"Gross."

"Oh my." She roots around in her purse for a smoke. "I had a great time and . . . my *God,* was her house tidy or what. You notice the picture on the TV?"

"No, Miss Detective," I reply. "I seemed to have missed it and if you haul it out of your purse, you're in big trouble, Missy."

There was a time, a long time ago, mind you, when I was a klepto-waitress. I used to grab huge cans of things like bean salad or creamed corn and chuck them into my conveniently enormous handbag. That was the seventies, when all I lived for was to disco dance at Fanny Hill. A girl could starve on what they paid you.

"The picture was of her and her husband, I'm sure it was." Ruby brings me back to the present. "They were so young and unsullied-looking. With that wide-open, innocent look. What a shame he left like that. In the picture she had the same hairstyle as now. Or should I say, until *we* came into the picture. I'm sure she was hanging on . . . to the past . . . to him. To what they were before." She sighs.

"She seems content—but searching," I say, thinking. "Let's give her a jingle when we get settled and have her up sometime."

"Of course, darling, that would be lovely." Ruby pauses for a moment. "Did you notice, on her dresser was a framed note from her husband. I only *happened* to read it." I thought *I* was nosy. "Marsha and you were chatting on about something or other. It was written on The Moose Head Lodge Motel stationery. The last sentence was, 'When thoughts flow to you, as they often do, I know love.' Says it all, doesn't it?" Ruby asks, petting Rocky and looking out the windshield.

"Yes." I'd frame that too.

We zoom on. It's later in the afternoon than we had planned, but I make up some of the time by going a pinch over the speed limit. We zip by a town called Haugen, then outside Trego we head northeast by picking up Highway 63. The day is crystal clear, made-to-order for a road trip. Several hours slide blissfully by.

"You tired, darling? I'd be more than happy to take the wheel."

"No way," I reply. "Thanks for asking, but I love to drive and this thing handles *way* easier than my van. Not as noisy, either."

"I do miss the little balls you have around the windshield though. I wonder if I should have hung on to my Buick. I'm rusty with a clutch . . . you may have to give me a review. That's all we had once upon a time, you know."

"It's simple."

"Why in the *world* would anyone in their right mind—no offense, darling—buy a brand-*new* car and then have one of those stick things and *not* an automatic is truly beyond me."

"My van is old. I don't think they even *made* VW vans with automatic back in those days. Some people *like* shifting. The big argument is you have more control and it saves on gas. It is one more thing to fuss with, though."

Ruby puts Irene Kral in the tape deck. As she sings "This Is Always," we relax into the afternoon. We pass through the former logging hamlets of Cable, Drummond and Grand View.

North of Benoit I turn right. We whiz through onto Highway 13 and then north into our port town, Bayfield.

"I can't believe we're back. I think Bayfield is one of the prettiest towns I've ever seen, isn't it? Damn, there are so many more *people* around this time of year. Let's park. Besides," I say with pursed lips, "I've got to pee."

"Why just *look* at all the people." Ruby pats Rocky's head as he stands on her lap looking out. "Isn't it wonderful how busy it is in the summer?"

"Today's been awesome. Sunshine, crispy-crunchy air and less roadkill." A little girl with pigtails crosses in front of us, pulling her dolls in a wagon. "How about I park this caravan here, there's no way in hell I could parallel park. We can walk into town for a bite to eat before our final leg across the lake." I pull alongside a Victorian cottage. A festival of color bursts from flowerpots on the porch.

"Now control yourself around any bad hair," Ruby warns. "Let's go to one of Ed's and my favorite haunts—Greunke's. They're famous for their Whitefish Liver Dinner. Then again there's always Maggie's. They have wonderful burgers. Or The Old Rittenhouse Inn. They tend to be spendy though; heaps of lace and—"

"The first one, however you say it—Grumpy's. I'm *not* going to have liver though and if you are, we can sit at different tables and wave." I scrunch my nose.

"I'd have to be very hungry, starving . . . desperate," Ruby says, scrunching up *her* face.

We stroll several blocks downhill on Rittenhouse Avenue, since Bayfield slants right smack down to the lake. We pass by antique shops, art galleries, taverns and restaurants spewing delicious smells into the street. The lane eventually ends at a pier, which juts out into the lake. The view is incredible.

"Classy." I read the pink neon sign above the two-story rambling house. "Greunke's Inn, Fine Food. God, if the food is anything like it smells out here . . ."

"You're going to get such a kick out of this." Ruby opens the door.

In we step, into the past, that is. The restaurant is a maze of cozy rooms. The walls are covered with pictures, mirrors, newspaper clippings, china plates, and kitchen lamps of all shapes, sizes and colors.

Every room is packed with people, so we get added to a waiting list. Taking seats at an old-fashioned soda fountain/bar, we order a glass of wine. I slip away to the world's smallest restroom while Patsy Cline sings "I Fall to Pieces" on a real jukebox blinking in the corner.

"Feel better, darling?" Ruby asks when I return. "I don't think a thing has changed here. I like that."

"This is a *gold* mine." I squish in next to her. "A waiting list, all this charm. Hey . . . get a load of that lady, a nice bob haircut, color's not bad either; could use a touch-up on those roots though." I can't help myself!

A tall, bone-slim blond woman zooms by. She's juggling water glasses in one hand and the other is clutching a stack of newspapers. I can overhear her ordering the gal in front of her to get her butt in gear. Has to be the owner, I can sense it from here. Looking closer at some of the photos on the wall in front of us, I recognize a younger her. She's climbing mountains, standing in the ocean, skiing down hills and quoted in an article for having a celebrity visit her joint.

"That's Judith—the owner," Ruby says. I nod and smile. "She pretty much lives here—used to anyway. Works her tail off. I don't think there's a husband."

"You can tell she runs a tight ship," I reply. "This is one business I wouldn't last a day in. The hours are a killer." I read a sign: "John Kennedy Jr. Ate Here." Such a shame, his plane crashing. Seemed like the only Kennedy that had some happiness."

"He was something to look at; beautiful wife too. How come everyone forgets she died as well?" Ruby asks. "Like Princess Diana. For us, they'll never get old. . . . Imagine."

"Imagine."

"Drink up! They called our name." Ruby hops off her stool. We follow Judith as she darts around tables, greeting people while leading us up and around into a cozy little nook.

"I know you from somewhere," Judith remarks over her shoulder. "You must have been here a while back—I never forget a face. But . . . let me think. Oh sure—you used to come in here with a really tall, handsome guy." She's tidying up the table next to us, resetting it and straightening a picture on the wall.

"Yes, that was my husband Ed. He passed away about five years back. We used to stop here on our way over to our cottage." Ruby scoots into the corner seat—church pew rather.

"Oh, I'm so sorry. I'm Judith, by the way." She doesn't offer a hand, as she hasn't a free one. "Nice to see you again. Ruby, right?"

"My goodness, what a memory. This is Eve." Ruby points in my direction.

"Hello, Eve. Try the whitefish liver. The fresh catch tonight is walleye, right off the boat and the soup is seafood bisque. Enjoy!" Off she sails across the room.

"She has more energy than a person ought to," Ruby says. "Wonder what kind of coffee *she* has in the morning."

"My God . . . look at this menu. Clever. It's a menu disguised as a newspaper—or a newspaper disguised as a menu," I say.

Ruby is discreetly running her finger across the top of a nearby picture frame. "Can't get over how clean it is. Must take *forever* to dust all this stuff." She's looking at an old black-and-white picture of Judy Garland.

"I wish I'd brought a bigger bag," I whisper. "I see several things I would love to . . . borrow."

"Eve, you are rotten to the core . . . Which ones?" Ruby whispers back, lifting her eyebrows.

Just then the waitress comes by for our order. We both exchange looks of, "Behave."

"That was wonderful." I slam the truck door. "I'm shocked by how reasonable the check was."

"There are so many memories in those rooms. I'm flattered she remembered Ed and me. You must have given the waitress one hell of a tip—you see her face?"

"She was *excellent* and I love to tip good service; it's so worth it. Hey, *I know tippers,* and in the Midwest—well there's not a lot of them." I shift the truck into gear and head down to the ferry.

"Rocky has been such a darling." Ruby lifts him into her lap. "He needs to stretch his little legs and I bet he could use some food too."

"Oh, I don't think he's ever going to run out of things to eat."

"He can't be expected to hunt mice *every* day and he doesn't actually *eat* them . . . does he?" Ruby asks while holding Rocky up so they're looking into each other's eyes. I nod.

We make it to the ferry at the last second. While it pulls away from the Bayfield dock, we hop onto the deck of the boat. Standing in the back of the ferry, we watch as Bayfield fades away. Then we rush to the front to watch as Madeline Island comes into view. It's bustling, with another ferry leaving, speedboats gassing up and groups of people strolling here and there.

The ferry pulls in and we drive off to the left, following the road and bypassing downtown La Pointe. Then I put the brakes on.

"Hey," I say in my "I Spy" voice, "how about stopping in that bar and checking out the jerk Dorothy was yammering about?"

"Oh I don't know if we—"

"I know you're just as curious as I am. Hang on and let me see if I can turn this sucker around."

I get halfway turned around and realize that there's not enough room. So I back up a teensy bit.

"Shit!" I share with all. "This road is too narrow, and now I'm, like, jammed in the middle. I really should have stuck to my *only-pull-in-and-drive-through* rule. Now what the hell am I going . . ." I'm really frustrated here. How come a semi driver can turn a corner and manage to miss your car by a hair and I can't manage a stupid rental truck—plus my van, of course.

"Well, darling, perhaps you'll be able to question the nice policeman who has just pulled up."

The policeman is nice enough, though he could lose about fifty pounds of tummy. He straightens things out and we head to the Liquor Lounge. Which, according to our handy, chocolate-smudged map, is on Main Street. This time I pull alongside and park on the street.

"Could use some paint." Ruby suggests.

"A wrecking ball," I offer. "Maybe a fire."

We push through a screen door, its various holes covered over with duct tape. It smacks closed behind us and everyone at the bar turns to take us in. The place is dark, damp and closed in. On closer inspection, it's got possibilities. Would need to be cleaned—no, scraped—first.

"Wanna order?" I half-whisper to Ruby.

"I don't think so . . . darling."

"What'll it be?" The bartender, his comb-over trying desperately to cover a shiny scalp, saunters over.

His bloodshot eyes take us in in that *ripping-off clothes* way, lingering way too long on my chest. I look down at my chest and straight back at him. The jerk *winks!*

"Hey Al," a man down the bar yells, "we playin' poker or what?"

Al turns to the guy and we turn and *run!*

"I don't think we'll be frequenting that place much," Ruby says as we drive away.

"He's too small to be of any danger," I respond. "I could handle that one—I think. But you never can tell." There was such a dullness in that man's eyes, like he was there, but wasn't. I need to clear my head.

I pop in a tape of Miles Davis and up and down hills we float. With the windows down, late-afternoon sunshine leads the way. Where the road takes a major right, I slow down and stop, pulling up to the vine-covered gate that leads to the cottage, the lake and beyond.

"What the hell?" I say. "Someone repainted the sign that said 'Prévost Place.'" Hopping down, I have a closer look. The background of the sun is now a brighter yellow. It reads EVE AND RUBY in raised letters painted a deep ruby red.

"Hope you like it, darling."

"Ruby . . . I love it . . . and you." I put my arm around her shoulders.

"We're home."

CHAPTER TEN

After several tries, *finally* I get the lock on the old gate to fall open. I drive through; we pull the gate shut, then hop back in. We look at each other and sit for a moment facing the rutted dark path with its tree-canopied tunnel.

Then Ruby says, "Now remember—there's potholes. It's narrow in places and I have no idea if this heap can . . ."

I shift the truck into "D." "Hang on, girl! Let's open this baby up. After all, we paid extra for the insurance." I punch the gas and off we lurch.

Low-hanging branches make scratching noises as they sweep and slap along the sides of the truck. Ruby curses up a storm, in between gasps of giggling. We bump and jostle down-hill; the tires clack over the rickety bridge. Up the incline we chug; then the trees part, opening up to the sunshine and it's gorgeous. I pull over by the barn, behind the cottage and shut the motor off.

"My God, Eve," Ruby says, laughing, out of breath. "For a moment there I thought for sure we'd end up in the creek!"

I pick up Rocky, who is fully awake now, and we head over to the back door. It's around sunset and there's an amazing golden light dancing all over the barn door, reflecting onto the windows of the cottage. We walk across the porch to stand at the bottom of the stoop. I set Rocky down. Ruby reaches up to unlock the arched door, then stops.

"You do it, darling." She hands me the keys. I reach up and the door creaks open before I so much as turn the lock.

"I can't imagine burglars way out here, can you? Do you have a gun or anything?" I whisper.

"That's odd it's open," Ruby says. "Perhaps you should in-vestigate while we"—she means herself and Rocky—"wait here." I give her a look that really could kill.

Carefully we push the door farther open, then slowly creep in—shoulder to shoulder. Just in case.

"Well I'll be . . . The boys must have come over. Look at all the flowers! Vases stuffed with wildflowers," Ruby says while Rocky leaps onto the stump table and paws at a note lying there. Ruby reads aloud.

"Hey Ladies,

   Howard got a new saw and has been desperate to clean up your sunset-sign for eons, since he and Ed made it years ago—and you must admit the facelift looks fabu-lous!

   We put some goodies in your fridge, something REALLY special in the freezer. We'd be glad to help unload your truck in the A.M. Give us a call, at a reasonable time, say, anytime after nine.

                                        Love,
                                        Johnny and Howard"

"Good grief." I go over to the fridge to have a look. "Hummus, olives stuffed with garlic, four flavors of yogurt, milk, eggs, a loaf of bread and look"—I pull down the freezer door—"Rocky Road ice cream!"

I mean—this is paydirt here. We don't have the guilt of knowingly buying the stuff and besides, everyone knows it goes bad *very* quickly.

The next day I awake to the aroma of coffee. Whipping on my robe, I glance outside—gray. Big angry-looking clouds are overwhelming the sky. They look as though a good cleaning is in order. Rocky and I head downstairs.

"Well there you are, darling." Ruby pours a mug. "So glad you slept in."

"Me too." I take the steamy mug. "Could've slept forever . . . such a cozy bed,"

"Why don't you turn right around and get dressed. I'll put together a lovely breakfast and we'll have it on the porch. I rang up the boys this morning and they'll be over later."

"That's just what I'll do." Over my shoulder I say, "Thank you."

Rooting through my suitcase in search of my favorite around-the-house-bra, I hear a scratching noise. I look around just in time to see a little tiny puff of fur scurry across the floor and dash under the bed. Seconds later, Rocky rushes through the door in hot pursuit. I'd rather not stick around for the final act, so I grab my clothes and make a beeline to the bathroom. Maybe mousetraps aren't such a bad idea after all. I click the doorlock, just because.

* * *

"Where are you ladies going to *put* all this?" Howard asks, surveying our packed-to-the-gills truck. Both hands on his hips.

"Go ahead—say it Howard," I respond. "We *did* bring too much. But we have room in the barn and—damn, we have too much stuff." I struggle with an armful of rugs, a floor lamp, cord dragging, and the top of my lava lamp. Some things you can't get rid of.

"Now Howard, darling," Ruby says, smooth as silk, "I don't want you throwing out that back of yours and *do* keep in mind that one person's things are another person's—"

"Shit!" Johnny finishes.

We all have a good laugh. But the truth is, I suppose we *could* have left a lot of this behind. Actually, it's not really the things, it's the memories surrounding the things.

Like this old lamp I'm carrying. Used to sit next to my father's falling-apart green chair. He'd come home from work, pour himself a drink and read the evening paper by the lamp's glow. I'd spy on him turning pages, occasionally getting a glimpse of his face. Sometimes he'd catch me and give me a toothy grin that would fill me right up. So—one person's stuff is another person's story.

"Ladies, where would you like this trunk?" Howard asks, wiping away sweat from his brow. "Is it full of books? Bricks maybe? Weighs a ton."

"Oh heavens . . . I would *love* it upstairs in my room. But it *is* heavy and I can't *imagine* how you'd get it up all those stairs." Ruby winks in my direction, working the situation. "It's filled with clothes I'd simply *hate* to leave out here in this horribly damp barn."

"We can do it, 'cause we are men," Johnny replies in a manly voice while whipping a mink stole around his neck. "You point the way little lady and leave the rest to us."

"Be careful, watch the corners, don't forget there's a step there and . . . Oh dear, I don't think I can watch." Ruby follows closely behind Howard and Johnny, watching every move they make.

Since the boss is gone, I walk around the side of the barn, which sits on a sandbank overlooking the creek. I watch the water as it meanders alongside the barn, then slips under the wooden bridge. On the other side it picks up speed and disappears around the far side of the boathouse, cascading into the lake.

The banks on either side of the creek are lush and green. Clumps of cattail leaves wave in the breeze. The air is rich with the scent of flowers and grass and wetness. A raven cackles in the woods somewhere, while a woodpecker taps away in the distance. I take in a deep breath, then sneeze.

Wandering down to the edge of the creek, I reach down and touch the surface: ice cold. I can see all the way to the rocky bottom. Leaning farther over, I look at my reflection before sitting back on my haunches *very slowly*. I spy a deer that has slipped from the trees on the other side of the creek and is now sipping water.

There's a rack of horns sprouting from his mushroom-colored fur. Beautiful dark round eyes stare into mine. A second deer slowly emerges from the woods. I'm certain she's his partner by the way she looks at him for a sign or a signal. I feel something communicated between them.

They take turns lapping out of the creek directly in front of me. I'm afraid to move. Before I know what's going on, he's no more than a foot away—then inches. We're gazing into each other's eyes.

Ever so slowly I reach out to touch his nose. He lowers his head, as though bowing. I reach farther. He steps back, looking me over; time freezes. Then—they fly away into the woods, the rustle of branches closing behind them. I can't believe what I just saw—and felt. This must be what it feels like to have touched something truly wondrous. Now that's not a word I normally would try on, but it's true and I feel it that way—wondrous. Is this something that happens all the time up here?

"There you are." Ruby comes down the path to the creek and thumps down beside me. "The boys managed to haul the whole lot upstairs and not *one* nick. Oodles of cursing though. You all right, darling? You look . . . odd."

"I'm fine." I put my arm around her shoulder and give it a squeeze.

"Hey, where's our lunch?" Howard asks, lumbering down to the edge of the creek. Bending, then squatting down, he scoops water to rinse off his sweaty face. "Sure can tell this is spring water, cold as a witch's—"

"Tit," Johnny finishes.

"I'll go see what I can manage," Ruby says, putting her hand on my shoulder, getting up. I turn, watching her and Johnny walk arm in arm back into the cottage. I smile, looking up at Howard.

"They make a cute couple, don't you think?" Howard asks.

"*Very* cute. Hey . . . thanks for the beautiful sign and flowers and food. . . ."

"Our pleasure. Ruby spent the better part of the morning thanking us too." He runs his hands through his mane. "Johnny sketched the letters and I cut them out on my latest obsession—my jigsaw."

"Well, it sure knocked me over. I like the sound of it . . . Eve and Ruby. Has a nice ring."

"I agree." Howard splashes me.

"Hey! That's cold!" I splash back and before you know it we're dousing each other, getting wetter by the minute.

Yelling and laughing, soaked to the skin, we suddenly notice Ruby and Johnny standing by the barn. Howard and I nod, then make a mad dash to catch them. We share cold, wet hugs and manage to soak them both, but good.

We're all huddled around the stump table in the kitchen, reviving our wet bodies with hot mugs of tomato soup.

"My goodness, we're a sight," Ruby says. "Good thing the neighbors are already here or I'm sure there would be rumors. Grabbing people and soaking them to the bone, the nerve." She elbows Howard in the ribs.

"You both deserved it," I say. "Looking all smug and dry. Besides, we didn't want you to feel left out or anything."

"Ruby tells me you're thinking of starting up some kind of business," Howard says.

"*Thinking* is the operative term at this point, don't you think, darling?" Ruby asks while ladling more soup into everyone's mug. I nod in agreement.

"I, for one, would love to be involved," Johnny volunteers. "Both of us. The summers here are wonderful, but the winters . . . Oh man, they drive us both a little buggy. We usually take long vacations."

"Let's brainstorm," Howard suggests.

"Rag rugs were a thought," I say. "But they'd take forever to make by hand."

"They would," Johnny agrees. "I *am* fast at sewing, though, with the help of a machine, that is. There must be something the world needs more of than rugs."

"Ruby sews too and I could learn." I pick up Rocky. "But what the hell *does* the world need more of? We need an idea that's not complicated but that's different . . . unusual. Why couldn't *I* have thought of lava lamps?" We also need to make money, I think. I look around; I wonder if this could be an inn. A brothel? Maybe a clinic for retired hairstylists—Nah.

"You know . . . now this may be too silly." Johnny lifts a flowered cloth apron from the countertop. "These could be—"

"Oh my God—this honestly could be *just* the thing." I take the apron from Johnny and put it on.

"Aprons?" We all say, kind of together, then laugh. Then it gets quiet.

"You know," I say, "you can't find *anything* unusual any more. Make the tie strings longer and wider since most gals are. *And* have a Web site." I shoot a look to Ruby.

"That's something *I* could do," Howard offers. "I'm not really the sewing type, but computers—I'm sure I could create a fantastic Web site."

"They could be artsy-fartsy," Johnny says. "They're simple to put together, not too many parts and all." He looks closely at Ruby's apron. "Use unique and beautiful fabrics. Hmmm . . ."

"What do you think, darling?" Ruby asks.

Everyone looks at me. "I think this could be *exactly* what

the world needs more of. We'll call them Ruby's Aprons," I say, handing it to Ruby, who ties it on. "This is *her* apron after all *and* the inspiration behind the concept. To Ruby's Aprons!"

"Cheers!" We all clink.

"Give it one more shove. There! Perfect," I say to Ruby. We slump down into the sofa in the living room.

"Why this is such a lovely idea, darling." Ruby turns a lamp next to her just so. "Ed was very particular about never moving a thing around. Now look at how much better this works."

"I am so glad you didn't get all up in arms." I sigh with relief.

"I realize I'm set in my ways, darling, but moving around the living room makes it much more ours now too. Don't you think?"

"Ruby, you keep surprising me." I honestly was thinking that she'd pitch a fit if I even suggested moving a lamp! Just goes to show me. At my age, I'm still tiptoeing around and all I had to do was ask.

"Before we dig into shuffling around the library," Ruby says, "tell me, what do you think of the apron idea—honestly."

"Well . . ." I stand and right a picture. "It does seem like it fell into our laps. That must be a sign of *some* sort. I'm thinking it could . . ."

"It could piss some women off!"

"*Ruby!* Such language." We laugh. "Who's to say men wouldn't like them as well? Besides, there's a whole bunch of us baby boomers who are slowing down—a little—and I bet a lot more of us will be spending more time cooking."

"I'm beginning to see your point. Being a . . . fringe boomer . . . myself." She gives me the evil eye, so I refrain from bursting out laughing.

"I say we give it a go."

"Let's do, darling."

Chapter Eleven

Standing in the second floor of the boathouse, facing a stuffed deer head hanging on the outside wall, I reach up and pull the jaw downward. I haven't a choice since this is where Ed installed the only phone out here. Strange guy.

Clearing my throat while the receiver slides slowly down a black cord and into my waiting hand, I let the jaw go. It snaps shut. Thank goodness he had the sense to put on ample cord. I'm able to walk into the kitchen area and use my notes that are laid out on the counter. I dial the handset.

"Hello? Is this the *Island Gazette?*" I ask quickly, as the line was picked up on the first hint of a ring.

"Yes."

"My name is Eve Moss. I've just moved out here on Madeline Island and—"

"You're staying at the Prévost Place on Steam Boat Point and you've been driving all over hell in that old floating bus scaring folks here to death, not to mention the fish," the woman says in one breath.

"I forget this is an island; I'm sorry if I—"

"I'm just giving you a hard time. Darlene Kravitz told me about you while she was checking me out over at the grocery store in Bayfield. There she was, out on her dock . . . nearly fell in when you and Ruby flew by. I personally think it's a free world and if you want to go around scaring folks half to—"

"Sorry. It's called a duck, by the way—and we were hardly moving. Look . . . the reason I'm calling is I'd like to place an ad . . . if that wouldn't be too much trouble."

"You wanting to sell something? Rent your cottage?"

"I'm wanting to hire some women to come and sew for us."

"Oh you must be putting up drapes. You know, when my *third* husband and I moved out here . . . that must have been back in—"

"No . . . a business. *Not* drapes," I inform her slowly, jiggling one leg, then the other; I have to pee and this phone doesn't reach the bathroom. Time to pick up the speed here. "Look, I'd like to place a want ad. Are you the person I should talk to or—"

"Yes sirree! I'm the ad person, editor in chief, and accounts payable *and* receivable. I also happen to write a column about local goings-on, *and* every Saturday's edition I do horoscopes."

"I would like it to read," I say in a controlled voice, " 'Wanted—' "

"Hold on . . . Okay, go ahead."

" **'Wanted'**—in bold across the top—'full-time seamstresses needed for Madeline Island business venture. Flexible hours, great pay, excellent working conditions, lunch included. Must have great hair.' " I pause. No laughter on the other end. Not a good sign. "That's a joke." I'm picturing myself sitting down on the toilet, the relief one feels.

"Oh, right . . . very funny. Scratch that . . . no lunch, right? Okay, got it."

"No, the lunch part is right. The hair part, scratch *that!*" My God. I'm about to pee my panties. " 'Call Eve Moss to set up an interview.' "

"Okay okay, got it." She reread the ad and our phone number back exactly right. "It'll run in the next issue which comes out in a day or so. Good timing. Can I do anything else for you? Hello?"

I'm yanking up my jeans, doing a little wiggly thing back to the phone I left hanging from the deer's mouth. "Oh hi. Had to turn the oven down, water was running over."

"Water? In the oven?"

"Never mind. Listen . . . you've been great. Thanks so much for your help. Look forward to meeting you sometime."

"You bet . . . Eve. Good luck with your business. What is it you're making again?"

"Drapes."

Over the next several days we begin cleaning the boathouse. I'm thrilled to have a workplace that has such a remarkable view of the lake. All this room here, and we'll be far enough away from the cottage that it will feel like we're "going to work" yet no commuting.

The boathouse perches on the northwestern corner of our property, facing the lake. Standing two stories high, the first floor is where you park the boat. It's been dug out so that it's actually lake water. By opening the doors facing the water, you make it possible to motor your boat in and park it. The second story is a charming two-bedroom cottage.

The living room has three French doors facing the lake that open onto a wraparound deck. The entire inside is paneled in yellowed knotty pine and is similar in design to the main cottage. There's a small open kitchen, two back bedrooms and a tiny, dark bathroom.

"What an awesome view. Feels as though we're sitting *in* the lake," I say, carrying one end of a long table we hauled down from the barn. Ruby is at the other end. "I think we should put the sewing machines up front, by the doors—perfect setting for inspiration."

"You have such a nose for this, darling," Ruby replies. "I would never have thought of turning this place into a factory. I bet we have buckets of people ringing for an interview."

"Ruby . . . the phone hasn't rung once."

"I know, darling; have patience. Things move a little slower up here."

"What was that? A buzzing or something; there it is again."

"That, patient one, is the *phone!*"

"Damn—the phone. I piled too much crap in front of the deer head!" I say, wildly pulling dusty curtain rods, a metal bed frame, brooms and what looks like a gun away from the phone's hiding place. "Hello?" I say, out of breath, holding a stuffed squirrel in my other hand. I pass him to Ruby.

"Hey, this Eve Moss? The drape lady?" a friendly male voice asks.

"Um . . . yes it is." I guess I asked for this.

"This is Charlie . . . Charlie Bruns. You must have given out the wrong number. Been getting all your calls . . . Ladies looking for you and all . . . A man, too."

"Oh really? I am so sorry. I should have double-checked the number." Shit shit shit.

"No harm done," he assures me kindly. "Things like this happen. Kept a list of who called for you."

"Thank you *so* much. . . . I really am grateful." Is this a nice guy or what?

"You renting Ruby's place for the fall or—"

"I live here . . . the Prévost Place. Used to be, anyway. What I mean is, yes, I *do* live here . . . with Ruby."

"Ruby Prévost? Well I'll be! Say . . . you wouldn't want to stop by, would you? Sure would enjoy visiting with her and meeting you, too."

"Oh sure . . . we'd *love* to come over. Thanks." I give a questioning look to Ruby, who nods. "We could stop by later this afternoon."

"That sure would be nice then. Yes sir, sure would. Should be around 'most all day."

"Okay, and listen, thanks again for being so understanding."

"Sure sure. No problem at all—my pleasure. 'Bye now."

"Okay then. 'Bye." I let the phone go and it slides upward, picking up speed until it snaps back into the deer's mouth, making a funny pop as the jaw clomps shut. I look over at Ruby; she lifts her shoulders and shrugs.

"Of all the people to . . ." Ruby says. "Charlie lives down the road a bit."

"I'm *positive* I gave the right phone number to that woman. His must be *really* similar. I should have insisted on seeing a proof before it went to press. He a friend of yours?"

"Charlie? Yes . . . yes, he was, is. *He's* very much alive, but his wife passed away quite a while ago," Ruby says, correcting her tenses. "He and Ed did a lot of fishing together. Such an odd fellow. Pleasant . . . but odd."

"Certainly *seems* nice and my God, what a deep voice," I say. "Might be fun for you to see him again."

"Oh yes indeed," Ruby says. "Ed always referred to him as the birdman. His yard is filled with the most remarkable bird-houses. He smokes . . . but not the legal stuff."

"Oh? Oh." I'm guessing Charlie must be one of those pot-smoking earthy types. "He's keeping a phone list for us; does-n't seem the least bit put out. I certainly got the feeling he's wanting to see you . . . us." Hmm, I wonder if he likes sassy Brits? Not to be a meddler, God forbid, but if they both lost their spouses . . . And that sexy voice.

"You know, darling," Ruby purrs, "let's take a break *now* and visit Charlie. We've been at it for hours and it's looking so much better. I should tidy up a bit, though."

"We should bring him something. You know, to thank him for being so . . . neighborly," I suggest. Then I lie, a white lie: "The van's out of gas . . . Not a drop . . . Fumes." My van is so unromantic, but a boat ride in that duck . . .

"Let's take the duck then," Ruby quickly says.

"We could pick him up and take him for a ride."

"Why not?" Ruby warms to the idea. "After all, he did help fix that thing."

"Might as well throw in lunch too." I wonder about her and

Charlie—together. "How about you gather some picnic goodies and I'll get the duck out."

"Lovely."

We head up the path to the cottage and around to the back
porch. Ruby and I lug the cooler into the kitchen and plop it
onto the stump table. We think better of it and put it on the
floor in front of the fridge since neither one of us could reach
into it up there on the stump table.

I dash upstairs, throw my filthy clothes in a corner and put
on an oversized T-shirt and baggy shorts, and throw some cold
water on my face. I look into the bathroom mirror and see the
gray hairs moving farther into my part. You know, I may just
ditch this hair-color thing. Maybe. Until I'm sure, I zigzag my
part, tie a big scarf to hold the ponytail and head down and out
to the barn to rev up the duck.

The afternoon is busy turning humid and sticky. I wipe
sweat from my brow while backing up the duck to the porch
door, then I hop out. Ruby, on the other hand, never perspires.
Me, I drip. Bitch.

We're fighting with the cooler, trying to lift it up the side of
the duck while balancing it on the ladder. Thank God the boys
come to the rescue.

"Damn. This thing weighs a ton!" Howard takes the cooler
off my shoulders and sets it up onto the side of the duck. "You
ladies simply do not believe in packing anything *lightly,* do
you?" He shakes his head while straightening out his back.

"Enough food for all of us, if you'd care to join an impromptu picnic," Ruby says, coming back out of the cottage,
looking fresh.

"Long story. Come aboard and we'll fill you in," I say over

the side of the duck. Ruby climbs up, followed by Howard. Johnny is last, so he pulls up the ladder. Rules of the road: last one in pulls up the ladder.

I put on a tape of Billie Holiday, who starts singing, "Trav'lin' Light." And off we go. Down the road, over the bridge and through the woods to find Charlie's place. This time I'm trying my best *not* to go so crazy fast. Keeping an eye peeled for the deer. Ruby is busy chatting up the boys, her bracelets jangling like crazy. She's one of those people that if you tied her hands together, she couldn't say a word. Hmm.

"Which way, Ruby?" I ask.

"Left, at the gate; then it's a mile or so down to where there's a bank of trailers. Watch for a birdhouse-mailbox. It marks the start of his driveway. You can't miss it, darling." She jumps right back into her chat.

I smile to myself. I do that too—carry on several conversations at the same time with different people. Oh maybe not catching every word in every situation, but one must edit anyway. Don't want to miss a thing. I've found that sometimes the best stuff is delivered in the least bit of speech.

"He's a woodcrafts man," Howard says. "You won't *believe* his yard."

"Ed knew him for years," Ruby replies. "But you know, he was the hardest man to figure—never spared many words."

"We're coming to some trailers," I inform whomever. I slow down, then turn left in front of a miniature Victorian-mansion, three-story, combination birdhouse-mailbox. All that fancy work to get bills and bird poop. Makes you think.

Charlie's driveway is a couple of ruts, like ours. The grass in the middle makes a scraping noise under the duck. The drive curves, then dips down a bit. I slow to a crawl; on either side of the road are birdhouses. Hundreds of them. They perch atop tall, thin poles, giving the illusion of floating. Some have hand-painted signs on them with names like Radcliff's Roost, Patty's Perch, Cat-less Crib and Shakespeare's Shack. (Are you getting the idea?) Every one is brightly colored.

Rounding a final bend, the drive leads up to a curious pink and chrome trailer surrounded by billowy willow trees. Bright red geraniums in flower boxes hang from every window. Wind chimes clang and sing in the breeze.

Around a far corner, a path leads off into the woods. The willow tree's branches, slinking over the trailer, sweep back and forth across the metal roof, making a rustling sound. Like an overweight woman's nylon-covered thighs rubbing together.

"Isn't this divine?" Ruby half-whispers. "Looks as though the ground is swallowing up his house."

We all climb down from the duck. The boys hang back a bit, admiring the carvings on the flower boxes. Ruby reaches up to knock, but before she can, it opens.

"Well, well . . . if it isn't Ruby Prévost. What a sight you are." Charlie comes out onto the small stoop.

As he steps into the sunshine, he seems to unfold. He's so darn tall. Setting down an enormous coffee-stained mug on the rail, he takes Ruby's hand with both of his. His gray hair is tightly pulled back into a ponytail that reaches to the middle of his back. Wearing a tank top and shorts, he's the picture of health. I couldn't begin to guess his age. Sixties? Seventies? A deep tan sets his brown eyes off. He's a fox.

"Charlie darling, so nice to see you," Ruby gushes. "We're *so* sorry about all those messages from—"

"Not another word. Glad it happened. Fact is, I should've come by myself. To pay respects and all. . . ." Charlie bows slightly to Ruby. "Now . . . this must be Eve."

"Hello there Charlie. Nice to meet you." I offer my hand. "You probably know Howard and Johnny." I point.

The boys nod their hellos. Charlie nods back, then walks over to the duck.

"Well I'll be. So she still runs. Not many of these around anymore. What a sight." Charlie chuckles. "I remember when Ed drove this tub up from some farm down south near Oshkosh. Took a whole summer just to get all the horseshit— horse crap—off her. The motor was a mess, too. But Ed and I fixed her all up." He pats the duck's underside with pride.

"We're hoping to take you on a lunch ride. To apologize and . . ." I start. Charlie raises his hand to protest. But his face gives him away.

"Like I said . . . really . . . no apology necessary. To be honest, I only got three or four calls—jotted them down somewhere. I sure will take you up on your offer of lunch and a ride, though. Let me go grab some sunglasses and let's go." He saunters back inside his trailer.

We look at one another. Ruby is checking her lips in a tiny mirror in her straw bag.

"Good heavens . . . he hasn't aged a minute," Ruby says with some disgust. "Hardly seems fair and did you see those arms?"

They are nice and lean, his arms, the kind that could hold

you an awfully long time. Ruby and he would make quite the
pair. In my head I sing a few bars of "Matchmaker."

Charlie is back seconds later. He's covered up with a white
shirt and a ratty gray fedora sits rakishly on his head. We all
clamber back up the ladder and into the duck. I turn us
around and slowly drive by the floating birdhouse city.

"Take a right on North Shore Drive," Charlie directs.
"Then another quick right down this driveway. Ease onto the
little beach over there. She still floats, right?"

"She sure as hell does!" I say with a laugh and hit the gas. I
drive straight into the lake, switch to the prop drive and off we
go.

Howard and Johnny are deep in a discussion. Ruby and
Charlie are carrying on like old friends. I put the duck into a
higher gear and head over to where the outer Apostle Islands
are. The lake is calm; our wake ripples across the mirrorlike
surface. The wide-open feeling is breathtaking.

I click on the microphone. "Our tour today features the
Apostle Islands, where an impromptu lunch shall be served,
compliments of none other than Miss Ruby. Please note that
the captain has turned *off* the no-smoking sign." At which
point Ruby and I both light up.

"You two—and smoking," Charlie slurps out of his coffee
mug. "That is one habit I am happy to say I have kicked for
good. No wonder you're both so short." I look into the
rearview mirror, winking at Ruby.

"We're thinking about *trying* to quit." I take a couple of
drags, then put my cigarette out, feeling suddenly conscious of
the fact that our smoke was flying right into everyone's face.

Ruby puts hers out, too. I snap shut the ashtray and make a mental note to clean it out and fill it with Reese's Peanut Butter Cups. Much better habit.

"I *used* to smoke cigarettes," Charlie says sadly. "Gave them up for good when the Missus passed. Feel as though I killed her, I do. She never smoked a day in her life, but inhaled my smoke. Sure do miss . . . Sorry." He stops talking, looking over at Ruby in apology. The rest of us look out to the lake in order to give him a moment.

"Now Charlie . . . isn't that taking on a bit much?" Ruby asks. "Didn't you go outside to have your smokes?"

"Nope. I told her it was *my* house and I'd be damned if I'd smoke anywhere but *in* my house. Stubborn fool." Charlie spits out "fool." "I still smoke, but not . . . never mind."

"Legal cigarettes." I try to let Charlie know I could care less. "*Should* be legal as far as I'm concerned."

"Why Eve Moss. You—radical," Ruby chides. "I had a lady friend in cancer treatment. Only thing that kept her eating—kept her alive—was her marijuana cigarettes."

"Well I haven't got cancer. Just enjoy it is all. Grow it myself too," Charlie boasts. "Silly it's not legal. Never understood it."

"I think it's all tied to the government," Johnny comments. "Control . . . taxing and, well . . . money. Everything's tied to money."

"If our friends with AIDS hadn't smoked it," Howard adds, "they would have died even sooner."

I catch Howard's eye in the rearview mirror and share a weak smile. The furrow in his brow eases; I like how you can care with a look.

"It's been years since I've . . ." Ruby says, and we all inhale and then laugh. "Honestly, when is the last time you read about a *high* driver killing anyone?"

"Once the government figures out how to tax it," I say, slowing down a bit, "you'll be able to buy it along with a bottle of now *legal* wine."

We're coming into a grouping of small islands. Some have rock ledges with pine trees hanging over the water.

"Let's see . . . if you pull around over to that cove area there . . ." Howard maneuvers up the aisle toward me. "On the right . . . slow down and let me get on the bow so I can watch for rocks."

"Rocks? What the hell?" I slow *way* down. I am not in the mood to sink!

"This entire area is full of rocks," Charlie says to my wide eyes reflecting in the rearview mirror. "Go slow and keep a sharp eye out."

"Wow—did you see that fish?" I ask as another huge fish shoots up into the air, then splashes down again.

"I don't know if I'd have a pot big enough for him," Ruby says. "He was bigger than me!"

"Okay, this looks good. . . . Let's pull around and into the lagoon there," Howard says, hopping down from the hood of the duck, walking back down the aisle. On the way he gives my shoulder a good squeeze.

I drive up onto the little beach area and park over on the edge of the sand, leaving us room to spread out. Charlie lowers the ladder, then helps us ladies off first. I look over to Johnny and Howard as I climb down. Howard is standing behind Johnny, watching us with his big arms wrapped around Johnny's waist. Those two.

The island is just big enough for the five of us—barely. The duck and a few scattered pine trees and that's it. The little beach we're on faces open lake. I read in a book, back at the cottage, how there are actually twenty-two islands out here. Yet some overzealous "island namer" decided to call them the Apostle Islands. Could this be one of the unnamed?

Everyone helps unpack the cooler. Ruby brought a red-and-white checkered cloth and I'm trying hard not to laugh as Johnny and she are wrestling it to the ground. A stubborn breeze keeps it dancing. Using all of our shoes, we finally tame it into a sloppy rectangle. The sun is high in the sky overhead and warm air swirls around us. I reach to undo my hair; I love the feeling of hair blowing all to hell. Who the hell cares if I have roots?

"You must be crazy about your grandkids," I say, as I help myself to one of Ruby's man-sized slices of wheat bread and slather it with peanut butter, jam and several long slices of banana. No more talking for me.

"I am," Charlie replies, with a light in his eyes. "They're still a big part of my life. Oh we don't get together as often. But in the summer they all come up for a visit."

"You must miss Margie," Ruby says softly. " I sure enjoyed her and oh my heavens, could she laugh."

"Yup. But . . . I do all right," Charlie says just to Ruby. "You learn to . . . *We* learn to."

"I'm sure the four of us could use some of your woodworking expertise from time to time," I slur through peanut butter goo. "That is, if we can *afford* you."

"It'd be my pleasure," Charlie says with a crooked grin.

"We could work out a dinner barter arrangement." He winks at me and things are looking good.

We munch and crunch through our yummy spread. In addition to the ingredients for my peanut butter/banana concoction, Ruby packed crackers, a veggie relish, sliced cheeses and a thermos full of cool well water, which rounds things out just right.

Eventually we repack, clamber up the ladder and back the duck into the water. I give it some gas and head us off to Madeline Island—to Charlie's trailer.

When I turn the duck into his driveway, he says, "Oh geez . . . I almost forgot to give you the list." He hands me a crumpled napkin with what looks like scratching on it. "Sorry, I'm not much in the writing department."

"Thanks. I had the number corrected for the next issue and if there's any more calls . . ." I pull up to his front door.

"I'll make sure and jot them down." Charlie climbs down the ladder. "Or better yet—I'll give them *your* number." He turns and waves us off.

"Sounds great, Charlie." I hand Ruby the list and we all wave back.

CHAPTER TWELVE

"What a lovely afternoon." Ruby pushes open the back door with her hip. "I'm delighted the newspaper woman mucked up the phone number. Charlie is such a love . . . we simply *must* have him for dinner."

"I think sooner rather than later," I suggest with a raised brow and a well-placed grin. "Perhaps when we *do* invite him over, I'll be out fishing or something."

"Don't be silly . . . a woman my age." Ruby opens and closes cupboard doors a bit too loudly. "He and I have both enjoyed long marriages—with other partners, of course. For heaven's sake, he was Ed's lake chum. Really!" she blusters out.

"Ruby, you aren't dead . . . or even near. All your parts are in order, and he *is* a stud *and* I don't think there are any such things as accidents." I fold my arms over my chest to establish my position.

"You mean this is a universal setup sort of thing?" Ruby considers this.

"Something like that."

"It was *only* lunch, for heaven's sake," Ruby says with a sigh. "I was thinking of our business venture. He *is* handsome though. Oh . . . listen to me."

"Pathetic, really." I shake my head. "I feel like your parent and I'm telling you to *go for it!*"

"Eve Moss!"

"You're blushing," I singsong. "My God, you're blushing." I pour a mug of cold coffee and head into the living room. "I'm going to the boathouse to give Marsha a call and return the ones from Charlie's list. Come down and join me. After you cool off, that is."

"Hi Marsha," I say into her machine. "Eve Moss here— your personal redo woman. Now if you're still interested . . ." I hear a soft click on the line. "Hello?"

"Hello, Eve? Is that you?"

"Yes, hi. How's it going?" I've got to figure out something to do with this phone. I'm really *over* looking into the eyes of that deer head. Turning my back on it, I yank some cord from its mouth and walk over to the kitchen to retrieve my lit cigarette.

"I'm actually playing hooky," Marsha says with a chuckle. "Have to screen my calls since you might have been Norske Nook and I'm just not in the mood to be around all that pie."

"I honestly think I can understand that." We giggle and I recall all those appliances lined up on her countertop just waiting to be turned on. "Are you still thinking of a career change? I don't know if the pay would be—"

"I am. Well, I mean . . . I wasn't. Then you and Ruby show

up and all I've *done* is think about it. I really don't need much to live on. My daughter's almost done with college. What's keeping me here?"

"Do *I* know what you mean." I stick my tongue out at the deer head.

"I checked with a friend of mine that has an empty cabin in LaPointe and they'd love to rent it to me real cheap."

"How are you with a sewing machine?"

"Made my very own wedding dress. Which I cut into tiny pieces on what would have been our tenth anniversary—the bastard."

"Oh my. Well you'd have no trouble with what we have in mind, then. We're just getting together a group. You thinking a month, or . . . ?"

"Something like that, I guess. I do want to give the restaurant a two-week notice and all—I've been there forever."

"That's great," I say. "Talk to you soon."

"Eve . . . thank *you*. Be sure and say hello to Ruby for me."

"I will." I hang up, letting out a satisfying cloud of smoke. I start down the list on the crumpled napkin. One phone number is disconnected. At the next one I leave a message. Then . . . "Hello? Is this Al? Al Smitters?" Oh man—is this that *Al* creature? I shudder and pull my chest in.

"Could be. Depends . . ." a man's raspy voice replies.

"This is Eve Moss. I ran an ad for seamstresses," I say, nice as pie 'cause he sounds paranoid. "But if I have the wrong number, I sure am sorry."

"Oh ya, sure, sure," I can hear muffled talking and some glasses clattering in the background. "My wife needs work. She can sew real good. Kind of shy is all."

"Can I speak with her? Is she there?" I detect a slur in his voice. This is really weird.

"You called me at my bar, the Liquor Lounge." It's him—shit. "We don't got a phone at our place till later in the week when I can get enough money together to rehook it up. Bonnie—that's my wife—every time I turn around, she's calling her sister in Chicago. *Every God damn—*"

"Have your wife give me a call when she can," I reply quickly. "She and I can set up an interview." Such a pleasant-sounding man.

"The pay good? She don't come free, you know. We need the cash. Going into winter and all." He starts clearing stubborn-sounding phlegm from his throat.

"Bonnie and I will discuss it. Have her give me a call, okay?"

"Sure, sure, hang on a minute." I can hear him cover the phone and yell something. "Okay, what's your number and you better give me your address, too, okay honey?"

My skin crawls when a man calls me "honey." I tell him and before I can say another word, the line goes dead.

The boathouse is beginning to take shape and look more like an apron-making shop. I can almost hear the hum of machines. I spend the rest of the afternoon getting a feel for the space and figuring out where things should go in my head. Ruby has gone into La Pointe for some much needed supplies, so it's just me and I'm done for the day. I'm sitting on the end of the dock, wrapped in a huge workout shirt. The sun is starting its dip down behind the horizon of trees. The water is slapping against the shore and I'm watching an enormous bird float on the wind . . . and wondering.

I wonder what the girls at the salon are up to and if they miss me. I miss them. Hair is such a funny business. It's one of the few jobs in which you actually touch someone—other than a doctor, of course. I miss Dorothy's laugh and how Watts was always making fun of her big hair. "Dot's do," she would chant while ratting it up to the ceiling for her. God—am I lonely? Do I need to have that? That and all the craziness too? I had no idea I would miss it this much. But I'm not the salon; I'm not a place. People are what counts and what really makes you you. I guess I'm feeling scared, too. I did this whole thing so damn fast and furious—have I made a major fuckup? My mother would gasp at the mention of that word. Then she'd say it herself and giggle.

But it's funny how quickly I've created a new world up here. I'm seeing how important it is to keep changing if you really want to grow—to become more. I was *way* overdue. But, then again, maybe this was exactly when I needed to do this.

I lift myself up from the dock and decide to head up to the barn and have a peek into the loft. Walking up the path to the front porch, then through the smacking screen door, I stroll through the living room. Stopping off in the kitchen, I scoop up Rocky, who's watching me from one of the wicker bar stools. I have a sip of water (I can't get over how delicious the well water is here) before we head out the back door, toward the barn.

Stepping through the side door, I hit the lights and marvel at all our junk piled at the far end. Ruby and Johnny had thrown sheets over everything. I walk around the duck, still holding Rocky, over to the far corner next to Ed's workbench and a wide staircase. I clomp up the dusty stairs leading up a flight, then around and up another, ending at the corner of a cavernous room.

"Holy cow, Rocky, look at this."

I set Rocky down on the wide-plank floor and walk toward a huge window. It looks down on the cottage and on to the lake. I turn back to the loft to do a little snooping.

Off to one side, tucked under the eaves, is a huge, sagging brown sofa flanked by a worn leather chair. On a coffee table made of crates is a jelly jar holding old cattails that long ago exploded their seeds. A wooden rolltop desk holds a jumble of dust-covered papers and folders. A pipe sits in an ashtray; I lift it and smell a faint odor of woodsy-cherry. A half-drunk bottle of Wild Turkey catches the sun's light, seeming as though lit from within. I lift a heart-shaped frame, swipe the dust away and study the handsome couple.

It's of Ed and Ruby, their faces close, blowing out candles on a heavily decorated cake. The sparkle in their eyes says it all. A lot of moments in life are like that. Like that sparkle—there are simply no words for them. It's knowingness, being right with the world. So many things I've seen or felt could never be mashed down into a single word. I like that. I slip the picture into my pocket.

Walking over to a canvas-covered table, I lift the edge to peek under. "What the hell?" Pulling the fabric off reveals, in exact proportion, a model of the entire island! Its three-dimensional detail is incredible. Trees, bushes, streams and curving drives lead to cabins nestled all along the lakeshore. Several farms have horses and cows; there's even a pond with ducks floating around. On one is a dock with a woman fishing!

I walk around and locate the cottage and barn. There's the creek, the boathouse and a little cabin hidden in the woods. I wonder just where that is. On one corner are some switches—of course I flip them.

"Holy cow!"

All over the model island, lights come on. Bending way over, peeking here and there, I can see some of the cottages are cut away, revealing equally meticulous interiors. They're furnished with chairs and tables set with dishes. Kitchen windows have tiny lace drapes over tiny sinks. Unbelievable. In the little town of La Pointe, where the ferry drops you off, are miniature cars unloading. This must have taken Ed years.

Under other tarps are hand tools, drill presses, several saws and a collection of paints. There's a hulking, windup record player and bins of heavy records. Finding one that says, "Fox Trots," I crank up the turntable. Tinny music fills the room.

Along one entire wall are floor-to-ceiling mirrors; waist-high runs one of those wooden ballet bars. A long time ago this must have been a dance studio. Standing in the center of the room, I can imagine it better. If all this stuff were moved to the end, over by the stairway, it would be a great place for a work-out room.

The record ends, and the repetitious scratching noise of the stuck needle is maddening. I lift up the arm of the record player and close the top. Peering out the window, I take one last look at the view. Rocky rubs my leg; a clump of dust is floating off the tip of his tail. Looking down at the back door of the cottage, I watch as a patched-together station wagon lurches to a halt. A woman with pink curlers hops out and heads for the back porch. I grab Rocky and move toward the stairs, taking them two at a time. Just as I'm coming out of the barn, she's getting back into her car, about to pull the door shut.

"Hello?" I say, breathless. "Can I help you or . . ."

"I'm Bonnie." The frail woman gets back out of her car. "Bonnie Smitters. Come to ask about the sewing job. If it's still open, that is."

I put Rocky down and move toward her. She's dressed in a dark sweatshirt with the sleeves shoved up to her elbows and baggy jeans, both of which seem to be hanging on her. Her tired eyes are the color of gray storm clouds.

I reach out to shake her hand. She stares at it for a second, then offers hers. It's worn and callused, but warm. I spy a bluish-green mark on her forearm. She sees me seeing and quickly pulls down her sleeve.

"Nice to meet you, Bonnie. I'm Eve . . . Eve Moss." I quickly let her hand go, as I can feel she needs it back. She takes it into the other one, cradling it.

"My husband came home, told me you called and said I best hightail it over here. Jobs are hard to come by here and—"

"Would you like some coffee . . . Bonnie?" I suddenly want to do something for her. It's those eyes *and* the pink curlers.

"Oh . . . I shouldn't, but if it's no trouble or . . ." Her voice is careful, timid.

"No trouble at all. Follow me." I lead her into the kitchen, where I busy myself with coffee-pouring.

"Nice place. I've cleaned a lot of cabins; this here is way

more . . ." She blows on her coffee, considering. "Homey. Plenty big, though."

"It is . . . thanks." I think I'd like to get to know her. Find out what's behind those eyes.

"What are you're wanting sewed?" Bonnie asks. "I sew, but not all that fast."

"A simple design. Speed's *not* the issue." I don't think I want to tell anyone what is to be sewn until our first day on the job. "If you could work four, maybe five days a week, and if you have a working sewing machine . . . ?"

I feel funny asking this, but I've got to keep a grip on expenses. My gut tells me this is going to work, and *finally,* I've learned to listen. Besides, maybe we're supposed to be here, meeting these people, helping each other.

"I can do that and I've got an okay machine. If you need references . . . last lady I cleaned for . . . she's dead, so . . ."

"Well I guess I can't call her now, can I?" She cracks a wry smile. "Haven't set a starting date yet, but . . ."

"With fall coming, most folks are closing up to head south, so I'm pretty open."

"If it sounds like something you'd like to do—you're hired!"

"Sure . . . but . . . that's it? Just like *that?*" She squints her eyes in disbelief.

"Yup. Just like that. You're hired." I smile and see a light behind the gray. "You wouldn't have any friends that sew, would you?"

"Nope, sorry," Bonnie says. "I keep pretty much to myself. I should be heading back; I need to start dinner and . . ." She

reaches up to touch her hair, hitting a curler instead. "Damn—
I forgot my damn curlers are still in." She smiles a tiny bit,
looking over at me. We chuckle. It's a start.

"I hired our second seamstress today—What the *hell* is
this?" I hold up a huge mushroom from one of the million
bags of groceries Ruby has heaped on the stump table.

"Portabella mushroom. Isn't it lovely?" Ruby beams with
shopper's pride, turning pages in her bible, *The Joy of Cooking.*
"I'm going to sauté it in olive oil and then make a lovely
roasted red pepper sauce out of these beauties." She holds up
a bag of deep red peppers. "I found the most divine roadside
market over in Bayfield."

"It's amazing." I give the mushroom a good sniff.

"The young man assured me they're a delicacy." Ruby
whisks by, snatching it out of my hand.

"Well, I'm the last one to question your cooking." And I
mean it.

"Cooking for us, darling"—Ruby fills the fridge—"is something I get such a kick out of. Especially since I get to have all
the fun and you clean up my mess!"

"I've never been interested and as long as you're cool with
it . . ."

"I'm *cool* with it," Ruby tries, but it still sounds so silly coming from her.

"You'll never in a thousand years guess who she is. You
should've seen this woman." I start folding grocery sacks.
"Thin, wispy hair in rollers and clothes that just hung on her
skinny little body."

"The poor dear," she says from inside the fridge. That

woman spends half her life with her head poked in there. "Are you going to tell me, or must I beg? I detest begging; I'll sing." She singsongs "sing." Let me tell you, that would be torture, having Ruby sing.

"It's that Al the creature's wife—Bonnie. What a small world. She's pretty, though, I can see it. Maybe a richer hair color and with a decent makeup job . . . all that eyeliner."

Ruby chuckles. "It's an *island* and you must remember, you can't save them all, darling."

"I was only saying . . . I can't help myself." I spin around on a stool. "I think how you present yourself to the world has a lot to do with how you're going to be treated."

"That may be true, darling," Ruby says. "But some people are so busy with children and family and . . . life, that it's not a priority. Me, I wouldn't be caught *dead* without my best face on."

"Do you know how that makes the rest of us feel?"

"Of course"—she sighs dramatically—"*someone* has to set the standards."

The oven door is open; our backs are to the heat. Perched on stools, Ruby and I blow on mugs of hot chocolate. The air is getting cooler at night, so we've started wearing sweaters.

"Do you really believe in ghosts?" I ask.

"Well . . ." Ruby thinks for a moment. "I'm not sure, exactly. I believe in the *possibility,* I think. I certainly think we go *somewhere* when we die."

"A faraway somewhere or near?" I ask.

"Oh, I don't know, darling . . . Near. Yes . . . near, I think."

"Me too."

"You've not been hanging out with Ed or anything, have you?" Ruby asks, half serious. "I can't imagine he'd haunt the cottage . . . though he did fancy it here."

"Used to think I'd meet an Ed. Someone who would sweep me into strong arms at all the right moments . . . arms that meant something." I sigh at my miserable luck.

"Not everyone needs someone to hold them up, darling."

"Is that what Ed did for you? Held you up? You don't strike me as in need of a holder-upper. Not a bit."

"That may be true," Ruby says. "No . . . not hold up, maybe to reassure you're you and that your thoughts and feelings matter. That your actions are, oh . . . in the best light of what you are . . . I think."

"That's nice."

"Things have changed though. I think some women, like you, darling"—she touches my hand—"are not as *dependent* as my generation, especially when I grew up in England. I don't mean that in a good *or* a bad way, just that being a woman is . . . *more* now."

"Things *have* changed," I reply. "And things have *not* changed."

"Oh heavens yes. But what I wouldn't give to have the grit women do now."

"Oh honey—you've got grit."

"What I mean is . . . things are better for women—men too. I'll never forget working nights so I could pay for nursing school. Think my parents would help their only child with tuition? Pah! College was for the boys. I ended up dropping out on account of marrying Ed. Most people had to choose back then. Now that he's gone . . . I wonder . . ."

"Regret?"

"Not a moment . . . no. But I wonder what I might have become. Think I would want to be more like you, darling."

"You are *not* serious . . . are you?"

"Oh, not *exactly* like you. But with your spirit . . . your way
of approaching the world. It's remarkable—exactly what I
need more of. Now, getting back to the *someone* part . . ."
Ruby pours us more hot chocolate.

I thought for a moment. "At this point in my life, I honestly
don't know if I even have *room* for a relationship. You get to a
place when you've taken up all the empty space that maybe another would have filled and . . . you fill it yourself! I've come to
the conclusion that Rocky is all the man I'll ever need. He
never makes me feel anything but loved." I pat his head to put
a period on it.

"That's really all I think any of us wants to feel, darling:
loved."

It's around midnight and a noisy rainstorm is pounding the
cottage, making it shudder and groan. The sound hitting the
roof is driving me crazy. It's always either lulled me to sleep or
made me think powerful thoughts. Since I'm stuck in the
thinking mode, I figure *what the hell* and crawl out from under
my covers.

In the dark, I search for my robe. I shake each slipper before putting it on since I would hate to shove my foot into a
sleeping mouse. Lifting Rocky into my arms, I quietly slither
downstairs with him. The occasional lightning burst guides my
way. Reaching under a fringe-shaded lamp in the living room, I
snap the light on. Now I can maneuver my way over into the

kitchen. A Reese's Peanut Butter Cup (or two) sounds just right. I lift down a fresh pack, then two. Which I realize makes four—give me a break.

I head down the hall, into the library. Pulling the door closed behind me, I feel as though I've left the cottage and entered a whole new world. I pull the metal chain on the dragonfly lamp sitting in the middle of a wooden table. It throws a greenish-yellow light on the walls and furniture.

I let Rocky down in order to drag a wingback chair closer to the light. There's a rich, serious feeling, with all the books lining the shelves. They help to make the room quieter, almost cavelike. I pull my legs up, unwrap and take a delicious bite. Heaven. Chewing the peanutty chocolate goo slowly, I reflect on all that's come to pass so far.

I see Dorothy and Watts at the salon. Ruby standing over a box that had burst open, spilling books everywhere. The crazy going-away party. Watts, tears in her eyes, taking the keys to the salon—then hugging me a good long time.

Looking around me, I see this magical place of toads, duck rides and that wooden dock. Popping in the last cup, I open the window and gaze out to the lake. A damp breeze flutters my hair, moonlit shadows dance across the yard, and *this* is where I want to be.

I have no idea how long I sit there, but I drift off to sleep for a while. Eventually Rocky's meow wakes me up. I scoop him into my arms, take a hardback copy of *Cross Creek* down from a bookshelf and head back to bed and dreaming and sleep.

CHAPTER THIRTEEN

We're dressed in Bayfield-day-out clothes. Nothing *too* flashy. I've got on a green blazer and jeans. My hair is loose and curly as hell, thanks to all this humidity.

Ruby is totally "Madeline Island Matriarch"—hair wrapped in a scarf, long dangle earrings, fancy jacket and matching slacks. Puffing on a newly lit smoke, she hunts in her Louis Vuitton for something.

"Our first formal excursion since we moved here," I point out.

"A good day for an outing, darling," Ruby says through a cloud of smoke. She leads the way out of the kitchen, toward the van, her purse snapping shut on the "outing" part. "You simply *must* teach me how to drive this thing."

"Get in—let's start now."

"Oh, how jolly exciting!" She hops into the driver's side of my VW van. "This has got to be the first time in history that I have *not* had to pull the seat up closer. It pays to hang around short people."

"Smart-ass. Push in the clutch, throw it into first and let's go!" I slam the door shut. I lift her hand off the stick and point out first gear on the knob's little diagram. Ruby hits *just* about that.

We lurch forward; then the van sputters and dies. Ruby turns it over again, pushes down the clutch, and before you can say "automatic transmission," we're chugging down the drive, over the bridge and through the woods to the gate. Branches swish by; several yellow goldfinch fly across our path and make a mad dash for cover.

"You're a quick study *and* a lead foot. There goes *my* insurance," I say, hopping out to unlatch the gate.

Ruby drives through and I pull the gate closed. I hesitate a second, taking in the sun sign. I've never had my name surrounded by a sun before.

"Okay," I say. "Now let's get to the ferry in one piece—please."

"Grab your seat; let's see what this jalopy can do!" She puts it into gear.

The van shudders—only for a moment—then begins to pick up speed. I reach over and push in a tape of Pearl Bailey. She belts out "Hit the Road to Dreamland." We fly up, over and around the island road, making our way to La Pointe.

After fueling up the van in town, we get in line for the next ferry to the mainland. Since it's a weekday, they're running every fifteen minutes. The gate opens, so Ruby drives us onto the deck. As the ferry pulls away from the pier, we stare at the slowly approaching shoreline, thinking our thoughts. We glide toward the landing, then drive off through the parking area and onto a side street of Bayfield. Funny how sometimes time stretches out and other times it races by, leaving you breathless.

I had read earlier, in the *Island Gazette,* that Bayfield is busy gearing up for the big Bayfield Apple Festival. That explains why there are a lot of folks out on the sidewalks—cleaning, painting, and tidying up this and that. Men on cranes are hanging banners and posters; the air is bristling with activity. We find a parking spot outside Maggie's Restaurant and hop out.

"What a beautiful day in Wisconsin," Ruby declares. "Let's head over to that bookstore and have a look around."

We walk down Manypenny Avenue, then head into the What Goes Around bookstore. It's rather unimpressive on the outside, but as soon as I squeeze through the door, I'm surprised by the roominess of the place. It's made up of many different levels of hardwood floors, wooden benches and chairs arranged around packed bookshelves. There are oodles of cozy little nooks to crawl into with a good book and a hot drink. I can smell the cinnamon cider; it wraps around you the minute you enter. In the back, two rickety French doors open onto a brick patio that's strewn with leaves. I reach down to pick up a fluffy white cat that's been rubbing against my ankles like crazy.

"Good morning, ladies. I see you've met Lucille." A well-dressed man approaches. I love his unruly gray hair and black-rimmed glasses. He smells of fruity pipe tobacco with a touch of Old Spice. I like anyone who accessorizes with a pipe and a book in hand.

"Hello there. Lovely shop. We'll take the cat." Ruby assesses the man with her razor-quick eyes.

We laugh and introduce ourselves. His name is Leslie Aschenbauer. I slip away; Ruby loves to chat with complete strangers. Besides, there are shelves to explore. Lucille and I start to look around. I step off into the crowded bookshelves, scanning the spines for familiar authors. I always seem to find myself in fiction. I overhear Ruby and Leslie chuckle. I'm positive Ruby's tapping into good old Leslie's knowledge of the "Bayfield pulse." I pull out a hardback copy of Elizabeth Berg's book, *The Pull of the Moon*. Lucille and I drift away into her brilliant writing.

"This isn't a library, young lady," Ruby proclaims—scaring me half to death so that I smack the book shut, which causes the cat to dart away.

"I was just trying this on to see if it was my size."

"And?"

"It's perfect—I'll take it." And I do.

"You two seemed to get along awfully well," I remark as we stroll along Second Street.

"He's had that shop for over thirty years . . . and remembers Ed," Ruby says.

"That was very sweet of him," I say. "Anything interesting going on?"

"He's *very* connected, of course, but also protective. I got a few juicy little tidbits. Let's see . . . Judith, over at Greunke's is trying to get ready for the festival and refuses to hire any more help. The IGA is thinking of expanding; someone at the Rittenhouse is nicking lace doilies right out from under their noses; and a local bakery owner is having an affair with the man who runs the new flower shop. A true *scandal* as the owner of the bakery is a *man*. Leslie's eyeballs practically popped out of his skull when he let that one slip. Poor darling."

"You did great!"

"The best part was when he asked how long my sister was staying with me."

"Sister?"

"I can't help it, darling, if I look so desperately young for my . . . ah . . . age," Ruby says, smirking.

"Thanks—I'm going to assume he meant we *both* look young and not that we're a couple of old hags killing time before the next happy hour kicks in."

"Let's do the market next," Ruby says, dismissing me. "We can't forget your—"

"Plugs," I finish for her, hunting through my bag for a lighter and thinking I should maybe carry a gun for times like these.

"Lovely. Right, then—I made a list of all the things we're either out of or haven't got at all or . . ." Ruby chats away while lighting my cigarette and checking her list. "This could take a while."

"Thanks. All that pipe smell made me crazy for a smoke."

"Let me help you with that." She takes my cigarette and has a puff. "We're nearly to the market." I snag it back and take one more puff before snubbing it out. Did I really need to have that? Now my breath is icky, too.

As we pass through the glass doors of Andy's IGA, we're enveloped by the fragrance of fresh-baked bread. It's a tidy little market all done in that old-fashioned green. Narrow isles are neatly packed solid with everything one could possibly ever need. It makes me think of the corner market of my childhood, where they knew your name and you could always get a candy necklace or fizzies on credit.

"Oh my," Ruby mutters. "I'd quite forgotten what a *real* market looks like."

"Can you believe how clean this place is?"

"Look at this lovely broccoli." Ruby lifts a big green bunch and we bag it in plastic. "Good heavens—collard greens and squash and zucchini!"

"Put that down and come on!" I was served that stuff every day for too many years in school. I fight to control our jerky shopping cart. I always seem to get the ones with the bent wheel. What's that all about? Or the one that only goes left. Love those.

Heading away from the produce section, we wheel into the snack aisle. Out of nowhere, a woman heads straight for us. She's so busy looking at all the bags of chips that she bumps right into us.

"Oh I *am* sorry," she says. "This stupid cart simply won't behave." The lady has a marvelous lisp, and she has Dorothy's nose, not to mention her hair. She's wearing a light overcoat, sparkling white tennis shoes and, again, has the most amazingly high, swirled hair, like Dorothy's (should I sing "It's A Small World"?). Rhinestone bifocals perch on her nose, attached to a glittery chain. She smiles and it's brilliant, but her teeth seem a bit too large. I imagine her teeth sitting next to her bed at night, smiling back through a flowered glass.

"These aisles are way too small." Ruby tries to save face for the woman's bad driving. "Should all be one-ways or something."

"I wasn't paying attention, I'm afraid to admit. I'm *desperate* for some Bar-B-Q potato chips," the woman confides, whispering.

"You know—when those cravings hit, you just have to jump." I think fondly of a fresh sixpack of Reese's Peanut Butter Cups.

"Where are you ladies from?" Heavenward-hair asks.

"We live on the island. I'm Ruby and this is my friend Eve."

"Oh how nice to meet the both of you. I'm Lilly. You're *living* out there? In the winter, too?" She reaches for a *third* bag of chips.

"You're Dorothy's cousin, aren't you?" I accuse her, since this is really so odd. Then I change my tone because Ruby is giving me *the look*. "She works, used to work for me in Eau Claire. I've teamed up with Ruby here and we're—"

"Why yes." Lilly adjusts her glasses to study us. "Dorothy and I are second cousins once removed. She's mentioned you many times. Loves doing hair. You know, I do my own," she says with pride, giving a pat for my admiration. I start to raise my eyebrows—her hair goes up *so* damn far. Ruby clears her throat.

"You had asked if we live on the island," Ruby says. "We do. And we're starting up a business—we hope it will keep us from killing each other." She chuckles.

"Well you know," Lilly confides, peering over the rim of her glasses, "most folks that live out there all year get a little crazy. You can't come or go for a month or so until the lake is all froze through." Her teeth click every so often.

"Well, I'm *sure* we'll be just fine. So nice meeting you Lilly. . . ." I attempt to push our stupid cart around her. I need a cigarette. I wonder who the hell else we're going to *run* into. Maybe this is what is meant by synchronicity. I make a mental note to see if Ed has any books on the subject.

"Oh my Lord in Heaven—you're the ones in the *Gazette!*" Lilly blurts out suddenly.

"Yes," we say together.

"Before my husband dropped dead—right in the middle of watching *Murder She Wrote,* mind you, I had a notions store right here in Bayfield. Did all my own sewing and made—"

"Let me guess." I hold up my hand. "Drapes."

"Land, you must have heard." Lilly's face lifts a bit. "I did all the window treatments over at the Rittenhouse and for many of the Islanders, but . . . after Lud died, I just slowed down a bit. Sold my shop and—"

"You still have a sewing machine?" I ask. I know from Mom, if you've sewn on a certain machine for a while, you get to know it.

"Oh lordy, sure I do now." Lilly nods her head. "I have three . . . or is it four . . . and bolts and bolts of fabric. Not to mention notions coming out of my ears. The basement is jammed full."

"Have you ever considered returning to the workforce, darling?" Ruby asks, giving me the arched-brow look.

"You mean . . . for you two? Oh, I . . . The grandkids *are* all grown, and I have so much time on my hands and . . . I hadn't thought." She absently tosses *another* bag of chips in.

"We sure could use the help and . . ." What am I saying? She has a certain appeal, though *and* that delicious lisp, not to mention the Dorothy part. Which, if you've been paying attention, I *have* mentioned.

"I bet you could sew circles around the both of us," Ruby offers. "Lilly . . . I lost my Ed a few years back. I know what . . ." she shares with a hushed, understanding tone.

"Oh I am sorry," Lilly says knowingly, patting Ruby's arm. "You know, I *have* thought of a job of sorts and I *do* love to sew and . . . Oh lordy, I'd love to." And that's that.

We spend the rest of the morning setting things up at the bank, taking out a small business loan and have worked up quite an appetite. Signing all those forms can be exhausting. I suggest we try Maggie's. With a name like that I figure it has to be good. I'm a little taken aback when we walk in though. Everywhere you look—pink flamingos. Made from every conceivable material and covering all the walls. Strings and strings of flamingo lights are wrapped around poles and hanging from the ceiling.

An older gal with hips that move all on their own, leads us to a nice booth with a view—of a wall. But hey, it's in the smoking section, so what do we care?

"This is so cozy in here," Ruby says. Meaning even *she* feels squished.

"That it is and from the looks of the menu—and the size of the line forming outside, the food is going to be delicious."

"Let's split something," Ruby suggests.

"Okay, sure . . . fine." I gaze out the window at our wall.

"What?"

"Just thinking. The Apple Festival is coming in October and . . . if we had a booth . . ." I dig in my bag for something to write on. "We have that Bonnie gal and now Lilly. Marsha will be here soon. All we really have to do is *make* the damn things!" I list thoughts on a pink-flamingo napkin. Our waitress swivels by with mugs of coffee and takes our order.

"After lunch let's try and find a fabric store," I suggest. "There must be one around here somewhere. We could fill the van with crazy patterned material . . . thread . . . whatnot and get our butts back to the cottage. This could be a great way to kind of test the waters, so to speak. What could be better than a festival? What?"

"We don't even have a pattern. How can we . . . ?" Ruby asks.

"I'll use your apron. We can take it apart and copy it."

"Ruby's Aprons is going to be a *smashing* success." We clink our mugs.

"I sure hope so," I add. "We've just about stretched our credit to the limit with the bank and with me not behind a chair and then there's the—"

"Eve, darling, what were you telling me just yesterday?"

"That sometimes you have to jump . . ."

"In order to fly," Ruby finishes for me.

Okay, I got it, it's one million trillion times easier to give out advice than to be the one that has to, like, do the stuff you're advising. I'm jumping folks! Damn it—I am.

We eat our iceberg-lettuce-crouton-crunchy-dripping-with-blue-cheese-salad with gusto. Then chase it down with way too much coffee so we can hit the road in search of a fabric store. Our waitress, Verna, suggested we try the Wal-Mart in Ashland.

With Ruby at the wheel and Dean Martin crooning "Volare," the van is pointed south. Heading down Highway

13, we weave our way along Lake Superior, the snaking road presenting us with perfect views of the water.

"I think I have this shifting thing down pat . . . again," Ruby proclaims proudly. "You can take your foot off your brake over there." We laugh.

"I was just helping." I relax my right leg and give my calf a rub. She's heavy on the gas, but—so am I. "Our first business lunch and this will be our first official business *road trip*."

"Oh the write-offs, how jolly marvelous," Ruby adds.

"I haven't ironed out all the details . . . but it's similar to having a salon, only no clients."

"No clients, no overbooking, no skipped lunches or perm smell, no hair spray flying . . ."

"No *kidding*!" I feel liberated. "So far we've managed to gather three employees and one suspicious husband."

"Don't forget the boys," Ruby adds. "They've already done so much."

"I consider them . . . family."

"I do too, darling."

"We're here already?" The WELCOME TO ASHLAND sign flies by my window. "I think you should slow down a bit . . . like soon!"

"Wal-Mart," Ruby announces. "Precisely where she said it would be."

Ruby clips the curb heading into the parking lot and just barely manages to miss getting hit by an RV rig trying to leave. We end up taking two parking spaces way in the back. All in all, we arrive in one piece, but my stomach feels as though it's somewhere out on Highway 13, flat on its back.

Wal-Mart is an unattractive cement chunk. Inside, the rows and aisles loom fully stocked and overwhelming as hell. They have *everything,* in every size, shape and color. From hair dryers and popcorn, a book section I'll have to resist, power tools, fuzzy slippers and cat toys. Armed with carts, we head in.

Way off in a distant corner, we find the fabric section. Bolts and bolts of material line the walls, are stacked on tables and shoved underneath. Rolling up our proverbial sleeves, we steer in closer and park.

"How much should we get?" Ruby holds up a bolt of brightly flowered material and wraps it around her waist.

"Any of these—all of them! If it looks like it might brighten up a kitchen, grab it!" I unroll a bolt of neon-yellow daisies being attacked by huge ladybugs—just the thing.

"Haven't you always wanted to shop like this, darling? Come to think of it—you *do* shop like this." She dumps an armload into her cart; it lands with a nice thump.

"What a riot!" I reach for spools of yellow, pink and green thread. Have I become a consumer junkie? "Do we want buttons on the front pockets? Nah—buttons mean buttonholes; too much work. Dumb idea."

"Dumb idea," Ruby echoes. "Sheer stupidity. Could simply sew them on—no hole. Might jazz them up a bit."

"I agree . . . big, colorful ones. Look . . . ruby red." I toss handfuls of the brightest shades into my cart.

"I can't fit another thing in here, darling. I hope there's not too much aisle traffic—could be dangerous." She starts to maneuver her cart toward the checkout.

"Hang on there missy—this may take a while. Let's head up

the center aisle and be—" I bump into a display of bone-shaped dog chews and helplessly watch them clatter to the floor, making a huge racket. "Shit."

Ruby rolls her cart over and helps me restack them. We shove on to the checkout.

"You sure you want *all* this girl?" A beautiful black check-out gal asks in a low, syrupy voice right out of Georgia.

She has long corn-rolled braids that are bursting out from under a teal headband; hoop earrings slap her cheeks as she rings up our piles. Her long fingernails click the keypad.

"Can you guess what we're going to make?" I'm thinking, she'll never come close, not in a hundred years.

"Looks to me like . . . aprons." She rings up several spools of thread, cool as punch.

Ruby's mouth drops open. "How did you . . . ?"

"Saw your ad in the *Gazette*. You two aren't from here and honey, there's things that I just *know,* is the way it is." She thumps a bolt of material down. Her name tag says "Sam." I consider this.

"Good . . . guess." I wonder how she knew. Could she be related to Dorothy too? I'm kidding.

"I see . . . you want both carts rung up together—huh?" She looks at Ruby—who still has her mouth open. I reach over and close it. Sam smiles. "My name is Sam and no"—she looks at me—"it's not a nickname for Samantha. You must be Eve. Nice to meet you." She gives me a wink.

"Oh heavens yes . . . yes, this is all together." Ruby finds her voice. "I'm Ruby." Both Ruby and Sam say "Ruby" at the same time. My eyebrows arch far into my forehead. Far.

"Don't mean to make you all paranoid—I've had the sight all my life, I should watch my manners though. Didn't mean to offend. I just *know* things. My mama called it 'the gift.' "

"You could make a fortune. . . ." I think of 1-800-Samsees and imagine dollar signs.

"Never have," Sam drawls, then mutters, "one-eight hundred" under her breath, chuckling. "Not many folks I share my sight with. I learned a long time ago that most of us need to go through, not around life." She whips and jerks her hands around with every word. I bet she couldn't say beans if her hands were tied up! I quickly banish this thought so as not to get in trouble.

But I'm thinking, she sure would add to our operation. Not to mention the fact that I feel as though I've met her before. You know, that feeling when someone you've only just been introduced to seems so familiar, comfortable?

"How attached to this job are you?" I hand back the signed slip and help Ruby reload our carts. "Unless you can see our venture falling flat or something."

"Can't see everything—thank God." She laughs. "I'm only part-time. I also work over at JJ's Body Shop. Give me a blowtorch and Lord, am I a happy woman." Her laugh is infectious. It's deep and really true. "I'll give it a thought. Haven't sewn in years . . . but aprons seem awful simple and it's going to be . . ."

"What?" we ask at the same time.

"Big. That's all I'm saying." She grins.

"Either way . . . Sam," I say. "Give us a jingle. Let's get together. Our number's in the—"

"The *wrong* number, you mean. I have it right here." She pulls out the *Gazette* with our ad circled in red. "Was going to call—then I saw you all were coming in and got that this here number isn't quite yours, anyway."

"Right, of course . . ." I try like hell to keep my mind clear, empty. Impossible.

"So lovely meeting you, darling," Ruby offers, giving Sam's hand a light pat, pushing her cart ever so lightly into my rear.

"My pleasure ladies—I'll be in touch." Sam waves us out the door.

Chapter Fourteen

"I don't know the last time I felt so *peculiar*." Ruby holds the boathouse screen door open with her hip. "It's not every day you meet someone who already knew you were going to meet *them*, for heaven's sake!"

"I thought the entire experience was like watching a movie and I was off somewhere in the corner observing." I plop an armload of fabric down on the counter. "Hope she calls . . . Something about her."

"She *will*, darling." Ruby puts her hands to her temple. "I see it."

"Well, here the two of you are," Johnny says through the screen door of the boathouse. "Can we come in?"

"What a lovely surprise. Get in here and have a look around," Ruby says. "We've been out shopping all morning and look!" She holds up a bolt of material with enormous pink flowers.

"Oh man, these are going to look . . . obnoxious. Where

did you *find* all this stuff?" Johnny roots through the fabric Ruby had just finished putting into tidy piles.

"We found more than *this,* I'll tell you." Ruby and I fill them in on Sam and her "gift" as well as the rest of our adventures in Bayfield.

"I'm impressed with . . . everything," Howard says. "Sam sounds intriguing, Lilly will be a hoot and my *God,* things are cooking," he adds with obvious glee, lifting up some of the bolts of fabric and shaking his head. "Women will want armloads of these."

"These are like, totally kitsch, Valley-girls," Johnny says. "This is so on-trend *and* Howard's got the web site coming along *and* I just finished making a cutout of the original Ruby-apron."

"Let me see those, darling." Ruby reaches for the cardboard cutouts. "I had no *idea* there were so many parts to an apron."

"I think some should have pockets—some with wider ties—you know . . . variations," I suggest. "The more we make . . . I'm sure they'll evolve."

"Johnny, you used your Ouija board box for these?" Ruby shows us the backside of one of the patterns.

"Haven't needed it for years now. Have all the magic I can handle right here." He drapes his arm around Howard.

"You two . . . It's getting really thick in here." I shake my head. "Sure do appreciate all you've done though."

"Honestly Eve"—Howard comes over and puts his arm around me—"it's been a while since Johnny and I have gotten such a kick out of . . . well . . . hanging out. Making things . . . being involved again."

"Even though you and Ruby are working us to death," Johnny adds.

"Of course we are," Ruby states matter-of-factly. "We've every intention of paying you . . . both of you. This is a company after all and our intentions are—"

"To be filthy rich," I throw in. "No . . . to make enough to cover everything, at *least* in the beginning. Then . . . who the hell knows? We *do* need to get things in gear, with the booth I've reserved and—"

"Wait a minute." Johnny holds up a well-manicured hand. "What booth?"

"I rented a booth. During the Bayfield Apple Festival in October. So . . . we're firing up on Monday. That'll give us well over a month, seeing as today is . . . I don't even know the day . . ."

"August twenty-second," Howard replies. "I think . . . with just the two of you . . . and the two of us . . . we'll need those women you told us about."

Ruby jumps in. "Then there's the float for the parade. And a schedule for who will work the booth, who will keep the aprons coming, lunches, more fabric, since we'll certainly run out in no time at all and—"

"What have we gotten ourselves into?" Howard asks Rocky, who's staring at us from the top of the fridge.

The boys eventually head back over to their place. I get on the deer-phone and leave messages for Lilly and Bonnie. If they can start next week, that would be awesome. I expect they will, since neither one of them is currently employed.

Just as I reach up to open the screen door and head up to the barn, the deer head rings. Pulling the jaw down, I grab the phone, giving it a good tug so I don't have to stare old stuffed-head in the eye.

"Eve's Salon—I mean . . . hello?" That's the first time that's happened.

"Hi there. Is this Eve?"

"Yes . . . who's this?"

"It's Ruby, you nitwit."

"Ruby? Where the hell are you?"

"Up at the cottage. All the phones here become an intercom if you dial eight, six, two, three, which spells toad, of course. Let's have a chat like old times. I realized the reason the phone doesn't ring like it did in Eau Claire is because we're both here. So . . . hi." I hear the familiar exhale and imagine the smoke ring she's just set free.

"You know . . . you're right."

"Of course I am, darling. How's it coming down there?"

"Looks wonderful . . . I hadn't realized you'd snuck off. I was scouring the bathroom sink."

"I should think it was a bit of a mess . . . you poor darling."

"Those iron stains are not going anywhere."

"Eve . . . things have gotten so stirred up, in a good way, mind you. The boathouse is beginning to look like what we thought it would, only a hell of a lot better and who knew?"

"No kidding." I nod to the deer head. "Not to mention the band of women we've hired. What a riot."

"I *do* hope they all show up," Ruby says. "If the Apple Festival proves to be a success . . . well I'd say—we're in business. *If* I do say so myself . . . and I *do*."

"If we make these babies really well—you know, quality stitching and all, catchy label, affordable price that's not *too* affordable—I'd say we're onto something. Or . . . we could get laughed out of town."

"Let 'em laugh," Ruby says.

"That, my dear, is exactly what we'll do. You're a genius."

"True, so true. Hey . . . I like these sketches you left up here for a label," Ruby says. "Seems like *your* name should be on it too though."

"Ruby's Aprons is simple. Has a nice ring to it . . . without trying to be too cute."

"I must admit, I've always *loved* my name."

"Me too," I say. "I love the *color* ruby, too. Wish my hair was still . . . but that's a whole other story. How about meeting me at the barn? I could use some help."

"Delighted."

"Delighted?" I ask the deer head.

Letting go of the phone, I watch as it flies up, a blackened tongue finding its way home. The screen door slaps shut behind me. Turning back, I peer through the mesh into the boathouse. Piles of bright floral material are heaped on tables and chairs. A shiny chrome percolator coffeepot and mugs wait in readiness on the counter, and spools of thread are stacked in the shape of a pyramid, compliments of Johnny. There's still a lot to do, but it's taking shape.

I take the wooden stairs down two at a time. Whistling, I walk up and around the cottage heading toward the barn. I can see the outline of Ruby standing in the barn's open doorway, hands on hips.

"Don't you look nice," I sputter, a little out of breath.

She's changed into a long gray dress that hangs clear to her ankles. Silver bracelets clang as she waves.

"Thought you'd never get up here," she says and smiles. "Had a lovely chat with a dear old friend of mine earlier. I was inspired—here." She hands me a framed napkin.

"What the . . . oh man. Should be worth millions one day," I say. It's the one from Maggie's, with the "Ruby's Aprons" logo I drew on it. A pink flamingo winks from a corner and my lipstick marks an O on the bottom. It's a simple sketch, really, an old-fashioned tie-at-the-waist apron, the ties floating out on either side, with a floral print design and "Ruby's Aprons" written in retro-style letters.

"While we were chatting, I remembered you framing my check that I wrote you the first day you opened Eve's Salon. I was so flattered . . . a little embarrassed too. I just thought . . ." She stammers a bit and I'm all the more touched.

"Thank you. This is great. Who knows where it will lead. You have to admit, so far it's been smooth sailing." I turn the frame over and read what Ruby's written: "To my dearest friend in the whole world—that's you, Eve—even way up here you've managed to make the sun shine a little brighter. Thank God all those years ago you had the good sense to say, 'I have time for you.' Love, Ruby." I sigh, feeling all mushy.

"Now then . . ." Ruby moves things along with her brisk manner. "The boys will be over in a bit so you should hustle on upstairs—take a nice hot shower, throw on a favorite frock and let's celebrate!"

"Are you saying that I smell?"

"Good heavens, yes—stink is more like it, darling."

"Don't hold anything back, you old . . ." I grin. "I *did* want to haul a table down and grab some other stuff, but I can have the boys help tomorrow. Maybe we can take the duck out for a spin tonight."

"Sounds lovely, darling. Now come along." She turns me around and we head toward the back door.

* * *

Pulling on a sweater and khakis, I glance at my reflection in the mirror. Rocky's lounging on my bed with not a care in his furry head. I wind my hair up and shove several pencils in the twist for good measure. Dab on lip gloss and feel revived. I grab Rocky and we head down the stairs, following our noses into the kitchen.

"Hey—look at you," Ruby tosses a huge salad in one of her mammoth bowls. "Be a love and pour us some wine."

"My pleasure." I set Rocky on the floor. "What smells so tasty? I'm famished."

"That must be the garlic bread I'm warming." We clink our goblets and take a sip. "We're having salad with smoked salmon and homemade cilantro dressing."

"Sounds delicious." I sit down on a stool and spin. "Feels good to sit. I love being this tired—when I do get to rest, there's not as much guilt involved."

"Does make you appreciate the simple things: like being cooked for, cleaned up after and . . . get off your rear and come over here and open this!" She points to the salmon wrapped tight-as-a-drum in saran wrap.

"Right." I carefully open drawers in search of a scissors. I do not want any more surprises leaping at me.

"It's going to be lovely having a job again," Ruby remarks over the drone of her electric mixing stick. "It's been years and I'm *so* looking forward to it."

"Me too. But you know—why is it that I can't be happy to just *sit?* All our lives we complain about . . . well just about everything and yet when I have a block of time to myself . . . I'd much rather be busy."

"Gives us structure, I should think. Having things to do. But too much work . . . Perhaps that's what's making people nowadays so miserable." She comes at me with a spoon to sample the dressing.

"I think you're right." I smack my lips in approval. "When I used to listen to clients, I was shocked by their work schedules. Late nights, weekends, carting kids around, no time to cook. A few of them—the at-home moms—they always seemed the happiest."

"I'd like to think that maybe the world is heading back to what you and I are heading into." She adds a pinch of something.

"You mean working at home? Or working together? Or . . ."

"Yes, to it all, darling. More than anything though . . . doing things together, sharing all the things that make a home. The simple act of making a meal together . . . chatting; I love the chatting."

"I do too."

"I don't think *he* was invited." Ruby reaches up to remove a spider hanging off one of the pencils in my hair and escorts it out the door.

She returns with Howard and Johnny, who are looking handsome, smelling fresh and clean. I get pecks on either cheek.

"Hey you two, great timing!" I hand Rocky to Johnny, then load Howard's arms up with plates and napkins.

"Guess the honeymoon is over," Howard says. "Where shall we dine tonight?" I push him out into the living room.

"Out on the porch; the sunset is just beginning," I suggest. "Get busy and set a nice table. Honeymoon! You and Johnny are going to be working so hard, you won't have time to complain."

"I brought a couple more cardboard apron patterns," Johnny says to no one in particular.

"Wonderful." I reach for them. "I've appointed myself chief fabric-cutter. I figure I can cut a mean haircut, so fabric shouldn't be *too* hard. The ladies and you can assemble."

"You're a mastermind," Johnny chides.

"True."

"This is fantastic!" Howard holds up the framed napkin with "Ruby's Aprons" on it. "It's great for the logo and the story behind it will personalize the Web site."

"It is lovely, isn't it," Ruby agrees. "You don't think it should say Eve and Ruby's or Eve's Aprons or—"

"*I* think it's charming." Howard grins. "Simple, old fashioned and besides, old names are in again."

"*Old* names? *old?*" Ruby stands there with the devil in her eyes and a loaded mixer in her hand.

"Oh boy . . . did I just put my size fourteen in my mouth again?" Howard asks, laying an arm around Ruby, pulling her close.

"I *love* the name," I comment quickly. "It's important to keep it simple. How about a toast to the official naming of our lakeside factory. Then let's talk about something *else* for a while."

"To Ruby's Aprons! To the birth of a brilliant concept in ladies' ready-to-wear *and* to three wonderful friends," Ruby says. We clink and sip, then I re-pour and we all sit around the stump table except for Ruby, who's tending the loaf of bread in the oven.

"I'll give Howard a hand and bring the plates and stuff back in here. What were we thinking?" I chuckle. The kitchen always seems like the best place to be.

"You two sure look beautiful," Howard says while I help him clear the table on the porch. "The island's working its magic." He set it all wrong anyway, fork on the right, knives facing the wrong way—really!

"Thank you." I loop my arm through Howard's, steering us back into the kitchen. "There's something in the air here."

"I love what it's done to Johnny . . . me, too," Howard comments.

"Are you two staying on the island through the winter or . . . ?" I ask tentatively.

"We usually stay until after Christmas and then hightail it down to Key West," Howard says while I unload his arms, setting the stump table. I do it exactly as Howard had. Who the hell cares what side the fork is on anyway?

"It would be wonderful if you stayed." Should I beg? "Everyone's been mentioning how lonely it can be here in the winter, but with you two and—"

"Lonely? Winter? What are you two talking about?" Johnny asks, being nosy. "What could be lonely with you two around—excuse me, three." A muffled meow is coming from inside the fridge. Ruby opens it and scolds Rocky good.

"*There's* a point to consider," Howard says. "But I was telling Eve here—"

"We wouldn't miss this for all the rum in Florida," Johnny breaks in. "To be honest, last winter we vowed would be our last. It's gotten way too crowded."

"I don't suppose anyone is hungry?" Ruby asks. "Rocky and I are ready to serve."

After eating, we gather around a crackling fire. Howard has his arm around Johnny's shoulder and Rocky's fast asleep in Ruby's lap. I have my feet up on the coffee table, getting all warm and cozy.

"How about coming for breakfast in the morning," Johnny suggests. "We can show you the site on Howard's computer."

"Look's like Howard is ready for La La Land," I say quietly, since Howard's head is resting on Johnny's shoulder. "Sleeping Beauty."

"He can fall asleep anywhere. *I* can't even nap." Johnny gives him a little shake.

"What did I miss? Sorry." Howard rubs his eyes. "What a dream."

"You were snoring and drooling and the *things* you said," Johnny says and giggles. "I'm kidding. You did fart, though." Howard tickles him.

"I dreamt that Ruby and Eve were on a gondola in Venice wearing huge pink flowered aprons on their heads and Rocky was at the helm singing and—"

"At least this time it wasn't *you* wearing the pink dress . . . dancing on tables," Johnny says. "I won't go into it tonight, but this is one repressed drag queen here."

"Off to bed with the lot of us." Ruby waves her hand and finishes up a serious yawn. "Tomorrow will be here soon enough."

We steer the boys through the kitchen. Ruby hands them a plastic container of goodies on the way out the back door. We watch them slowly amble through the yard, hand in hand. The bright moonlight colors them silver. Right before they disappear into the path, they turn and wave.

"They are gems," Ruby says as we both step back into the warmth of the kitchen.

"Kind of gives you hope that love is very much alive in all its shapes and kinds." I scoop up Rocky.

"A glass of sherry, darling?" Ruby moves a curl out of my face, gives Rocky's head a pat. "My loves."

"Read my mind. I'll put more wood on the fire and let's have some of those gorgeous chocolates the boys brought over, BT McElrath's I think. That is, if you haven't *eaten* them all."

"Just *one* more chunk," I say through the goo sticking to the roof of my mouth.

"What could be more delicious . . . sherry and chocolate," Ruby replies.

"Wish we could offer the ladies health benefits—too expensive right now. It's on my wish list though. It took me a long time before I could afford it for Watts and Dorothy. I wonder how they're doing?"

"I'm sure you're missed, darling," Ruby says, reading my mind. "Ruby's Aprons. Ed would be impressed, not to mention surprised as hell."

"Surprised? How so?" I sink into the cozy sofa and pull a quilt up to my neck.

"No offense, darling, but I never thought at the ripe . . . *young* . . . age of . . . sixty-or-so, I would be starting up a business, living year-round on an island and having so much fun."

"I was raised to believe that work was right up there with pain and suffering," I add.

"Me too, darling; now let's take these tired bodies to bed."

"Good idea."

We say our good nights and part at the top of the stairs. Just as I turn to go into my room, something swoops through my hair.

"What the hell?" I say as Rocky comes streaking into the room, his tail whipping the air. *Not* a good sign.

Then a little black flying *thing* races around, smashes into the window, and tips over a lotion jar, sending it crashing to the floor! Ruby dashes down the hall.

"Are you all right, darling?" Ruby ducks just as the dark, soaring shape zips between us.

"What in the world?" Then it dawns on me. *"Bat!"*

"Oh—*bloody hell!*" Ruby screeches, as it flies into my hair and gets stuck. "I detest the buggery creatures!"

Reaching into my hair, I yank out the pencils and swing my head around like crazy. I'm screaming "Holy hell" and "Fucking bat!" Bending over, I give my head a violent shake, then lift and bring my head up and swing it back. The damn thing soars out of my hair, across the room and slams against the wall. In slow motion it slides to the floor, landing with a thud.

"Little bastard!" I want desperately to take my hair off and throw the entire mess into the washing machine.

I grab Rocky. We tiptoe over to the pile of black fur and peer down at it. Eyes very wide—ours, that is.

"Is it dead?" I ask in a half-whisper.

"I don't think so . . . the tummy is moving," Ruby replies. We can hear pounding at the back door.

"I think I prefer mice," I say, half kidding.

"The boys must have heard us. I'll let them in; you keep an eye on our visitor."

"I need something to defend myself with. Here—take Rocky or I think he'll eat it and catch something horrible." I hand Rocky over, looking around my room for a bat-killer weapon.

"This umbrella should do the trick. If it moves, run it through!" Ruby does a run-through demo with my floral-print umbrella. "I'll be right back." She leaves me with *it!*

The boys come running up the stairs with Ruby close behind. They crowd into my bedroom. Before any of us can think, Rocky dashes between Howard's legs and pounces on it. In a flash, it comes to life! Letting out a horrible squeaky-squeal, it flies into the air.

Insanity! We're all pawing at the air—jumping around. Johnny leaps on my bed, Howard tries to swish it out the window with a handful of my bras and I'm defending Ruby with my trusty umbrella.

Then, all on its own, it zooms out the window and into the night. My umbrella decides it's time to snap open—and so it does. We look at each other, then at Johnny standing on my bed and burst into laughter.

I hand my open umbrella to Howard and he gives me my bras as if handing me a string of fish.

CHAPTER FIFTEEN

"What a spread!" With my arms open wide, I'm trying to absorb the "Martha Stewart" breakfast goodies laid out on the flawlessly coordinated table. Denim blue stoneware, matching placemats with linen napkins folded just so. "This is so nice of you guys."

Their cabin (as they refer to it) is enormous, tastefully rustic and filled with pottery. Arts-and-crafts furnishings give it a manly feel, while floor-to-ceiling windows fill the great-room with sunshine and warmth.

Johnny places a platter of heart-shaped waffles on the table. We're informed we have hot maple syrup or whipped cream for toppings.

"Coffee smells *scrumptious*," Ruby says. "Your table is lovely and *how* did you manage fresh raspberries?"

"Out back," Howard says. "There's a big clump of bushes along the north side of our shed."

"This sure is a sweet place you two have." I plop down into a love seat that's overflowing with cushy pillows. "Where in the world did you find all this McCoy pottery?" I get up and move toward a small yellow vase perched on a shelf.

My mother had collected this stuff and I catch my breath recognizing this vase, identical to the one I broke as a little girl. . . . Mom ran over—hearing the crash—and instead of yelling at me she took me in her arms. She said she had buckets full of vases but only one little girl. Besides, now there was one less thing to dust. I smile and carefully put the vase back on the shelf.

"Mostly antique shops. Some pieces are from an aunt—she's the one that got me hooked," Johnny remarks from the kitchen. "I *have* gotten some pieces on eBay—but that feels too much like cheating. So we pick up a piece here and there."

"It's an amazing collection," I say.

"After we finish brunch, we'll show you the Web site." Johnny beckons us to sit around the table and we dig in. I wonder if there's a Weight Watchers group on the island.

Howard starts clicking his mouse, so we move in closer around him. Ruby maneuvers her way into the middle. There are pictures of the boathouse, the cottage, several of Rocky and one of Ed's smiling grandparents standing near to a beautiful speedboat next to the dock. The best one is a close-up of Ruby's actual apron.

"You've done so much," I marvel. "And so fast. It's great. What do you think about an eight-hundred number? Maybe set it up so people can buy directly from the site too?"

"Sure!" Howard sits back, folds his arms over his chest. "No problem—I can easily set up an eight-hundred number as well as a shopping cart."

"We were wondering"—Johnny clicks back to the picture of Gustave and Adeline—"did you two notice how *long* that boat is?"

"You know," Ruby says, putting her nose about an inch from the screen, "it *is* rather long. How in the world did they get it so close to shore? I mean, we could hardly get the duck that close in and it's much shorter—and look here." She points to the boathouse doors that are open in the background.

"Do you still have the originals?" I ask.

Johnny hands me a stack of photos, I sort through them looking for the dock shot and notice how the cottage changes over the years: the addition of the wraparound porch, a picture of the boathouse being built. Then I come to the one of Gustave and Adeline.

"Oh look." Ruby points out a side window that faces our cottage. "A cardinal is sitting right there on the path. How lovely."

"Let's walk over to the boathouse and say hello to the little feller," I suggest as I snap out of my thoughts. "I have to say, you and Johnny have done so much. We're really grateful." The boys both smile with "aw shucks" all over their faces.

Keeping an eye on the bird as it sails ahead of us, we stroll along the path leading through the birch trees to our cottage. The bird follows the shoreline with us, and not until I reach the boathouse does it flit away into the woods.

"What a wonderful day," I proclaim, starting up the wooden stairs to the second floor of the boathouse. "Just the right amount of chill to get the blood moving."

Johnny and Howard open doors and Ruby gets the coffeepot loaded. I sort through all the tapes I brought down and realize we haven't anything to play them with. While over at the boys' cabin I had put together a list of things that need looking after. I add a tape player.

"Howard and I can build some shelves along this wall for the bolts of fabric." Johnny points to the far wall where the deer head is mounted. "What are you going to do with the bedrooms?"

"The beds need to be moved out." I head in one bedroom and then the other for a look. "We can use the dressers for storage. One room will be an office and break room combination and the other will be . . . shipping and whatnot."

"This really is the ideal setup, Eve," Ruby says, smiling. "We need a microwave, some nice dishes for lunch, chairs out on the deck for cigarette breaks and . . . I *must* tidy up this old fridge and stove a bit more—Good Lord!"

"How about if Ruby and I head up to the barn and poke around for chairs and a desk. You two can start taking apart the beds," I say to the boys.

"Sounds good to me," Johnny replies. Howard nods.

We start out the door. As the screen door slaps shut, Howard says to Johnny, "I want a raise!"

"*I'll* give you a raise," Johnny chides. They giggle.

Soon Ruby and I are digging through our pile of *very* carefully stacked items from Eau Claire.

"I'm so glad we kept my microwave." I pull it out. "We must have enough sets of dishes for . . . 'Course you *can* always use another plate, you know," I offer, seeing Ruby's guilty look.

"I should have gotten rid of the whole lot," she says, exasperated. "I'm a dish junkie, so I've ended up with all this!" She points to a stack of boxes as high as her.

"Oh *hell*, Ruby—it's something you enjoy collecting. How many sets you think you have there?" I raise my eyebrows, counting. "That many . . ." I'm wondering how she snuck some of these in. Sly dish junkie.

"I've only got *four* Christmas sets, so that's a saving grace, wouldn't you say?"

"Well . . . sure I would. I got rid of my stereo though." I change the subject, realizing it's a lost cause and who cares, anyway. "The speakers alone weighed a ton, but I'll *die* if I can't play music down there. This is serious."

"The stereo in the living room is too enormous to move," Ruby observes. "You know, Ed had a system in the library."

"Wonderful . . . Besides, quiet in a library is best." I head into the cottage.

"Good morning sleepyhead." I pick up Rocky from the stump table. "You never used to get up on the table at . . . This is home now and you need to keep your paws on the floor. Come with me, young man."

We walk toward the library; the toad-window casts a green-ish glow on the floor and walls. Turning into the library, I stand in the middle of the room and inhale the calm.

Opening windows to let in morning air, I look around, try-ing to figure out just where this stereo is. Since I did all the wiring for a music system at my salon, I know how you can hide them, but for the life of me I can't see a thing. So I start opening some of the cupboards that run underneath the book-shelves.

Most of them are loaded with more books, some have magazines, one's filled with a collection of rocks. I run my hand over a few and decide to have a look at them another time. I get to the end of one wall and am about to look into the cupboards under the window, when I notice the wall is much thicker than the window frame. Yet there's no door or shelves. Standing back, I study the entire wall. On either side of the window, it's built out, but there doesn't seem to be an opening. I go over to the left side of the window and start tapping it with my knuckles. Then I try pushing the entire wall and—violà! The wall snaps open. Ruby breezes in holding two mugs of steaming something.

"I forgot all about those closets." She hands me a mug. I can smell the chocolate. "I've been meaning to give them a look and you found them all on your own."

"Here's the stereo." I start pulling it out.

"This is one of the speakers, dear." Ruby holds up a tiny black box.

"I'll be! So small." We gather up our find, then head back to the kitchen.

"All we've left to do is find chairs and a desk." I put the dusty speakers on the stump table. "If you'd snazz these up a bit, I'd be grateful."

"Certainly. Rocky can assist," Ruby suggests as Rocky leaps from my arms, racing out of the kitchen.

I open the barn doors to let the sun in. The boys are coming up from the boathouse carrying a bed frame over their heads. Ruby comes out on the back porch holding the speakers and a ball of gray fur.

"Now, what's in this barn that we can use down there?" Howard asks as we all walk in to "shop."

"There's some furniture stacked by the workbench," I say. "Must be a desk somewhere."

"Here . . . under this." Howard points to an enormous moose head. "Doesn't everyone have a moose in their barn?"

"It's a great desk. I love the paint splatters—adds character," I say. "Wrap it up! These club chairs could go in the office, and *look* here—all these wooden folding chairs!" I point to a stack under the staircase to the loft.

"Just right for the deck," Ruby adds. "It's lovely to put all these things to use again."

Johnny backs up my van into the barn to load it with our finds. Then we head down to the boathouse. Howard takes the stereo upstairs and puts on an old Gloria Estefan tape and soon we're cleaning, hauling, and doing the mambo to "one-two-three-four." We leave everything to sit in the sun to "freshen up a bit," as Ruby puts it, and join the boys upstairs.

"This is awesome." I look over the bedrooms. "I'm sure we'll do some moving around later on—but it's feeling very factory-ish in here. Hey . . . I thought you said there was only the fireplace for heat. Look at this." I point to a heater vent in the floor. "So there's *got* to be a furnace. Where the hell is it?"

"Good question," Ruby says. "When guests stayed here it was always in the summertime. Where could one hide a *bloody* furnace?"

We go into the soon-to-be shipping room directly behind the kitchen. Besides the dressers, there's only a closet. It takes up the entire wall. We slide the doors open and—nothing. Not even a hanger.

"I wonder . . ." I push on the back of the closet. "I just bet there's a little spot behind here like up in the library . . . . Hmmm—nope. Let's try the other bedroom."

"You, of course mean the office, darling," Ruby corrects me.

"What the hell are you two banging on the walls for?" Howard asks, coming out of the bathroom. Ruby and I are all the way into the closet, rapping on the wall.

Ruby's bracelets are making such a racket! Then Ruby exclaims, "Bingo!"

"Well I'll be damned," Howard says. He and Johnny crowd into the closet and peer over our shoulders, which is an easy thing for them to do.

The back of the closet door opens, revealing a small room. Cool air escapes, sweeping by us. No wonder the bathroom is so small and dark; this room is directly behind the shower.

A trapdoor is built into the floor. I lift a round ring and pull up—locked. Ruby hands me the ring of keys and I try a few that look about right. After the ninth try, the lock clicks, allowing me to lift up the metal door. A whoosh of chilly air comes with it. Smells of iron-y water and decay follow. Peering down into the hole, I can barely make out the handrail of a metal spiral staircase.

"There must be a room at the back of the boathouse down there," I say. "I just thought it was all water in there. Shall we?"

"I'll go first," Howard states in a commanding, take-charge voice that for some reason rubs me the wrong way. "Could be bats, you know."

"Not on your life, buster," I reply quickly. "I can see more light down there. It can't be very large and if there *are* any bats they better watch their hairy little rears 'cause we are coming down!" I yell this last part to ensure everyone is aware of my position and—mostly to convince myself.

"I'll be . . ." Ruby mutters.

I start down. With each step of my Keds I feel the dankness on my bare ankles. Ruby is close behind, followed by the boys. I get to the bottom of the stairs and find myself standing on a stone ledge. By the light of several dusty bulbs, I spot three switches next to an old furnace. Its pipes reach up into the ceiling. I flip the first switch.

"This is incredible," Howard announces, coming down the stairs. His voice echoes off the walls.

The ledge we're standing on leads farther back into the earth. I can see a long, narrow room with a wooden door at the end. Directly in front of us is water.

"This is all making sense now," Howard muses, while moving slowly down the ledge, toward the wooden door.

"I think I have an idea of what . . ." It dawns on me. I flick the next switch. A motor in the center of the wall to our left whirs to life, throwing out a dusty electrical odor. The wall slowly parts in the middle and folds in two until finally it's flush against either side. We're now looking into the front of the boathouse and out to the lake.

"Oh, good heavens!" Ruby wipes cobwebs from her hair.

"No kidding," Johnny adds dryly.

"My God—this is a *brilliant* setup," Howard says with admiration. "From this loading area in the back here and now that the waterway has become several times longer . . ."

"I think I see, but . . ." I say.

"There's a door built into the wall over here and it's hung on wheels." Howard gestures toward it. We join him in the back of the cavelike room. "This is one heck of a secure door and . . ." He gives the door a yank in the direction of the track above it. "It's locked tight."

"Perhaps this . . ." Ruby hands him the toad-key we'd found in Ed's notebook. "I have a feeling . . ."

Howard inserts the key, turns it this way and that—suddenly it clicks. "Fantastic! Give me a hand, Johnny ol' boy."

Together they pull the heavy door to the side, revealing a large low-ceilinged room. On the wall inside is yet another switch.

"Shall I?" Howard asks. We nod. He snaps the switch, filling the room with light.

The tunnel is crammed on either side with huge wooden barrels. A narrow aisle down the center leads back, ending at a spiral staircase.

"My God, this is so . . ." I say.

"It's quite simple, darling—Ed explained a few things in his journal," Ruby says, "Canada is north . . . across the lake . . . During Prohibition, let's see, what years?"

"It began in nineteen twenty-one and lasted until thirty-three," Howard informs us as we gather around Ruby.

"Thank you, darling." She's *totally* enjoying this. "Gustave had a trucking company already, with a network to Chicago, New York and Philadelphia. He had a long and fast Chris-Craft boat, the one in the photo. It made late-night trips under the cover of night."

"What a sneak," I say in awe. He must have been *very* interesting. "Then they'd zip in here, close the doors, load these from the boat into trucks and be off."

"Something like that, darling," Ruby says. "It was bottled either here somewhere or in a larger city. Gustave's lot was called—"

"Toad Tea!" Johnny points to a faded toad on the wall with gilded letters underneath.

"How clever . . . It's the toad from upstairs!" I say. Ruby nods.

"He was never caught. They simply closed down in thirty-three . . . and that was that," Ruby says, and we all kind of go, "Oh."

"The staircase at the end of the aisle down there?" I ask, pretty sure of the answer. "Takes us to the cottage basement, I bet."

"Let's check it out," Howard suggests.

At the base of the stairs are several wooden cases. Johnny reaches in one and pulls up a brown bottle. He blows the dust off and reads out loud, "Toad Tea—the magic's in the tea; the toad's for luck."

The toad in the picture on the bottle is winking. "I can't get over the fact that this is here still," I say with wonder. "It's not like you could just sell the stuff or . . ."

"No, the enforcement agents, or 'Revenuers,' as Ed referenced them in his book"—Ruby puts her lecturer hat on again—"they searched high and low many years after Prohibition—since so many families had made fortunes. There were back taxes to be collected, so it was best to simply shut down."

"Let's get on up these and see where the hell we come out!" Johnny impatiently suggests.

We head up. At the top of the stairs, Johnny pushes the door open and we're all standing in the basement of the cottage. In the wine cellar, to be exact.

"Nothing like a back entry to round things off," I say.

"I think we need to give it a taste sometime," Howard suggests. "I mean, there's enough there for—"

"Perhaps later boys. All this excitement makes a girl hungry," Ruby says. "But one thing you all must promise . . . and that's to keep this *our* little secret. Otherwise . . . I'll have to kill you," she calmly adds.

We chuckle and quickly agree. The boys head back down to the boathouse. We go in the opposite direction to put together a snack.

"Well don't just stand there, darling," Ruby says to me. I follow her up the stairs, into the kitchen.

"My heavens, what a super find!" Ruby pulls things out of the fridge. "Ed only gave me a few hints in his journal. But when we found the room and he *had* explained about his grandfather. . . ."

"It's history," I say. "I mean, this is a big deal. But you're right, we can't let it out. This place may have been paid for with—"

"Dirty money," Ruby finishes for me dramatically. "How divine! Now hand me a tray."

"I'm sure the boys won't tell anyone about Ed's grandfather's past. We *could* threaten them . . . 'Course as you so nicely put it"—we say the next words together—"we may have to kill them." We then laugh like hell, remembering the looks on their faces.

"Really darling, no one's past is truly all that squeaky clean. Let's see here now . . . I have some Gouda, a spot of Brie with crackers would be lovely and some bars perhaps."

"That is plenty." I marvel at how she comes up with all this food. "To think that all we were doing was looking for the damn furnace."

"I'm just as surprised, darling." Ruby pats Rocky on the head as she whizzes by. "Can't be many more secrets left. Not *physical* ones, anyway." She adds napkins to the tray, and we head back downstairs to see if it's a quicker route through the tunnel versus the path.

"These shoes *used* to be white," Ruby remarks, peering down at her gray—but I'm certain expensive—canvas slip-ons. "We must consider installing a lift. This is simply too many steps in one day." We amble down the staircase, through the tunnel and then up another staircase into the office.

"Hello boys." I come out of the closet with goodies. "The office looks like . . . an office! Thanks for hauling all this in here—tight, but cozy."

"I wonder if it's safe to drink this?" I hold up one of the newly discovered bottles. "What a cool label."

"I bet it's fine," Howard says. "What are these?" He holds up a square of chocolate-chip yummy-ness.

"Eat it fast or Eve will and I'm not kidding," Ruby says. I harrumph for effect.

"I'll pour coffee all around. Give me a hand, will you Johnny?" Ruby brings the pot in from the kitchen and hands Johnny a cat mug with eyes that move. "Special brew . . . no flavors, no extra smells . . . pure coffee."

"So, Eve . . ." Howard smirks. "There's this rumor that you and Ruby truly are planning to kill us."

"So, Ruby," Johnny adds, "how dirty *is* the money?"

"What the hell?" I ask, looking at Ruby with a blank face. "I, ah . . ."

"How in the world could you have heard us? It's all the way down . . . and up, around corners . . . ?" Ruby asks, a little breathless.

"You would not *believe* how clearly we heard you," Howard says. "Every word—like the sounds were amplified or something. I have a feeling it was designed that way."

"We didn't hear *you* . . . Nothing." I'm amazed; embarrassed too. "When you guys headed around the corner, that was it. We never heard another sound. Weird."

"I imagine it was done for security measures," Ruby states around a mouthful of cheese and cracker. "If the revenuers found the tunnel in the cottage basement . . ."

"You could grab your wife and kids, hop in the boat and get the hell off the island," Johnny offers.

"Thank God it's legal now," I say. Everyone nods. "Seems so silly."

"Yes it does, darling. But we're slow learners, you know."

CHAPTER SIXTEEN

We spend the rest of the afternoon cleaning and scrubbing, our energy renewed due to Ruby's strong coffee; and of course, all that adventure stuff helps too. Johnny brought over some old disco tapes, so the boathouse is thumping to the rhythms of Donna Summer belting out "MacArthur Park." There's nothing like good disco to clean up an old boathouse

All the drapes are out on the deck, hanging along the banisters to get some fresh air. They're fifties' floral prints with tiger lilies and leaves as big as my head. Ruby and I go through the shipping room and office, dusting, sweeping, shaking rugs and mopping floors. Since the kitchen is open into the living room, we can all chat in between Howard's pounding.

"The shutters I found in the barn will make great shelves," Howard says, nails in his mouth. "Should work perfect for the bolts of fabric. Then I'll start on the wiring for the sewing machines. I'll bring the electricity up from the furnace room," he adds, heading down the newly discovered spiral staircase. "This is fantastic—there are enough circuits down here to light the island!" His voice echoes up, loud as all get out.

"Is there anything he *can't* do?" Ruby asks Johnny from the stool she's standing on while wiping the top of the mint green fridge.

"Cook. He is a *disaster* in the kitchen," Johnny comments, shoving tables around. "He can burn and melt."

Later, the four of us are sitting out on the balcony with our feet up, enjoying the view of the lake. The boathouse is all set to go. We have all day tomorrow to shore up any details. Since we're supplying lunch for the crew, we're hoping it will evolve into a potluck concept. This *is* the Midwest, after all. Ruby likes to cook, but I don't want to push it.

"The sound of the waves is the best tension reliever." I sigh. "That and a nice smoke."

"I thought you two were quitting." Johnny bats my smoke ring away. "It's really a disgusting habit, you know."

"I'm hoping to be just too darn busy to think about it," Ruby says. "You're completely right; it's a *disgusting* habit."

"Expensive as hell too," I add. "Do we dare make this a nonsmoking workplace?"

"Seems to me," Howard says, "it's against Wisconsin law . . . *some* law, anyway . . . to smoke in a workplace. Only in designated areas. Something like that."

"This could be the push we need," I say, and Ruby nods. "Could you look into it on your computer, Howard?"

"Our pleasure," Howard and Johnny say at the same time, then laugh.

"I think we're going to head on home and clean up." Howard yawns. "I need to get out of these filthy clothes and maybe even take a nap." He grins slyly at Johnny.

"Shall we gather for dinner?" Johnny asks as they get up to go. "We also need to do some sampling of Toad Tea."

"Let's make it a couple of hours from now," Ruby says. "I'm sure there's something in the freezer that needs to be eaten."

"Thanks for all your hard work today and look—it's a factory!" I announce as we walk back into the living-room-turned-sewing-room. "Who *wouldn't* want to work here?"

"Hello? Ruby? Eve? Hello?" A voice is coming from the closet. We all look at one another.

"You weren't kidding . . . Must be someone up at the cottage," Ruby says. "Eve . . . you take the tunnel and I'll dash up the hill."

"You want us to hang around?" Howard asks.

"Heavens no; scoot on home." Ruby waves her hand, then she's off, out the door, heading up the hill.

"Hello? Is anyone here? It's Marsha from Rice Lake." The boys follow Ruby out the door, heading toward their cabin.

Pulling the French doors closed and scooping up Rocky, I head down the spiral stairs.

"Hi there," Marsha says from the top of the basement steps.

"How are you? I didn't expect to see you *this* soon." I come up the basement stairs and set Rocky on a stool.

"I am doing wonderfully," Marsha gushes as Ruby comes in the back door. "Hello Ruby. What a lovely cabin. I know you didn't expect me for a week or two, but I just got to thinking . . . what *am* I waiting for?" She walks into the living room and oohs and ahs.

"Where are you staying, darling?" Ruby asks while rooting around in a drawer.

"In an adorable little cottage in La Pointe." Marsha sits down next to Rocky. "It's the carriage house of a much larger main house. I just love it here. I've already met a few of the locals."

"What did you decide to do with your house in Rice Lake?" I ask, setting a mug of coffee in front of her.

"I cleaned it from top to bottom—threw out a lifetime of junk—loaded up my Jeep and headed here. I'm not going to sell it. It's long paid for and maybe someday I'll want to move back, or maybe my daughter might want it." She blows on her coffee and turns the mug around to look at the front of it.

"I brought my entire cat-mug collection," I say apologetically. "Ruby and I need to clean up; then we're having some friends over for dinner and—"

"You're more than welcome to join us," Ruby breaks in. "And we can give you a proper tour."

"Thank you so much, but I still have some unpacking to do and I don't want to intrude on your plans."

"Don't be silly," I say. "We're going to be working together come Monday anyway. That is, if you're game?"

"I am so ready to do something other than asking, 'And what'll it be today?' What's the rush though?"

"There's the Bayfield Apple Festival in October and we've rented a booth for our apron collection," Ruby informs from the freezer. "Oh shoot, I thought I had a chicken in here."

"I've been going to it for years; lots and *lots* of people. Apron collection?" Marsha asks, raising an exceptionally arched brow.

"What do you think?" I ask. "Easy to make . . . We found all this wild fabric at Wal-Mart and who doesn't need a cool, snappy . . . *handmade* apron?"

"I think it's . . . well, I'm not sure," Marsha says. "I *do* hate the ones you find now. Not much to look at and certainly nothing like the fancy ones my mother wore."

"Kiss the cook," Ruby and I say together.

One Christmas years ago, I got five 'kiss-the-cook' aprons from clients. Ruby and I found them tucked away in a corner of my apartment when we were packing me up and had a good laugh.

"We're going to give it a shot," I say. "The festival will be sort of a *test* market."

"I have a feeling that whatever you two put your minds to—it works," Marsha says. "I'm going to pass on your dinner invitation. Thanks, though. You know, I never figured I'd consider leaving Rice Lake. 'Course I kept the house in case I change my mind, but I wonder what would have become of me if I'd never met you two."

"Who's to say? We're glad you're here." I give her shoulder a little squish. "Though I doubt there's much social life here in the winters. Do you drink, Marsha?"

"A little."

"You'll be fine," I say, and we wave her out the door. Ruby shakes her head.

"There you are," Ruby says. "That old scarf suits you. To think I used to put my hair up in rollers every day and covered them up in that."

"It dresses up this top I've had forever." I lift a lid off one of the many pots on the stove and have a whiff. "What can I do for you, oh, mistress of the cooking cauldron?"

"I need you to stir a few things. But first, how about getting a bottle of Toad Tea up from the basement. The boys left a few in the wine closet."

"Sure." I pull open the basement door and turn on the light. "We have to remember not to go disappearing into the closet when we're all down at the boathouse." I head downstairs with Rocky in the lead.

While opening the metal door to the wine closet (which also leads to the tunnel), I hear Rocky growl and hiss off in a corner. Switching on the light inside, I call him a few times: no Rocky, no sound. I find the bottles and am turning to leave when he flies right between my legs and up the stairs, in a gray flash.

"No problem buster; I'll get the lights." Pushing the door shut with my rear, I head upstairs.

Ruby yells, "Eve! Eve come quick!"

I quickly scuttle back into the kitchen. Ruby is on top of a stool and Rocky's looking up at her with curiosity, his tail twitching like crazy.

"What the hell?" I ask, trying to catch my breath. "Not two seconds ago he was in the basement and . . ." I follow Ruby's pointing spoon to the floor, next to the stove. Putting the bottles down, I cautiously peer around the corner of the stump table.

"Oh my God. It's *huge*. Rats? We have rats?" I ask with disgust. "My God—let's open a zoo. This is getting old."

"I believe . . . now that I'm in a better viewing position of course, our *new* friend is no longer of this plane," Ruby says quietly. She squats down to have a closer look—but not too close.

"You mean the little fucker's dead?"

"Well put."

Using long vegetable tongs and wearing oven mitts—on both hands—I carefully approach the victim. After the bat coming back to life, I'm not taking any chances here. Ruby is two inches behind me. I nudge the creature a smidgen, to make sure it's really dead. Nothing. I lift it *very* slowly, using both hands since the damn thing is heavy. Deadweight, you know.

"A squirrel . . . for God's sake. Look . . . a tail was tucked underneath." I turn to Ruby, showing her the evidence, tail and all. It sways in my shaky tongs.

"Poor darling." Ruby takes a closer look. "You know . . . I could be mistaken, but I think its bloody eye moved!" She takes careful steps backward toward the sink.

Then the damn thing starts to squirm. Here I am in the kitchen with this undulating rabid-filled furball. Suddenly it makes a horrible squawking sound! Rocky, of course, joins in, meowing like a banshee.

I'm yelling at Ruby to open the "God-damned" back door while she's shouting to "Stay calm!" (Right.) Finally we manage to get it out of the kitchen before it leaps off my trusty tongs, landing on all four feet, claws making a scratching sound on the porch chair cushion. I make a mental note to never sit there—gross.

Head shaking, the creature looks around. Ruby and I, shoulder to shoulder, step backward into the kitchen. We don't want to stick around and welcome it back to the food chain. 'Course, I have no idea what in the world would consider a squirrel a treat. I slam the door shut and lock it. We push aside the lace curtain, trying to get a look—the chair's empty. We turn to glare at Rocky—gone.

* * *

"Knock knock," Howard announces as he and Johnny come into the kitchen. "You must have unknowingly let a squirrel into the porch, but he's free now. Hey, what smells so good?"

They're dressed in baggy jeans and flannel shirts. A lock of Howard's silver hair falls into his eyes; Johnny reaches up to move it aside.

"You're smelling the beautiful loaf of basil bread Ruby's baking in the oven," I say, rinsing a blue porcelain colander overflowing with steamy pasta. "Have a seat. We'll tell you about our little visitor. The latest, I should say."

"I am *quite* sure, not the last," Ruby adds,

"I've come to the conclusion that Rocky only *stuns* his furry playmates, leaving the actual killing decisions to us," I say after filling in the boys on the details of our latest animal adventure.

"He *does* bring us mice that are no longer alive," Ruby comments. "At least I think they're dead. I should *hope* they're dead."

"Many critters freeze when in danger," Johnny says. "Maybe the same goes for mice."

"Well that means I've drowned quite a few in the toilet. I really don't feel any regret *at all*." I hand Howard cat-faced placemats and paper napkins with cheery pumpkins and point to the stump table. Ruby has a drawer filled with packages of paper napkins printed with every holiday design and color combination. When we've used them all up, we're switching to cloth napkins. Save the trees!

"It's part of living up here." Johnny gives Rocky's belly a good rub. "You should be forewarned that when winter sets in

. . . more little heart attacks might be assisted by our bud here, Rocky the Man."

"Hard to imagine such a 'nice little guy' is also a cold-hearted killer." I glare at Rocky.

"Oh, it's not like he's walking around thinking murderous thoughts," Ruby says protectively. I smile. "It's *instinctual*—he's no idea what to do once he's *got* them though."

"We could stockpile a bunch, make mice potpie," I suggest to a group response of "gross," "disgusting" and "you are so sick." Which is true.

"Well . . . shall we eat?" Ruby asks. We look at each other. "In a minute then."

"I know," I say. "Since I just crushed our appetites, how about if we give the tea a taste?"

"Lovely idea, darling." Ruby puts the platter of spinach pasta into the oven to keep warm. "Howard love, would you get down some glasses?"

"My pleasure," he replies.

"Now . . . we have no idea if this is drinkable." I attempt to open one of the bottles, then hand it to Johnny. "Make yourself useful—pull!"

Johnny tugs a bit and the cork breaks off. "Damn—sorry." He hands the bottle and broken-off bit back to me.

"I'm far more experienced with twist-offs." I set to work trying to hook the broken-off piece and get to the bootleg. "Got it!" I show the half-cork on the end of the opener.

Ruby smells it, scrunching her nose. "My word—strong."

"Pour!" I pass the bottle to Howard, who hands out amber-filled highballs all around.

We look at one another for sipping cues. I pour big glasses of water since I'm sure we're going to need a chaser.

"I say"—Ruby raises her highball—"to Toad Tea!"

We clink our glasses and take cautious sips. Everyone reaches for water. Johnny gasps. Ruby's face turns scarlet. Howard tips his glass and finishes every drop. Me, I follow Howard's lead and empty my glass. The fire starts in my belly and travels everywhere real quick. There must be smoke shooting from my ears.

"Mmmmm," I say with tears running down my cheeks.

"You drank the whole lot?" Ruby asks, her voice rising in disbelief.

"Yup." Howard decants more into his glass.

"Jesus." Johnny gasps, chokes, then gulps down his glass of water followed by Howard's.

"Well," Ruby says. "Perhaps now we can have dinner, but let's have some of Ed's wine. I think that this"—she points—"should be mixed with a great deal of—"

"Mix," we all reply.

While Howard and Ruby are washing the dishes after our feast, Johnny and I take a stroll down the hall, finally cozying up in the library. A cool breeze is slipping in the open windows and moonlight illuminates the toad-window, filling the hall with a silvery green.

"This is a great room to sneak off to and do some serious thinking," Johnny says. "I know that Ed used to practically live in here."

"I wish I could have known him better." I sit down in one of the wingback chairs facing the potbellied stove.

"He was very . . . intellectual," Johnny says. "But in a subtle way. He just knew things, but didn't make you feel bad if *you* didn't. Ruby and Ed mostly kept to themselves."

"I know he was crazy about his Ruby." I get up and light the gas fire with a long wooden match, then close the door. "She misses him."

"He looked at her with such . . . love," Johnny says real dreamy-like. "They were always hand in hand or arm in arm."

"How sweet. It sucks though, him dying and all."

"How about you, Eve? Anyone ever hold *your* hand?"

"Oh, I really . . . no, I mean . . . Growing up, I was short, overweight. A redheaded only child with parents who were much older than anyone else's. I guess you could say I had . . . issues."

"Thank God you still have the red hair and I'm afraid you *are* short, but I'll tell you what, you're very beautiful. *And* I think it's just a matter of time—okay, maybe a long time—before we, as a culture, realize that beauty isn't just about high cheekbones and perky breasts." He reaches over and we clink glasses.

"Thank you. You're good for a girl's ego, but what the hell's wrong with my cheekbones?"

"Oh . . . I didn't mean . . ."

"I'm kidding." I've never liked talking too much about myself, so humor usually takes the spotlight off me. Usually.

"What else Eve?" Johnny prods gently. "That Toad Tea has made me brave. . . . You seem to have a something in your eyes, I'm not sure what. Something. I don't mean to pry, but . . . I was a hairstylist too, you know." We laugh. A good hairstylist works on what's *inside* the head as well as what's on top of it.

"I made some hormonally driven, stupid choices and ended

up pregnant," I say quickly. I can't believe I'm sharing this. But along with all the other changes in my life, it's high time to open up a little. I need to, and you know what? It doesn't hurt a bit.

There are some things that I've never shared with anyone, and I sometimes wonder if that makes those experiences less or more real. Like how you feel when nature hands you a beautiful deer to admire or what a certain smell reminds you of. It's sometimes just you and that thought, and off you go in your head to that place that's only yours. Does everyone dash around through thoughts in the middle of a meaningful conversation?

"Abortion?"

"Adoption." Do I dare look for her again?

"How long ago? If you don't mind me . . ."

"I was seventeen. . . ." I take a sip for strength. "My parents drove me to a *convent* and picked me up six months later when it was . . . after she was born." A single tear sneaks down my cheek, but Johnny doesn't see.

"Damn," he says, and we're quiet for a moment and that calms the air. "You try and find her or . . . ?"

"A while ago I did, but never heard a word back." I want to *not* talk about it anymore.

"We could help. If you ever decide to . . . you know . . . look for her again."

"Thanks." I *really* want to change the subject to, say, fly fishing or flatulence issues. How about menopause? I suppose that's on the way. One more thing I'll never be able to ask my mother about.

"Thank *you*," Johnny says before I say something really

ridiculous. "Takes guts to share something so personal like that. . . . I'm flattered."

"I never thought of it that way," I say. "How about you, Johnny? What is it that's behind *your* eyes? There's something sad there."

"Oh . . . well . . . that's pretty easy. AIDS. It cleared out—gutted—wiped out—my entire circle of friends. Every last one of them. I'm forty-eight and there was a time when Howard and I were going to more funerals than dinner parties. It's this haunting guilt."

"I'm so sorry." I look over at him. "Guilt?"

"Because *they* got it and *we* didn't and they're dead and gone. I know guilt. I'm Catholic." He tries to laugh, but it doesn't come out right.

"I don't know what to . . ."

"Knock knock." Howard peeks into the library. I look over to Johnny; he smiles and gives me a knowing nod.

"Come in; join the circle," I offer. Howard drags a chair over. "What did you do with Ruby?"

"She's fiddling in the kitchen still." Howard sits down next to Johnny. "Hard to keep up with that woman. And bossy?"

"Here you all are." Ruby enters the library, carrying Rocky and a half-filled wineglass. "This is so cozy and if you're talking about Eve . . . she *is* bossy."

"Come have a seat and put your feet up," I say. She thumps into a chair with a big sigh. "I can't budge."

CHAPTER SEVENTEEN

I wake up to the magical sound of rain pitter-pattering gently on the roof. My cat-clock, rhinestone-swinging tail, eyes that move, says "six" on the nose—literally. Rocky is sprawled on my chest, between my girls. It gets chilly during the night, so I don't mind.

"Hey, lazybones . . . time to rise and shine . . . buster."

I give him a little kiss, *never* on the mouse-tainted lips. Off he dashes out the door, down the stairs. I pull on my robe and slippers to follow.

Mornings here are something. Not a sound. Oh, the old fridge in the kitchen whines and groans a bit, but no planes overhead, no cars rumbling past, shaking the whole place all to hell. I wonder how many humans in the world have ever heard all there is to hear in silence?

In the kitchen I put two rocks from Eau Claire on the windowsill and they look *just* right. Then I root around for some instant coffee. A few scoops, hot water and violà. I have a slurp; it hits my stomach and I feel the oomph start to work its way around. Instant's not my favorite, but sometimes I just need to get a move on! I feed Rocky, then head back up to change.

The rain has let up a bit. Now it's turned misty, like a huge walk-in facial. Pulling the back door closed behind me, I head around the cottage toward the boathouse. Taking two steps at a time, I scuttle up the wooden stairs and pull open the screen door. As I cross over the threshold, I glance toward the lake and see the sun starting to shine on the water, bringing warmth along with some brilliant yellows and oranges. Taking a deep breath of deliciously damp air, I listen to the sounds of the lake lapping the dock and birds announcing a fresh day. Damn— this is living.

Putting "Vivaldi: The Four Seasons" on the tape player, I fill up the electric percolating coffeepot for any joiners that may wander in. Looking around, imagining what lies ahead, I sigh and feel my stomach knot. What if this crazy apron thing falls flat and all is for nothing? It won't.

The deer-phone rings, bringing me out of my thoughts.

"Ruby's Aprons . . . Eve speaking," I say.

"Yes hello there, this is Cook, Mrs. Prévost, speaking *clearly* into her mouthpiece. I was wondering what Eve Moss would like on her toast?" Ruby says in a nasally Brit tone that makes me smile.

"Peanut butter . . . with butter, please."

"I should think . . . that's exactly what I have here, but you best get your rear in gear as I may be tempted to have a bite or two."

"Okay, okay, don't do anything drastic. You know . . .

there's really not much to be done here. It looks . . . *fantastic*,"
I say, thinking of Howard and Johnny.

"I think we all need a break," Ruby says, and I can hear
Rocky meowing in the background. "Not a bat in sight, nor
squirrel or mouse, or—"

"I'm on my way," I say, chuckling.

I let the phone slip up into the deer mouth. I light up a cigarette and step onto the balcony, facing the lake. Whatever
happens happens. I snub out my stupid smoke, take in a gulp
of fresh air and head up the path, humming all the way.

"If I could only eat *smells*," I say, coming into the kitchen.
"I wouldn't *ever* worry about fat grams or calorie counting or
points!"

"Yes you would, darling." Ruby slides eggs onto plates and
we sit down at the stump table.

"True." I take a sip of orange juice. "This basil bread is even
better toasted, but I don't think it would work with peanut
butter."

"Oh, I . . . No, it wouldn't, darling," Ruby agrees.

"I had the nicest chat with Johnny last night. He's so . . .
deep and has more intuition than most *women* I know."

"That's lovely. He and Howard share such a bond and have
been together for—I don't know how long, to be honest. At
least since they moved next door and that's a long time now."

"I like how they treat each other." I dab at my mouth with a
Christmas-tree napkin. "Such good friends—and they laugh."

"They do, don't they." Ruby pours coffee. "You know, I
simply have taken it for a given—they've always been a part of

our summers up here. Howard and Johnny, the two of them constantly coming and going. In a way, it's as if I'd not been away."

"Was Ed uncomfortable with them? You know . . . them being gay?"

"Good heavens, darling." Ruby's brows rise. "He could have cared *less,* and to be honest, I rather think he enjoyed them admiring his bum."

"Who wouldn't?"

It's around one. The boys spent the better part of the morning finishing the wiring for the sewing machines and Howard was able to get my mom's Singer going, too. Ruby and I have reorganized the fabrics for the hundredth time and now are in the office setting up the desk and trying to get my laptop to behave.

"There! Done. You can run scores of machines and not worry about an overload on the circuits," Howard says.

"Thank you, Howard darling," Ruby says. "The sky is still not sure if it wants to be sunny or cloudy today."

"Good day to lie around and relax," Howard suggests. "Anything else we can do before the big day tomorrow?"

"Not a thing." I look up from my computer. "I'm going to call the ladies to make sure everyone is on for the morning. Then it's full steam ahead." He and Johnny good-bye and head out the door.

"What say you and I have a girls' day," Ruby suggests with a glint in her eye. "A late lunch, followed by cool showers. Then we can brew a spot of tea and do each other's nails over a lovely fireside chat."

"You—my partner-in-aprons—are on!"

"Oh double drat . . . it's raining cats and bats."

"Shut the lights off and follow me," I say.

"We haven't umbrellas. The tunnel?"

"Don't be such a nudge. Come on."

"Oh . . . super," she says less than enthusiastically. I ignore this and grab her hand and give her a yank.

Down the wooden stairs and into the now torrential rain two crazy women scoot! Between my laughter and Ruby's cackle, we make enough noise to wake the dead. I pull Ruby along the path to the cottage: by the time we reach the back porch, we're soaked to the skin—feels wonderful.

"Oh my God," Ruby says between gasps of laughter, "I am frozen clear to the *bone*!"

"Me too. What a marvelous rain."

We're wrapped in fuzzy robes, yellow tissue between our toes. Our feet are happily warming in front of a crackling fire in the living room. Our toenails are a gleaming red. We've managed to polish off a kettle of tea. Our jaws are busy munching on a frozen chocolate bar that still has some of the wrapper stuck to it. I'm filing my fingernails while Ruby braids my hair.

"Now that we know Ed's grandfather's money was made from bootlegging," I say, "what in the world will we ever do with all that booze down there? I mean, we can't sell it . . . can we?"

"I have no idea, darling." Ruby gives the fire a poke. "It obviously keeps well. Pity it's not wine though. The hard stuff is so—"

"Strong." I wince at the memory of tasting it. "They sure went to a lot of trouble. What a riot."

Looking into the mirror underneath the stairs, I check out Ruby's handiwork. She has braided my hair into a thick rope that travels from the top of my head all the way to my nape, ending in three braids down my back. How in the world am I going to get this out? I do like the way it pulls my face back tight. Who needs a face-lift?

"Oh Ruby," I singsong, heading into the glow of the kitchen and the clatter of pans.

CHAPTER EIGHTEEN

Down at the boathouse, Ruby and Johnny are fussing in the kitchen. Howard is working in the office. Me, I'm having a smoke out on the deck. It's nearly nine; I'm beginning to think that maybe no one's coming. Then I hear a knock.

Looking up to the sky, I say. "Thank you." Turning into the boathouse, I announce to everyone, just like I used to in the salon as the first client of the day came in, "It's Show Time!" Before reaching for the screen door, I give everyone a thumbs-up. Howard and Johnny offer it back. Ruby's eyes twinkle.

I pull open the door. There stands Sam, dressed in bright yellow, with Bonnie close behind. "Well, look at you girl," Sam says through sensuous lips. "I have chucked my Wal-Mart gig and decided you need me *far* worse than *those* folks. I *will* miss the discount though. Hello—you-all must be Johnny and Howard." Sam hands me her sewing machine and saunters over to the boys, extending a hand. A waft of Sandalwood floats behind her.

"I sure hope . . ." Bonnie says, snubbing out a cigarette on her hiking-boot heel and dropping the remains into her jeans pocket. ". . . I'm not late. Al, my *husband,* woke up with a hangover and wasn't too thrilled he had to drive me over. He left before I could grab my sewing machine."

"I'm sure someone can give you a lift home," I say. "I'm *really* glad to see you." Ruby comes forward, offering her hand. "I'm Ruby." She clasps her other hand over Bonnie's. "Nice to meet you, darling."

"Hello? Hello?" A shrill voice calls from outside.

Walking over to the edge of the balcony, I look down and see Lilly. She has on the same trench coat. Her glasses are perched on her nose at half-mast, silver-white hair looking as though it's being sucked up to heaven. I wave her up.

Marsha's following down the path, I hurry over to the top of the stairs in time to take Lilly's machine and wait for Marsha to catch up. Letting the screen door smack behind me, I reach up to push my hair away, then smile, remembering the braids. The boathouse is alive with gabbing women and an occasional cackle from Johnny or Sam—hard to tell the difference.

"Good morning." I walk over, stand next to Ruby and face the group. "It's wonderful to see . . . well . . . everyone." The assemblage regards one another. "How about we start with something to sip, then take a seat and we'll get acquainted before I *crack* the whip."

After everyone gets coffee and finds a chair, I lean on the edge of a table up front. "In a nutshell, for the next"—I look under the deer head, checking the Chippendale calendar Johnny placed there—"month or so, we're going to be making

. . . aprons. Not just ordinary aprons, mind you, but aprons with—"

"Attitude!" Ruby offers, lifting her chin for emphasis. Laughter.

"Ex—actly," I continue while walking slowly around the room. "It's a simple pattern, not too many pieces and . . . we're planning on selling them at the Apple Festival in October. We're also going to offer them online—but our goal is to get them around as many waists as possible and we think the festival will be the ideal testing ground."

Sam claps her hands together. "Girl . . ." she drawls, "you are going to *take* that town."

"Thank you, Sam." I take a slug of coffee. "*This* is how we'd like to run things." I set down my mug and look around the room. "Pay is fifteen an hour." There's an approving murmur. "An hour for lunch . . . *we* provide. You can bring a dish tomorrow, if you like. I need a commitment of at least four days a week. *no* overtime and maybe someday soon I can offer you health benefits of some sort."

Lilly raises her hand. "In all fairness and seeing as the morning is getting on . . ." Her half-moon glasses enlarge her eyes. "Let's get started!"

There's an overall nodding of heads, then we hear the clomp of footsteps coming up the stairs. The screen door smacks open and a man steps into the room carrying a sewing case and breathing heavily. It's Al. Our eyes lock and I feel this queer chill run down my spine. He nods ever so slightly in recognition. I squint my eyes in return.

Sam shakes her head, then says in a low voice, "Mmm, mmm. Trouble has just come a knockin', yes sir."

He's dressed in tight jeans, a beer belly straining his shirt buttons. He reaches up to flop back in place his greasy, combed-over hair. I don't think a new do could help this guy. 'Course, if the comb-over went; lose the belly *and* new clothes— Nah, hopeless.

He pants out, "Looking for Bonnie . . . she forgot this." He looks around, catches her eye and he clumsily sets the machine down. Turning to leave, he says, "You know I close late tonight, so you gotta find a ride—"

"Don't you fret about your wife, Mr. Smitters," Sam assures him. "I'll be more than happy to bring her home."

"Fine by me. . . ." The door smacks. His footsteps fade down the stairs along with the smell of liquor and a sweet/sour cologne odor.

"Thank you," Bonnie says to Sam, who pats her on the hand. "Sorry about . . . him."

"Well . . . as I was saying"—I arch my brows a touch—"before that charming young man interrupted us, let's get started, shall we?"

Everyone moves around, looking over the fabric, exploring the back rooms and setting up their sewing machines. I crank up Ella Fitzgerald, who belts out, "They Can't Take That Away from Me."

Purses are put away, windows and doors are opened and bolts of fabric are being unrolled. An order falls into place as each gal creates a space to work in. Johnny, Sam and Lilly look over the cardboard apron pieces while Marsha and Bonnie thread their machines. Howard heads back into the office.

"Who was that?" Johnny asks, following me into the kitchen area.

"Bonnie's husband," I say.

"Oh yeah," Johnny says. "Owner of the Liquor Lounge. *That's* the wife? She's too pretty for—"

"Meow."

"Lovely, isn't it, darling." Ruby comes over beside me. "I think Sam's right, you know. We're going to *take* this town!"

"You know, I think she is too." I head back to the office to check on Howard.

"Hey, Eve." He leans back, clasping his muscular arms behind his head. "Have a seat and *listen.*"

I thump down into one of the chairs opposite him. We overhear Sam and Lilly deciding just who should cut the pieces out and who should assemble. Lilly declares she's an okay cutter, but "Eve's probably faster," and then we hear the buzz of her electric scissors going at it. One by one, sewing machines rev to life, and the drone makes my stomach vibrate. Howard and I chat about the hundred and one details concerning the festival.

Johnny appears in the office doorway looking suspicious and I notice the silence out in the workroom.

"We have something to show you two," he says, and we follow him to the front.

The four women are grinning—Rocky's sprawled out on the table in front of Sam's machine, wrapped in a colorful apron covered with ladybugs and flowers. It's silent for a beat, then Rocky meows and his tail slaps the table.

"This what you had in mind?" Sam asks, and all eyes are on me.

"Oh *yes!*" I lift Rocky into my arms, unwind the apron and admire it.

"Honey," Sam drawls, "the day we met I felt something powerful special about you and this is just the beginning, child." She looks deeply into my eyes.

Then all four ladies stand up. Ruby comes around the counter and everyone shows off their fancy aprons! Johnny comes over and ties one around my waist. A tear trickles down my cheek.

I clear my throat. "I'll take it!" Everyone laughs.

Ruby gives my shoulder a nice pat and heads back into the kitchen area. After some minor task adjustments, the team jumps into production again. I take over cutting fabric after a few lessons from Lilly. With five sewing machines roaring away, not to mention these fancy cutters of Lilly's, the room is filled with life. I hand a stack of apron ties to Johnny and we grin. Several hours whiz by before my stomach starts to growl.

"Lunch," Ruby announces right on time. The sewing machines go silent. "Pick up a plate and help yourself. Let's eat out on the balcony. No sense in letting all that sunshine go to waste."

Chairs scrape as everyone stands to stretch, Rocky included. Ruby has set out a tasteful buffet of sourdough baguettes, thinly sliced cold meats, cheeses, salad fixings and several pans of gooey desert treats. Are we good bosses or what?

"My land." Sam takes a plate from Ruby. "Wal-Mart, with all their money, only ever gave us coffee. You are going to spoil us something fierce."

"Totally fat-free desserts." I nod to Ruby. "Just don't swallow."

"Ha ha, very funny," Lilly says over her glasses. "I'd better try one of these—well, one of each maybe, to make sure they're—"

"Safe," Johnny finishes.

"No one's fallen dead . . . yet," Ruby remarks.

"Hmm, now *there's* a thought." Bonnie takes a bit of this and that. "Food poisoning."

I try to picture Al with that beer belly and her scrawny little body naked and then cough to clear my mind. Maybe a class on nutrition would help; we could convert the loft into a yoga/workout room. I'd have to start with yours truly. But Reese's Peanut Butter Cups must have *some* health benefits. I've read the label a thousand times and at least I *recognize* the ingredients.

We spend a quiet lunch chewing and enjoying the sun. After everyone finishes eating, Sam, Lilly, Bonnie and Marsha all go back into the boathouse. Seconds later they return with purses, root around in them and produce cigarettes. Oh boy.

"This is *not* a good sign," Sam says through a cloud of smoke. "I think besides yoga, we need something to help us kick this nasty habit." I blush, remembering her "gift."

Ruby and I join in the smoking. The boys retreat into the boathouse, where the air is cleaner, but not before Johnny makes several comments about lung disease, the horrible smell in one's clothes, hair and on one's breath. He has a way with words.

"This really is pathetic." I blow smoke out of my nose. Cute huh?

"I've smoked since I was ten and—" Bonnie offers.

"Ten!" Sam declares. "You must have come into this world

smoking, girl. I picked it up when I moved up here. Never touched one before and that's the God's honest truth."

"When was that?" I ask.

"I moved up here about . . . twenty years ago, I guess." Sam ponders this.

"I think it must have been when Lud died that I really got the hang of it," Lilly says. "If I didn't smoke, I'd be big as a house. It keeps my mouth busy. 'Course I'd rather be crunching."

"Crunching?" Marsha asks, putting her cigarette out, checking her makeup in a tiny mirror.

"Chips . . . I am addicted to potato chips," Lilly proclaims with pride, holding open her enormous purse, showing us all several chip bags in various states of consumption.

"You know," I say rather conspiratorially, "there's something about a good crunch that—"

"Beats sex cold," Sam throws in and we giggle. "I'd rather be crunching with Lilly here than dealing with men."

"You ever been married, Sam?" Ruby asks, handing her a fish-shaped ashtray quickly filling with lipstick-coated butts.

"No, ma'm, never have and I can't imagine I will. Nothing against it, mind you. I just never had any *use* for it. Doesn't seem right, spending your life with just one other person. Besides, with the sight I got gifted with, well, I see too much as it is."

"What do you mean . . . sight?" Lilly asks. Marsha and Bonnie move in closer.

"Oh, it's nothing really; everyone has it," Sam says apologetically. "Most folks are too busy *thinking* about the future—

not *living* in the present. Gives me room to take a look around in their heads."

"You can see into my *head?*" Lilly asks, her eyes wide.

"Only if I'm invited, if it's in your best interest. That's what my momma told me, anyway." Sam shakes her head. "Sometimes though, I see things that make me *so* sad. Guess that's why I like living up here at the end of the world. Folks here seem to have mostly found their peace." I notice her casting a worried look in Bonnie's direction, but it quickly vanishes.

"I had my palm read by a woman once and she had everything all mixed up. Charged me twenty bucks for nothing," Marsha says, giving her hair a pat. "I believe I have spent half my life thinking about the past, what *might* have been if my husband hadn't gone off and left."

"Oh, there's nothing wrong with remembering, wondering now and again," Sam observes. "It's when you sit there in your head and don't see what's in front of you—that's the rub."

"Lordy," Lilly says, getting to her feet. "We have talked right through an hour out here and it's high time we hit the machines . . . ladies." She heads back into the boathouse.

"You can root around in my head anytime the feeling hits you, darling," Ruby says. "Just be forewarned, I can't be held responsible for what you find in there." Sam smiles.

We move back inside and everyone digs right back in. Around four o'clock the sewing machines all come to a halt for the day.

"Well, that's that and what a *that* it's been," Ruby announces to the group and I nod. "The way you all moved today . . . was super! Won't be long and we'll have hundreds of aprons for the festival."

"I'm afraid I'm not very fast," Bonnie apologizes to the group. "It's been a long time since I've sewn anything with more than a couple pieces."

"Not to worry, child." Sam waves her hands around for emphasis. "In no time at all you'll be sewing up a storm just like Miss Lilly there." She has a sizable pile of aprons next to her machine.

"I've sewn drapes to dresses and even worked with upholstery," says Lilly, adjusting her glasses. "Takes time and experience. You're doing fine, dear."

"Maybe some of us should sew certain sections and others, other ones," Marsha suggests. "I bet we could get more done if we each get real good at putting together the same parts."

"Excellent idea," I say from the kitchen. "If you can work out what you'd like to sew yourselves . . ."

"Oh, sure we can," Sam drawls. "Can't we, ladies—and man?"

Everyone nods in agreement and this is how our first day comes to a close. Sam and Bonnie leave together. Marsha and Lilly exchange phone numbers and go out laughing about how they can't wait to see Mr. September seeing as Mr. August is such a "hot number." I go over to the deer head where the calendar is tacked up and have a peek myself. Oh my.

"It's a shame the festival is so far away." Ruby lifts an apron from a pile on Sam's table. " 'Course, we do need time to get all the kinks worked out, but, *Good God,* they're quick!"

"If we price the aprons cheap enough, people will buy more than one," I say. " 'Course, on the other hand, people may take one look at these, laugh and keep walking! We could have our heads up our—"

"Eve Moss, have some confidence," Ruby commands. "There's not a reason in the world this can't work. It's brilliant—*we're* brilliant!"

"I . . . think so too. I wonder if this is how Mary Kay started." When will I not worry about every little thing? Why is it I can't let things be and not wonder myself silly?

"Johnny," Ruby says. "He created a shampoo and lord knows the world certainly had enough of *that* to go around, and look how well *they* did."

"You're right . . . I'm getting caught up in negative stuff. It's my nature, and I really need to—"

"Loosen up," Ruby says, and I agree.

Chapter Nineteen

All four ladies are down at the boathouse, busy at their machines, when Ruby and I walk in the following morning. There's an air of camaraderie, and I know Sam's had a big part in it. When the screen door slaps closed, the women look up and "good morning" us.

Johnny winks from the cutting table, then motions me over, handing me the electric sheers. I dig in. When I have a stack of parts cut out, Johnny, Marsha and Bonnie sew them together. They in turn pass that assembly to Sam, who sews on the tie-strings and pockets. Then she hands the result to Lilly, who adds lace to the bottom and to the pockets and finally all five of them take time out from using their machines to sew on buttons—by hand, no less! This also is when everyone chews the fat.

"Not a lick of sense in that man . . . His brakes were shot all to hell and he wouldn't listen, no sir. No woman was going to tell *him* nothing about his macho-man truck," Sam says while the ladies tsk-tsk. "Sure enough, he got a couple miles down the highway and had to run into a pile of brush to stop. A call come in . . . I knew it was him, so I let JJ answer it."

"Well?" Marsha asks while pulling a long black thread through a button and biting the end off with her teeth. I walk over and hand her a scissors.

"I told JJ—he owns the body shop—that I would be more than *happy* to run over and tow Mr. So and So's butt back to the garage." Sam chuckles. "I drove up in that big old tow rig, started chaining up his truck—had his tail between his skinny legs. I asked him if he would be wanting his brakes fixed now and he thought that would be *real* nice."

"My my . . . I sure admire you, Miss Sam," Lilly lisps, peering over her glasses. "I lift the hood of my car and wonder how all that metal and tubes and filth gets me from one place to another." Bonnie and Johnny nod their heads in agreement.

"I learned it all from a man I nearly *did* marry once," Sam says to a suddenly still room. "Got to my senses at the last moment and not a minute too soon, either. Seems he liked my best girlfriend same as me. Walked in on the both of them doing their *finest* right there in my bed. Can you believe?" She shakes her head.

"My husband—Lud." Lilly looks down at her work. "He was a wonderful man and I wouldn't trade the years we shared for . . ." She looks over to the calendar of nearly naked men. "Well, for our Mr. August, I might." We laugh.

"You are very lucky to have those memories, darling," Ruby says sweetly.

"Looks like I'm the only one married," Bonnie's apologetic face glances at Johnny and he shrugs.

We all look at him; Sam says, "Don't seem right—folks like Johnny and Howard can't be."

"When I married Al . . ." Bonnie pauses.

"Have you been together a long time?" I ask.

"Met Al in *fourth* grade. We were sweet on each other all the way through until high school," Bonnie says. "Then he got two other girls pregnant and—"

"Two!" Marsha, Lilly and I say at the same time.

"He *was* good-looking and a charmer and . . . he made me laugh. We used to laugh," Bonnie says as if to defend him. "Neither one of them ever *had* their babies, though."

"Mmm mmm," Sam murmurs.

"What in the *world* happened?" Lilly asks.

"Susan Beckerd was killed in a car crash and Laurie Fleming . . . she went away for a weekend with Al and came back with her belly flat as a pancake."

"She give it up, or . . . ?" Marsha asks, her voice rising a bit.

"She wasn't all that far along. Al said later she wasn't even carrying . . . But everyone knew," Bonnie says, and I feel my eyebrows lurch.

"How in the world did you ever end up *marrying* him?" Lilly asks. "After getting two . . . I just can't imagine."

"It was a long time ago and honestly . . . he used to be . . . someone else. He started drinking and it's changed him," Bonnie says.

"Child, his hold over you is all he's got left." Sam pulls tight her yellow headband. "The anger he dishes out is festering like hot coals. Could burn you up if you don't be careful."

Bonnie nods in agreement. "I don't know how to . . ."

"Are you in any danger, darling?" Ruby asks kindly and we all lean in as I think everyone is wondering the same thing.

"I can take care of myself. No, Al . . . he's nothing to be afraid of . . . except when he's smashed."

"Oh boy." I feel kind of sick. Knowing from listening to too many women over the years, booze can make a man danger-ous.

Sam reaches over and pats Bonnie's arm. "Things are going to change for you, sister. You just keep strong, baby. Things are going to be *just* fine."

Before anyone can question Sam, as *I* sure as hell would like to, Lilly-the-taskmaster puts the pedal to the metal and every-one follows suit. I crank up Dean Martin and go into the kitchen area to help Ruby get lunch together. Everyone brought a dish to pass and from the looks of everything, we'll *always* have leftovers!

Later, that night, Ruby and I are sitting around the stump table relaxing with a glass of wine after dinner.

"Hello?" I say into the yellow phone that hangs in the kitchen. I untwist the cord a bit so I can sit back down.

"Eve? It's Bonnie. I . . ." she stammers and I can hear her take a sip of something that requires the tinkle of ice cubes. "Al's over to his bar and I . . ."

"Oh boy," I utter and mouth Bonnie's name to Ruby. "You okay over there?"

"Oh sure . . . yeah . . . fine. I just was wondering if I could ask you something. About Al and all."

"Sure. Of course." I motion for Ruby to freshen my glass of wine pronto. "What's on your mind?"

"I don't have all your . . . well . . . strength. Wish I did, but I'm not made that way. But I've been having these thoughts and . . ."

"What kind of thoughts?"

"Like of doing to Al what he's been doing . . ." Bonnie sputters out, then gathers herself up again, speaking more gravely. "He hurts me . . . sometimes, see? And I don't know if I can take it much more. Sometimes it's real bad and I—"

"Bonnie—Christ! There are places you can go—safe places— aren't there? I mean no one needs to put up with that kind of—"

"You don't know him; you have no idea who he knows, what he could do. He'd find me; he told me. He would."

"Bonnie, you can stay *here,* or go to the mainland, or . . . how about family?" I'm wrapped up in the phone cord and Ruby has to help me get my legs untied as I take a puff from her cigarette.

"I don't have family *or* close friends, never been social, and Al keeps a tight rope on me." She speaks in a scoffing tone, but it comes out broken and way too old-sounding for such a young woman. "I needed to talk is all. Hey, thanks for the job and . . ." I hear her take a deep breath. "For listening."

"Anytime. You call here *anytime,* you hear me? You sure you're okay?"

"Yes, I'm fine, just fine now; good night then."

"Good night, Bonnie. See you in the morning." I hang up and pace. "She's not safe there and now that we know her and all, I can't help feeling responsible. . . ."

"You were bloody marvelous, darling. Sometimes just to talk is enough."

"He's hurting her, you know that." I hold my stomach, feeling it churn at the thought of him hitting her. "I don't know what to do."

"Do? Oh, you can't *fix* everything. All we can do is *be* here and let her know that she's safe talking with us. That was very hard for her to do, ring us and talk about it. It's a start. I'm not saying what's going on over there is right, but it has to be up to her."

"I don't get it." I feel helpless. "There are choices, there are . . ."

Choices? Like I had any all those years ago. A hot time with dream boy and I get secreted away without so much as a "see ya later, I'll miss you, only daughter of mine." Sure I loved my parents, but that's one wound that still burns. No, hurts like hell is more like it. Bonnie isn't a little girl and neither am I. Yet why do I feel this same helplessness I felt so long ago. Some memories I really would like to chuck.

"Love is such an odd mix of things, darling. She may see the man he was when he's—"

"Beating the shit out of her!" I want to bust *his* greasy face. "You know, I need some fresh air. You want to maybe take a spin in the duck?"

"Love to."

I stomp over to the barn and give the green button a good smack. The barn door slides open, I climb into the duck and pull it over to the back porch. Parking it, I head back into the kitchen where Ruby is waiting, wrapped in a sweater. Her hair is up in a scarf and she's holding an armful of blankets. She hands me a pullover.

"What took you so long?" Ruby asks.

"Well, don't just stand there . . . get your fanny in the duck and let's find us an island with no men!"

"Let's."

We're parked on a small island facing out to the lake. Which means it seems as though we're all alone out here. I've built a nice fire and since Ruby thought to bring blankets, we're all warm and snuggly.

"I can't stop thinking about that bastard." I poke the fire into higher flames.

"Well, I can't change your thoughts." Ruby digs into her pricey, zipped-up vest pocket. "But Sam said to bring this with tonight—and here . . ." She hands me a small envelope. "Open it."

I tear it open and out falls a joint and a book of matches with JJ'S BODY SHOP on the front. "Oh for God's sake—look what that rotten woman sent us!" I hold up the evidence. "I haven't gotten high in . . . years." We laugh. I look at her, then back at the joint. "What the hell." I light it up, take a cautious puff, hand it to her. "Oh man," I say and let out the smoke, real slow.

"She said we might be *needing* it." Ruby holds up the joint as if it may bite. She takes a hefty puff. "I'm not sure I'll ever get used to the idea of her always being a step or two ahead of the game," she says in that strange voice you make when holding in a breath. (You know the one.)

"I had no *idea* you smoked. Pot, I mean." I take it from her and have another toke.

"Oh, Ed and I tried it," Ruby admits with dignity. "As I recall . . . we'd always end up in the bedroom."

For some reason this is so funny that we both burst out giggling. I straighten up my back and have another. "I had no idea what pot even *was* until Watts left a joint at the shop once. It must have slid out of her bag and there it was on the floor in the break room." I take the smoked-to-the-quick joint from her for a final hit. "What could I do? I couldn't leave it there for *Dorothy* to find."

"No darling, that would have been a *horrible* thing indeed!" Ruby nods way too much, then snorts. "Can you imagine Dorothy, with her glasses and all that hair . . . stoned? Oh my heavens and those bangs catching fire and . . ." We cackle into the starry-night air.

"What can we do for Bonnie?"

"Sometimes you have to surrender to life and let it *take* you." Ruby repositions her scarf.

"Surrender?" I prod the fire more. It snaps and shoots a flame into the air. "I push and pull at life. Have *forever* and maybe I need to let things . . ."

"Unfold," Ruby says for me. "We're taught that life is something we need to wrestle and fight against. As I get older, I realize you can kick and punch all you like but things ultimately turn out as they're supposed to . . . regardless."

"Okay, so I'm a slow learner."

"No, most of us *never* learn. We plod along in a state of . . . oh, I don't know . . . sleepwalking."

The fire fades to glowing embers. Chilly night air moves in around us. We kick sand to cover over the fire and giggle into the duck. There's not a cloud above—the moon is hanging huge and low in the sky. The duck is equipped with intense headlights, so the drive home is easy as pie. The thought of pie makes me realize—oh, no *munchies!* I pull us into the barn; we dash through the backyard and into the kitchen.

"Thank God you don't get a hangover from smoking weed." I open cupboards, pull out several bags of chips and open a jar of pickles Ruby just pulled from the fridge.

She adds a plate of cookies *and* a round tin filled to the top with Reese's Peanut Butter Cups. I thump down at the table with a glass of milk. Ruby has a pickle hanging out of her mouth like a cigarette. Rocky is sprawled out on a side counter, his tail flapping, watching us with mild interest.

"These are better with a dab more peanut butter." I slather on a gob. "I think I need extra protein . . . seem to crave it." I start to giggle, goo dribbling down my chin.

"Well . . . well." Ruby's eyes have become slits. We yawn. "I think we're crashing—darling."

"How about you head up to bed and let me deal with this." I point to the remnants of our munch-fest.

"Good thinking." Ruby kisses the top of my head, then drifts away.

I roll the tops of chip bags and secure them with clothes-pins, snap the lid back on the peanut butter cups and put everything away. As I climb the stairs, I notice that one of the pictures of Adeline and Gustave is crooked. While straightening it and thinking that some things should really be packed away, I notice that in the picture they're standing next to a lit-tle log cabin. Where have I seen . . . ? I remember the model. There must be a cabin back in the woods somewhere.

I drift into my room, snap on the lamp next to my bed and thump into the pillows. My God, what a day. Poor Bonnie, why can't women just—There doesn't seem to be an easy answer. Never is, not really. Things are so much more complicated when you lift all the edges up and really look. Smiling, I recall her in those pink curlers.

I hope *my* daughter's not in that kind of a situation. Sounds so odd: "my daughter"—Amy. Wonder if the new mom kept that name. I wonder myself to sleep.

CHAPTER TWENTY

I open my eyes, look over to the cat-clock and see it's only a bit past seven. Getting up, putting Rocky on the floor, I hunt for my robe. The smell of coffee lures me to the kitchen. On the stairway, I hear Ruby's voice coming from down below.

"... Not to worry, darling ... Yes, yes, I'm sure it will pass over and ... All right, then ... Good-bye." Ruby hands me the phone to hang up as I walk into the kitchen.

"Sam rang up to tell us she and Lilly will be a little late this morning. There's a storm brewing, so she thought the ferries might be running late." She pours coffee.

"I thought I heard some thunder earlier this morning." I sit down at the stump table and spin on a squeaky stool.

"Sam said something else I thought a bit odd." Ruby sits down next to me. "That Bonnie is going to be needing—"

Just then the phone rings. "Hello?"

"Eve ... it's Bonnie." She sounds odd. "There's been an ... accident ... and Al ..." Now she starts sobbing and not making any sense whatsoever. I'm getting really bad vibes here.

"Did he . . . *hurt* you?" I manage to stammer out while standing up, then slamming down my mug. Ruby heads over with a dishrag in one hand and Rocky slung over her other arm.

"He tried to . . ." She's gasping for air and I feel my skin go clammy. "He wanted to . . ." She snivels, sighs long and slow and then nothing—silence. She whispers in a voice I doubt I'll ever forget: "He'll never, *ever* hurt me again. Never." The finality of that sends chills through me. I tighten my robe.

"Oh no . . . Bonnie." I sit back down. "Is . . . he there *now*?" Something tells me I don't want an answer to this.

"Yes . . . but . . . no."

"Oh, boy . . . oh shit." I let Ruby know I need a smoke. She lights up two and puts one in my mouth. "Just where *is* Al— exactly?"

"Facedown, next to the stove." I gasp. "He hasn't moved. I felt his neck . . . nothing there but . . . *cold.*"

"Cold?" My stomach roils.

"Well, see . . ." Bonnie's voice rises and she starts talking really fast. "He came home this morning stinking drunk. It's not that unusual for him to pass out at his bar and then crawl home the next day."

"Oh Bonnie." The poor thing.

"So he comes in and I'm vacuuming, and he gets all hands and dirty words and grabbing at me and calling me a good-for-nothing, dried-up bitch! And you know, something happened—something snapped inside of me and I wasn't *me* anymore. I wasn't there anymore . . . . It was like I was watching from the ceiling. He kept shoving and pushing me, so I hit him with the vacuum cleaner tube and . . ." Her voice begins to squeak. "I honestly didn't hit him *that* hard. I'm not very strong, you know. But then . . . this weird look came over his face and his eyes went white-like and he . . . he . . . he went . . . like . . . it seemed like . . . he wasn't there anymore and then he just kind of melted onto the floor."

She takes a deep breath and sobs out, "I don't know how . . . I feel like I broke apart and part of me went away and part of me didn't and *that* part . . . that part . . . watched. I couldn't stop watching. I—" She breaks off sobbing in big mournful heaves.

"Oh . . . my . . . God." The picture plays out in my mind. Ruby is shaking my arm, telling me to listen for a second. "Um . . . hang on, Bonnie," I say gently. "Don't go anywhere, okay?"

"Okay," Bonnie whispers. I cup the mouthpiece and am pacing—thinking. My skin is clammy and I have the worst dry mouth ever. I feel sick.

"I can't *believe* this. This is too much. I've never . . . What the *hell* are we going to do? I have to think; I . . . what?" A tear slides down my cheek.

"Sam said not to let Bonnie do anything *rash,* to tell her we'll be over there as soon as we can." Ruby's eyes bug out of her head. "She knew . . ." We exchange a look. I frantically take a puff, looking in amazement at how my hand shakes.

"This is *so* nuts! What the *hell* should I tell Bonnie? To put on a nice outfit, brew a fresh pot of coffee and we'll be right over? Come on over and have some coffee . . . with a *dead body*?" My voice cracks.

"Tell her to *wait* and we'll ring her back in a moment or two. Tell her not to ring *anyone* until she speaks with us. Do it!" Ruby says with more oomph than I knew she had.

"Bonnie . . . listen . . . Ruby and I need to think here. We'll call you back in a few minutes, okay?"

"Okay . . . but hurry. I'm so afraid," she chokes out in a desperate voice.

"I promise, okay?"

"Sure . . . okay."

"Oh, and Bonnie?"

"Yes."

"Don't do anything crazy, like leave or . . . Just sit tight, all right?"

"Okay . . . 'Bye." The phone goes dead.

I hang it up and it rings the second it hits the wall. "Eve . . . Sam here." I shoot a look at Ruby.

"How the hell? . . . Oh . . . right." I shake my head, wondering when I'm going to wake up and realize this is all a dream.

"This is *not* a dream, girl. Now listen up: Bonnie is going to be just fine, but we all got to support her with this thing."

"Oh, Sam . . . I don't know . . ." I put my cigarette out in my coffee, take a sip and gag.

"*Girl,* I have been down this lonely road of drunk womanizers *plenty*. Besides . . . it *wasn't anything that Bonnie did.* You got that?"

"Okay, okay . . . but Jesus . . . he's dead . . . Couldn't be from her vacuum cleaner?"

"Not likely. Now listen up!"

"I'm listening." I wish I was drinking something stronger than coffee.

"Stick to coffee. Now, it's pretty simple as to what's going to come down. You and Ruby get over to Bonnie's and—"

"My God—won't we be considered accomplices or something? What a fucking *nightmare*!"

"It's been *her* nightmare for a long time and now . . . it's about over," Sam says in a way I have to take notice of—like it *had* to be this way. "I got Lilly coming in the door here and we'll be there soon as we can."

"But . . . shouldn't someone tell the cops? Shouldn't we call . . ."

"Eve, would you let me finish?"

"Sorry. Right . . . sure. Go ahead."

"Soon as you calm down Bonnie, call nine-one-one and just tell them Al Smitters needs an ambulance."

"But . . . what about Bonnie and her vacuum and . . ."

"Don't you worry none about that. Just tell them to come get . . . him. You understand me?"

"Yes, I do."

"Good. Now we're on our way, but it's going to be a bit, so . . . so you call back Bonnie soon as we're done here and then get on over there so she's not alone—with him. It may be a while before an ambulance can get over from Bayfield."

"Right. You and Lilly meet us over to Bonnie's then . . . And Sam?"

"Yes child."

"Bonnie's going to be all right . . . isn't she?"

"For the first time, both her and that lost soul of a man . . . I think peace has come for both their tired souls. We just gotta help Bonnie be strong now, that's all."

"See you at Bonnie's then." We good-bye and I hand the phone to Ruby.

"Oh Lord . . . I just want to wake up all over again." I sit down and light up a fresh smoke. "Let's see if I have this straight . . ." Adjusting my robe and pushing my hair up out of the way, I explain. "Bonnie was cleaning her house—correction: *vacuuming* her house—when Al comes at her all hot and horny, not to mention drunk out of his mind. I figure he grabbed her, threw her around a bit . . . maybe slugged her too." Ruby gasps.

I continue with my description of the scene. "They fight . . . he swings . . . she runs . . . he grabs . . . she struggles and then BLAM! She freaks out and after holding in all that hate and fear for all those years—she hits him back with her trusty Hoover . . . maybe the thing's even running . . . but it sounds like . . . like it was his time and that she was supposed to be there. It's so weird. Then afterwards . . . after she knows he's . . . gone . . ." I take a deep breath and say very slowly, "She sighs and sighs and sighs."

I slowly exhale, imagining the scene: the whir of the vacuum competing with Bonnie's sobbing and Al, lying there, all his meanness finally gone. Bonnie, in slow motion, sliding slowly to the floor, wondering, "When did things get so bad."

"Good heavens, Eve." Ruby adjusts her necklace for the hundredth time since I began my story. "Horrible—horrible—simply horrible. The poor woman."

"God . . . can you imagine? Right in front of you—just like that. Poof and he's toast." I get up and move around, nervously picking up a spoon and walking around the entire stump table tapping the pots and pans hanging above it for therapy. I feel like exploding. I feel—I just wonder how she feels. Then I realize we need to be there with her.

"Sam is on her way with Lilly. I'm to call back Bonnie and let her know we're on our way over and then Sam says we should call nine-one-one and tell them we need an ambulance for Mr. Smitters."

"Well I think that sounds logical. Considering. Don't you?"

"But Sam didn't say anything about Bonnie hitting him back and—"

"I should think the less said about that, the better." Ruby shrugs and we look at one another like we're guilty and . . . are we?

"But I heard Bonnie say . . ." I stammer, trying to make sense out of this.

"I think"—Ruby rises, takes our mugs to the sink, then turns to face me—"I think that we should support Bonnie and leave the entire affair up to the authorities."

"No kidding." I turn toward the living room. Then turn back.

"I'll get dressed now, ring Bonnie and tell her we're on our way over. Scoot!"

"Jesus . . . but, well . . . you know he's been drinking for years. Why even Dorothy's heard about him way down in Eau Claire." Ruby shakes her head. "Let me call her back—I feel it should be me." I dial the phone; Bonnie picks up on the first hint of a ring.

"Yes—hello." Her voice is so small.

"It's me, Eve . . . Um . . . you doing all right there, Bonnie?" I'm picturing Al slumped over on the floor with the tube from the vacuum nearby. I shake my head and—the image is gone.

"Yes . . . fine. Considering." She laughs weakly.

"Ruby and I are on our way over—okay?"

"Sure." There's a pause while she takes a big breath. "Thank you Eve; thank you." The line goes dead.

I hand the phone to Ruby, who gives me a Reese's Peanut Butter Cup and for the first time in my entire life, I set it down on the counter. So she gently places Rocky into my arms and we dash upstairs to change.

Ruby and I are heading down our winding drive on our way to Bonnie's place. I'm letting her drive; I just feel so odd. I'm seeing my mom's face again. Her death was so peaceful, but you never forget the goneness afterward. I sat there holding her hand until a nurse came and slipped it from mine. I instinctively am holding my own hand now and realize it and try to relax the thoughts away and to . . .

"You all right, darling?" Ruby asks as the van clumps into gear. We're passing over the little wooden bridge. The creek has a mist floating above it and for a moment, off in the trees, I swear I see the shape of a woman. I shake my head and look again—nothing.

"I'm just remembering . . . dead stuff. Like in that stupid movie that gave us the creeps for weeks."

"I see dead people!" We say at the same time, then laugh and boy does that feel good.

"Now be a love and unlatch the gate, hmm?"

"Right." I hop out of the van, open the gate, then close it after Ruby pulls the van over next to the sun sign. I slam the door closed and suddenly feel better, stronger.

"Put the pedal to the metal," I say, and she does and of course it takes the van a bit to get going, but we do. I root around, find my tape of Michael Franks and pop it in. His voice is so soothing. He softly croons "Dragonfly Summer." We head south along North Shore Drive toward La Pointe.

"Oh look." Ruby points to her left and toots the horn. "Charlie's out fussing with one of his birdhouses." We wave to the handsome man and he—paintbrush in hand—waves back.

"What will her life be like?" I ponder out loud. "Bonnie's been with Al since fricking high school. Can you imagine?"

"I think perhaps we should focus on the present situation of Al not yet even in his grave, for God's sake! He was a man . . . a human . . . a person with . . . I simply can't bring myself to speak ill of the dead. Not yet. Those poor people."

"No kidding—you're right," I agree, but with little conviction. I mean, I *saw* the bruises and what about the wounds on the *inside?* I know Ruby though and this *is* really a very sad day.

"You know"—I have my head half in my shoulder bag— "I'm not exactly sure just where the hell Bonnie and Al live— lived. I mean . . ." I light a cigarette and feel the cancer-causing serenity. These things are going to kill me. I take one more puff and put it out.

"I don't think it'll be too awfully difficult to find," Ruby notes. "We've only to keep a lookout for that dreadful station wagon of hers."

"Hey, this isn't exactly a limo here." I snap the visor on my side up and the yellow fringe with little hanging balls I tucked around the windshield comes undone. We chuckle.

"I know it's a few blocks from the Liquor Lounge, so turn here." I point down a side street off Main and sure enough, there's Bonnie's wagon parked outside a tired-looking faded yellow bungalow. The white shutters on one window are just about to slip off. But there's a neatness to the yard—not a leaf out of place. We pull up along the street and hop out.

"The sky is getting awfully dark." Ruby gasps as a bolt of lightning snaps and crackles across the sky directly above the house. Oh boy.

I reach up to knock but change my mind and try the door instead. "Hello? Bonnie, it's—"

Bonnie rushes out of the darkness, grabbing me in a tight hug. She's so frail, even though much taller than I. There's just a hint of a woman wrapped up tight in a big blue sweater that I notice is inside out.

"Oh Eve." Bonnie's voice is a hoarse whisper; her eyes are red and puffy as hell. I pull away and she immediately crosses her arms in front of her, pulling herself in. She "Hellos" Ruby, then steps aside for us to enter.

I'm surprised by how charming the living room is—small and sparse, but I can see there are good bones here. It's a typical Craftsman-style house with open rooms and lots of wooden built-ins. Everywhere you look—covering the mantle, on shelves and in several hutches—are trophies. Tons and tons of trophies. I'm doing everything I can to avoid looking down— but where the hell is . . . he?

"I'd offer you something, but he's . . ." Bonnie snivels, brushes hair from her face and then adjusts her body. She becomes a bit taller. "He's in the kitchen, in front of the refrigerator." She stammers this fact. Ruby and I exchange a look of, "Now what?"

I sigh. "Where's the phone?" Bonnie points toward the

back of the house. "Not in the kitchen?" I accuse, then think better of myself and grab Ruby by the wrist and we head off through the dining room and around and into—the kitchen. If I think too much about all this, I'll . . . I don't know . . . throw up maybe. The air in here is so tight.

"Watch for Sam; we're just going to call the sheriff or police or . . ." I manage to say over my shoulder while hauling Ruby beside me. We stand on the threshold of the tidy little kitchen and both of us stop short. Ruby smacks into me and I nearly trip over the big lump lying on top of a fuzzy green rug. The offending vacuum is parked neatly over in a corner. The phone seems to be miles away, over by the back door, which I really would like to dash out of.

"Thank heavens she thought to cover him." Ruby sidesteps the pink chenille–covered Al, and joins me at the phone.

"I really can't get over how everyone has these old dial phones here," I remark to the black plastic phone, its curly cord is all twisted.

"If you haven't a direct line when the power goes," Ruby says while wrestling to open the back door, "then you're shit out of luck!" The door yanks open and we both gladly gulp in the damp, stormy air.

"Hello, I'd like to . . . There's been a vacuum . . . I mean . . . accident . . ." Ruby snatches the phone from me and explains the situation. In her clipped Brit way it sounds so less awful, like reporting the accidental demise of a soufflé that up and fell.

"There—that's done. Someone from the police station will be here shortly as well as an ambulance. The ambulance will be a bit as they've got to take the ferry over from Bayfield."

"Let's go out front and see how Bonnie's doing," I exit the kitchen with Ruby on my heels.

Bonnie rises from a rocking chair, quickly crossing the room toward us.

"I don't know why I didn't just call them myself. I wasn't sure what . . ." Her frightened eyes implore me to what? Forgive her? "I simply didn't—He's always had this power over me. I can't explain it."

"Dear child." Ruby reaches for Bonnie's hands. Holds them like a precious treasure. "You needn't be afraid any longer."

Then the dam lets loose and Bonnie crumples into Ruby's tiny arms. Ruby leads her over to her couch, carefully sitting next to her, cradling her convulsing body.

I head over to the large picture window and sling open the drapes. The storm is still in the brewing stage. A few rumbles of thunder but no rain. My God, how in the world did I get myself wrapped up in all this? How do people get so twisted up together, and how is it that somehow you survive. Ruby's a big fan of the "surrender" concept and—I look over at them— it seems to work for her, but me, I'm just not really made that way.

Yet I do see how so much crap in life can land in your lap and you have to either accept it and move on, so to speak, or jump up and either run, or at least try to change things. I guess it boils down to whether you're the victim or not. Can you be a victim and still be a hero? Being a woman—hell, being a human—is such a drag sometimes.

"Hey," I say too loudly. I've never been so relieved. "Here comes the ambulance with Sam and Lilly right behind." I look down and notice that in my rush I put on one green and one blue Ked.

"Thank heavens," Ruby remarks. "You let us handle things; you're in no shape . . ."

Bonnie closes her eyes for a moment and I'm sure she's going to pass out or something. Instead she pulls herself up. Pushes her hair back, out of the way and accepting a tissue from Ruby, blows her nose ever so politely.

"I'm fine." Her voice is stronger. I look at Ruby and we shrug. "I'm really fine now." She takes a deep breath and all three of us head toward the front door.

The ambulance has hauled Al away. He was declared dead by a very kind young man who gently gave the news to Bonnie. She mumbled a tearful "I know," and they left with him. The young man also offered her something to calm her down, but she declined. I had all I could do not to butt in and ask for several somethings for myself. Ruby saw me step forward and shot me one of her looks.

"Lilly and me"—Sam motions for Lilly to follow—"we gonna brew up a big pot of Jamaican coffee." They head back to Bonnie's kitchen and we hear drawers and cupboards being opened and closed.

"Exactly what's *in* Jamaican coffee?" I ask. Both Bonnie and Ruby shrug.

The smell of coffee starts to permeate the living room and draws us back into the kitchen. The three of us stand in the dining room and peer into the kitchen where Sam and Lilly have set up a lovely table. I notice the green rug where Al—

never mind—but the rug is in the shape of a big lily pad with a red dragonfly in the middle. I smile and realize the vacuum has been put away as well. Good.

A knock at the front door is followed by a creak and a slam. Marsha rushes into the kitchen all out of breath, her hair dripping wet.

"I was in the shower"—Sam hands her a towel—"when my machine picked up and the man I rent from told me he was looking at something with his telescope and was watching an ambulance pull up to Bonnie's and . . . What the hell happened? You okay?"

"Pull up a chair sister," Sam directs. We all find chairs here and there, reassembling around the worn Formica table. "A mug of this and things are gonna smooth out a bit." After pouring all around, she plunks the pot down in the center and we reach and lift and tentatively sip.

"Oh my." Ruby blinks her eyes a bit. "I believe I'm going to enjoy this."

"This is . . . strong," Lilly lisps. We nod agreement. "Would you mind if . . ." Lilly disappears into the living room and returns with her shiny purse. She snaps it open, roots around inside, then holds up a crumpled pack. "If I smoke?"

"Al never allowed it in—" Bonnie catches herself. Clears her throat, pulls a plastic orange ashtray out of a drawer and puts it in the middle of the table. "Could I have one of those?"

Needless to say, everyone but Marsha lights up. She's trying to quit—who isn't? Looking around the table and feeling calmer all the time, thanks to Sam's "brew," I am grateful to be here. Grateful and more than that, I'm realizing that this bunch of women, in all our different shapes and sizes, are a family.

"Listen, Bonnie," Marsha says, waving away smoke. "I'll help with the—you know—arrangements and—"

"We'll all help," I break in and mean it. "I've got an idea."

"Oh dear," Ruby says with a sigh.

"By any chance have you got a big trunk?" I ask Bonnie. I put out my cigarette.

"No," Bonnie answers. "Wait a minute. In the living room. Al brought it home when he emptied his parents' trailer."

"I bet you're not very attached to it." I get up, push in my chair and suggest we adjourn to the living room.

Bonnie liberates the steamer trunk, which used to be their coffee table. The thing is enormous, but after several bangs with my trusty Ked, the stubborn hasp falls, allowing me to open it all the way. An odor of damp and old seeps out. Thunder shakes the house and the lights dim but come right back up. Thank God.

"I was thinking"—I reach for one of the gazillion trophies—"that maybe these need—"

"To go!" Bonnie announces, louder than I've ever heard her speak. We all marvel. She stands and takes the trophy from me. With great care, she sets it gently down inside the trunk.

I hand another to her; it's dropped with a resounding clang and we're off. All the gals get up and start chucking trophies. From the buffet and builtins, side tables and wooden hutches, Al's bowling trophies clump and clang into the trunk.

"We *sure* can't be forgetting this." Sam lifts the pink vacuum up. She places it onto the pile of trophies. Lilly pulls the lid up and over and down. It thuds closed.

"There's just one thing left to do," I announce. Thunder booms in agreement.

I'm backing up my van to Bonnie's front door, Ruby is directing me this way and that.

"Not too much farther, darling. There! Perfect."

"We can push it out," I direct the group. "Thank goodness it's on this rug."

With Sam and Lilly on one side and Marsha and me on the other, we grunt the trunk into my van. Bonnie and Ruby push the doors closed.

"Lilly," I suggest, "how 'bout you and Sam give Marsha and Bonnie a lift back to our cottage."

"Sure thing." Lilly cocks her head toward her Lincoln. She takes something out of her purse, gives it a shake and unfolds it over her towering hairdo. It's one of those plastic pleated rain hats.

"C'mon," I say to Ruby. We climb in my van and head out of town.

"I didn't tell the boys"—Ruby dabs color onto her lips—"exactly what was *in* this trunk, just that we would appreciate the help of two big strong men."

"We'll tell them eventually," I say. "Of all people, they'd understand the symbolism. My God, talk about good anchor material. But you know, I didn't really see anything of hers. Like she wasn't really there."

"Perhaps she wasn't." Ruby sighs.

We drive on in silence, the morning's goings-on receding little by little. A soft rain begins. I spy Lilly's car in the rearview mirror, give my hair a push here and there and signal to turn left down our winding driveway.

"Wish I had Lilly's hat," Ruby remarks, hopping out of the van in order to open the gate.

She thumps back in and pulls the door shut. "It's a lovely rain."

The van chugs up the final little knoll before reaching the back door to the cottage. Lights are on in the kitchen. As we pull up, Johnny and Howard wave us over.

"Too cute," I comment. "Matching yellow slickers."

The rain starts coming down harder. We make a mad dash for the back-porch door that Johnny is gallantly holding open. Bonnie's the last in. I see that she's got on one of Lilly's plastic scarf-hats.

Ruby herds the ladies into the warm kitchen while I explain what happened to Al and also what I want them to do. I assure them there's no one actually *in* the trunk, but Johnny still takes a peek inside, shows Howard and then they close it again. They walk toward the barn, shaking their heads. Maybe I'll just let them wonder—I mean think about it: a trunk of trophies and a pink vacuum. Hmmm.

I hear the toot of my van horn, our agreed upon signal. Those guys are so great. I told them we needed to do this without any testosterone around. But I did have to promise them a complete explanation over dinner later tonight.

"Okay ladies," I announce to the group huddled around the stump table. "Time to roll." As they pass the basement door on the way to the barn, I hand each one of them an umbrella from the pegs. I watch four round puffs of color appear outside as they pop open. Bonnie's is the only one with bright flowers on it. The other three are dull shades of red, yellow and brown. I put my arm around Ruby's shoulder and give her a good squeeze.

"Shall we?" I hand her a bright red one and decide on a basic black. We follow the line of color.

The ladies are gathered around the side door waiting for me to unlatch it. I open it and in we traipse. All the umbrellas close real slowly. Then I punch the big green button and the barn doors swing open.

The boys had hefted the trunk up onto the very back of the duck and tied it on. I get in first, start up the engine and pull up to the door. One by one the ladies climb aboard. I come over to the side to give Sam an extra tug.

"Suppose you're wondering," she gasps out, "if the trunk or me weighs more—hmm?"

"Of course not," I lie. "I'm sure *you* do. Now sit down so Ruby can climb aboard."

"Thank heavens," Ruby says, plopping down beside me, "this thing has a top on it or we'd all get soaked to the skin. Should we even be out in this rain?"

"Probably not." I click on the lights and pull out of the barn.

Since the boys are back at their place, I drive us down the hill leading to the boathouse. We travel past it toward the dock. I head us into the lake, switch on the outboard and off to the east we float. I decide music would seem inappropriate. I look into the rearview mirror and watch Bonnie. She's going to be okay now.

"How about here?" I ask no one in particular. "There's no cottages in sight and we're far from the shore."

"This'll do just fine," Sam says.

I cut the motor. We all turn to look back at Bonnie and the trunk perched on the lip of the duck. She stands, figures out the rope and unties it. Then she looks back at us.

"I feel like I should say a prayer or . . ." Bonnie says, her voice mixing with the sound of the water lapping against the sides of the duck. "But for the life of me, nothing comes to mind. Except"—she turns to the trunk, steps back and then lunges at it with all her might—"bon voyage!" The trunk sails off the duck and lands in the water with a huge splash that leaps up and drenches Bonnie.

She laughs and laughs and we join in and it feels just right.

We're cozy around a crackling fire. The boys are wrapped in an afghan on the couch and Ruby and I are each snuggled in big shawls. Cups of chamomile tea are steaming on the coffee table. Rocky's tail is the only movement in the room. I scratch his belly and he purrs deep and reassuringly. We've been filling in the boys on all the goings-on of our disastrous day.

"Soon as we left your place," Johnny says, "and headed home, the post-lady stopped us and told us that Al Smitters was dead. Something about a man with a telescope?"

"That would be Marsha's landlord," I suggest, then sigh. Could someone be spying on us here? "*I* bet he had a heart attack, or one of those annual things that can burst."

"Aneurysm," Howard corrects me. "I had a friend complain of a headache, went and lied down and—"

"Gone," Johnny finishes. "Not a bad way to go, if you ask me."

"Such a peculiar day," Ruby adds. "Al and Bonnie and all that lot and my *heavens,* what a sight when all that bloody water came splashing all over—"

"What?" both the boys say at once, sitting up real quick.

"Oh heavens," Ruby admonishes with a small chuckle. "Not *bloody*-bloody. Really, you two can be so daft."

Rocky meows huge and big with a yawn thrown in and we chuckle and sigh into our thoughts.

CHAPTER TWENTY-ONE

Days . . . endless days. Like molasses they slugged along as we waited for the final results of the autopsy. From what the emergency-room doctor could tell, it looked like a natural death: heart attack, massive stroke or the like. There was no mention of foul (vacuum cleaner–like) play, but he did point out that even without doing any fancy tests he could tell that the man had either recently used whisky as a mouthwash or had been very drunk at the time of his death. Sometimes I think too much information is just too much, or was that ER humor?

Bonnie was so relieved she hadn't even *remotely* been the cause of his death that she stood in the lobby of the Memorial Medical Center of Ashland and broke out into a very hysterical laughter. She couldn't stop though, so the comedian-doctor gave her an injection that made her laugh even more. I wanted some too. Poor thing had to identify Al "for the record," and she in turn shared the fact that he was buck naked and "Good

Lord, you should have seen how white his skin was." She was about to share other interesting details, but Sam cut her off.

Later the coroner revealed to Bonnie that Al's blood alcohol level was off the charts. He also had an enlarged liver, spots on his lungs and a clogged valve in his heart. But it turned out I was right after all—he died of an aneurysm.

Bonnie told us that unbeknownst to her, Al had life insurance. Not millions, but enough for her to gut his crummy bar and reopen it as a swanky restaurant. She's considering naming it Al's Place. She figures it's the least she can do.

Marsha's been hired away from Ruby's Aprons since Bonnie needs a *professional* waitress. Marsha says sewing really wasn't her bag anyway and besides, Lilly and Sam sew so damn fast it gives her a headache. Bonnie already looks ten years younger, is eating better and thinking of growing her hair out. I'm considering turning one of the bedrooms in the cottage into a tiny salon; these women need me! And the hell with going gray, I'm sticking to my *natural* red. What was I thinking?

So after Al's funeral we all spent the better part of a week helping Bonnie. Believe it or not, when we were cleaning, Ruby found more bowling trophies in a shed behind Al's Place. This time we just tossed them into the mega-Dumpster Sam hauled over.

Every so often I catch Bonnie's eye and there's something different there now: hope.

Since the Bayfield Apple Festival starts tomorrow and we've long passed our goal of five hundred aprons, I'm sending Sam and Lilly home early. We have to be up at dawn and at our booth to set up at the ungodly hour of seven A.M.! I boot

Howard and Johnny out as well, as they've been right by our sides the entire day. Even Rocky has had it; I have to lug him up to the cottage. Ruby and I root around in the fridge, eating leftovers.

"I am *so* looking forward to this weekend," I say through crunches. "Just hope the weather holds . . . people come . . . that we don't run out of anything and . . ."

"Eve, darling," Ruby offers. "Everything will be super!"

"I guess you're right and *really,* this should be the fun part, but . . ."

"What?" she asks, clearing away our dishes, filling the sink with steamy water. "What in the world is so complicated about selling overpriced aprons? Howard got his way in the end, didn't he?"

"Of course." I take a plate from her and dry it. "He's right though. We *have* to cover expenses and if we make more, a nice chunk is going to be donated to Bayfield's Shelter for Women."

"That's such a lovely gesture, darling."

"Isn't it kind of embarrassing . . . we think as a culture we're so advanced and yet the symbolism . . ."

"What?"

"That Ruby's Aprons—an apron—*still* is a symbol for women, for domestication. That we're still 'tied' like apron strings to a societal expectation of how to be. And we're helping a few *un*tie. Freeing them from some situation that was . . ."

"*Not* helping them."

"Exactly," I say, and we untie our aprons.

I open my eyes to the sound of curtains being thrown open by a stylishly dressed Ruby. Looking over at my cat-clock and realizing it's five in the morning, I moan.

"It's daylight in the swamp. Chop, chop," Ruby proclaims, breezing by my bed and out the door. She turns at the threshold. "Lilly and Sam are driving over in your van. Should be here any minute. Sam's finished fixing the clutch and says you owe her a fortune."

"How in the world can you look so fresh . . . at this hour?" I push sleep out of my eyes.

"Coffee, darling, lots of coffee. There's a cup on your night table. Now snap to it."

"Okay already." I disappear into my bathroom with it.

After a quick shower I dash around trying to figure out what in the world to wear to an apple festival. I decide on a yellow top, navy Capris and my favorite two-inch wedgies. I do a soft, curly up-do, grab some hoop earrings and clomp down into the kitchen.

"Well, good morning Sam—Lilly," I say to the women perched around the stump table. "You're so quiet I had no idea anyone else was here except Captain Ruby."

Sam is decked out in a muumuu of bright teal with a matching turban wrapped smartly around her head. Lilly is in a pretty green floral housedress and has puffed her white hair up a good foot. Her reading glasses are perched on the tip of her nose and she regards me over their rims. I never can tell if she's winking at me or if it's a twitch.

"Howard and Johnny are down at the boathouse loading the van," Ruby reports while refilling mugs. "Did you mean to put your top on inside out, dear?"

"Shit!" I go into the living room and redress. "I'm still half awake," I say when I return. "I went back down to the boathouse after you went to bed last night and rechecked every-thing—twice."

"Child . . . you are the biggest worrywart I have *ever* . . ." Sam remarks deep and low. "Like I told you right off, this is going to be a big ol' . . ."

"Wait!" I hold up my hand. "Don't tell me. I want to get as much mileage out of my worrying as I can." Everyone laughs as Howard and Johnny come banging in the back door.

"Hey, ladies," Howard booms. "It's a gorgeous day out and not a cloud in the sky."

"The van's packed." Johnny gently removes Rocky from a bar stool and thumps down in his place. "We can take Sam and Lilly over in our Jeep as there's only room for Eve and Ruby in there now."

"I say we have a toast," Ruby suggests, handing Howard and Johnny a mug of coffee. "To a *smashing* success!"

We raise our mugs and meet in the middle, clinking—then sipping. Rocky meows and that seems to round things out. We march out the back door, into vehicles, and off we drive with Ruby and me in the lead.

"Charlie said he'd be able to bring more aprons over to Bayfield as we need them," Ruby says while checking her lips in the visor mirror. "I simply press this button here." She shows me the red button on the two-way radio. "And he'll dash them to us just like that!"

Just then the radio makes a scratching noise; we hear Charlie's voice. "That you, lamb chop?" Ruby takes in a deep breath and blusters a little. I shake my head.

"Hello there," Ruby yells. "I'm in the van with Eve and—"

"Don't need to shout!" Charlie shouts back. "Just give a holler if you need anything. I hope you all make a *killing* today." We look at each other with wide eyes, then sigh.

"All right then, darling," Ruby replies. She tosses the radio into her purse.

"All right—darling?" I mimic back. She pretends not to notice, but smiles just the same. Grins.

I glance over at her and notice how snazzy she looks, all decked out in a pricey pantsuit that's supposed to look casual. Passing by Charlie's driveway, I honk a few times. I push in a tape of Harry Belafonte. He blasts into the van singing "Day-O" from "The Banana Boat Song" and of course, we sing along until we jiggle onto the ferry and have to clamber out to stand in front with the others. Bayfield slowly comes into view. Even from the lake we can see the hustle and bustle of people; white tents cover the shoreline.

We drive off the ferry and park by Maggie's Restaurant as that's close to where our booth is. The roads are all blocked off, so people are busy hauling their wares into the tents that line both sides of the streets. *Everything* is for sale. Hand-painted signs, beaded jewelry, pottery, wood carvings, candles and all things "apple." There's apple bratwurst, ciders, jams and jellies, turnovers, mustards, pies, and fritters and, of course, wine. The smell of hot apple cider fills the air.

The festival runs for four days, ending on Sunday with the famous "Apple Parade," featuring floats, performers, clowns, and regional marching bands playing "On Wisconsin." What a hoot.

The boys are off snooping around, so it's just the four of us busting our butts putting the booth together. I stand in the street and look back, making sure the signs Sam and Johnny made are hung straight on either side. We all tie on an apron and when the boys stroll by, I ask the nice lady next to us, selling flags, if she'd take a group shot of the six of us. She does and after that the boys head home to the island with instructions to return before dark.

The streets fill with people; women cluster around our booth three deep. I am one happy woman. They giggle at the outlandish patterns, no one buys just one, and before too long Ruby is in the back yelling into her purse to Charlie that we "need more *bloody* aprons and step on it!"

Sam puts her arm around my shoulder. "Now don't you go and stir up any trouble on my account," she says in my ear.

"What the . . ." I say, then spy a newly hung Confederate flag in the booth next to ours. I know it wasn't there earlier. I feel something twitch in my stomach. My mouth goes dry.

I've learned that life is about choices and either you let things be—or open your mouth and do something. I look at Sam, who's now chuckling with a customer. I know it's a free country and all—but that's a symbol that belongs in the past, not here.

"It's going so well, darling," Ruby says, handing a woman a sack and some change. "You okay, dear? Oh no . . . you have that look in your eye."

"It's that flag," I spit out. Sam steps over to me.

"You chill now, honey . . ."

I lift Sam's arm off my shoulder and stroll next door all cool and collected.

"Excuse me," I say to the lady who earlier had taken our picture, "but what are you doing selling *Confederate flags?*" I ask in my above-the-blow-dryer-noise voice, knowing full well she and all the folks milling around can hear.

"We always run out of the American ones," she replies feebly as a man in faded jeans with a scraggly ponytail comes forward, standing beside her.

"Do you know what this symbolizes?" I hold up one of the offending flags while Sam tsk-tsks. "You have any *idea* how this flag pisses me *off*?" A small crowd gathers.

"In America, anyone has the right to sell . . ." the man sputters, then swipes sweat from his brow. "We have the *right* to—"

"To sell every one of them to me *right* this minute," Ruby quickly adds, coming over next to me. "How much for the whole lot of these *vile* things?" She waves around her Gold American Express card. The crowd murmurs in approval.

"We don't *take* American Express, *lady!*" he yells, his face turning a marvelous red.

"Well, then . . ." Sam says, her voice silencing everyone. "You *must* take Masta' card," she drawls, stepping in between Ruby and me. She plops an arm around each of us.

The crowd whoops with laughter. The man just melts, hands the pile over to a laughing Sam and retreats to the back.

"I think I've peed in my dress," Sam says. Ruby about splits a gut. I look over to Lilly and she's wearing such a smile. Damn—that felt good!

The parade route begins at the top of the hill, then meanders down Rittenhouse Avenue, the main street of Bayfield. Seeing as there are hundreds of people in the parade, we have to get a number and get in line before it actually begins.

Ruby and I are decked out in our flowing gowns with specially made (by Lilly) frilly aprons tied around our waist. We're sprawled out on either side of the duck's hood, tossing Reese's Peanut Butter Cups (with our business card stapled on) to the cheering crowds lined up on the sidewalks. Howard is driving with Johnny sitting next to him, both in bright white T-shirts that say STAFF in bold letters stretching across their muscular chests. We took the awning and all the rest of the seats out of the duck in order to create a stage area for the three gals and Charlie to accompany Sam.

Lilly, Marsha and Bonnie are wearing ruby red house-dresses and matching aprons. The trio is singing harmony underneath illegally high, swirled-to-death up-dos that would make Dorothy proud! Charlie, fedora hat askew, is in a snazzy suit, blowing jazz out of a clarinet. The background music is from an old tape I used to play at the salon a lot.

Sam stands tall and gorgeous, draped in a flashy yellow African-styled gown, her turban piled high on her head, huge hoop earrings glinting in the afternoon sun. She holds a microphone that's rigged to the boat's speakers—though she doesn't really even need one as her rich and soulful voice has a power that can make your heart swell. She's belting out "Easy Street," and I'm singing along.

The throngs on either side of the street are singing and clapping—even Watts and Dorothy have come and they scream and yell like hell! They follow us and eventually we end up parking in front of Greunke's Restaurant. We join in with Judith and staff for her famous fishboil. There are introductions to Dorothy and Watts, more singing and of course, a great deal of eating. We have a magical—wonderful—time. I even spy Charlie giving Ruby the sweetest peck on her cheek. I catch her eye and we share a grin.

* * *

It's late at night and a full moon shines over Madeline Island. Ruby and I are snuggled in huge itchy sweaters, sitting on pillows out at the end of the dock.

"I still can't get over how much money we hauled in," I comment to the sky.

"It was super!" Ruby agrees. "The check to that shelter was a lovely gift."

"And Sam—that woman took the parade and moved it right on down the hill!" I pour (compliments of Judith) some bubbly into fancy goblets and hand one to Ruby. "She would have made Pearl Bailey so proud." We clink and sip and— sigh.

"I think she's *full* of surprises, darling." The glow of Ruby's cigarette is bright as she takes a puff.

"What a surprise to see Watts and Dorothy. I had no idea . . . Hey, *wait* a minute! Did you?"

"My lips are sealed . . . Oh blast! Of course I rang them up. I figured we needed some crowd motivators. My word, that Watts can project."

"She's probably the closest I've ever come to a mother-daughter relationship. I mean . . . it was a lot of working to-gether too, but offering her the job of managing the salon made me feel something . . . maternal. You know?"

"I think I do, darling."

"Too bad they had to get back to Eau Claire," I say, plump-ing a pillow. "I made them promise to come visit."

"Lovely. Oh my heavens—I nearly forgot, what with all the excitement and all. Watts found this letter along with a stack of

ancient beauty magazines when she and Dorothy were cleaning."

Ruby hands me a wrinkled envelope postmarked over
seventeen years ago marked CONFIDENTIAL TO BE OPENED BY
ADDRESSEE ONLY in bold black letters.

"This couldn't . . ." I mutter, then open it. "Thank *God* for
this moonlight—Dear Evelyn Moss . . . Jesus . . ." I whip
through the note, looking for the meat of it. Knowing.

"It can't be bad news," Ruby advises. "It's *far* too old for
that."

"It's from the detective I hired *years* ago. He said that if
there was any information he'd mail . . . I just assumed . . .
maybe was relieved in a way . . . you know? But they did find
her, or at least there was a trail. He says that the convent was
closed down—the one in Chippewa Falls where I was—and all
the records were sent to Sacred Heart Hospital and to contact
them . . . . Oh my God. Do you know what this could mean?"

"It *means* we need to plan a trip to Sacred Heart Hospital
and ask some questions."

"I wonder if Amy has red hair . . ." I say, and for the first
time in such a long time, feel hope. I hold the letter close to my
heart.

"I know a wrench-carrying jazz singer who just might be
able to tell you."

The moon shines a little brighter—then we watch as a star
shoots across the sky.

A Special Chat with Jay Gilbertson

I HAD to write this book. If I didn't, well, I would have burst!

You see, for years now I've been listening to stories and tales and—life. I run a hairdressing salon and my clients are an eclectic mixture of the finest and most attractive folks around and I'm not just talking about their hair either. The majority of them are women, I love the way they see things and share and seem to have a far different sense of life. Women simply experience things differently than men do.

Within my marvelous client roster is something even more interesting and for me curious—the number of single women. Now these aren't the "Sex-and-the-City" types; desperately searching for Mr. Right while agonizing over just what top goes with what shoes. Oh no, these gals are business-savvy, highly successful, not-to-mention sassy-haired women who are HAPPY being single. Imagine that.

Not so shocking is that these very same gals all have a strength that's refreshing to me. Family seems to play a large role in their lives, as well as a solid collection of friends; friends that really—are family. Even though the literal definition of family is parents and children, that definition needs some updating because so many people out there are creating family that's anything *but* parents and children.

Usually the problem isn't with the women, it's with the rest of us. Instead of honoring the fact that they're happy, some of us are busy trying to find them mates. We all just need to get over it. What I've found is that yes, I believe most people would like to find someone to share sunsets with, but why in the world should one "settle" for someone that's just an *okay* fit? I think that's the crux of this new phenomenon—women aren't as willing to put up with the crap that, say, their mothers did! And why should they? Okay, so that's basically why I chose to create Eve Moss. I wanted to honor women like her, to give them a voice.

Setting is actually a character to me, that's why it's so important to my story. I love visiting people's homes—seeing what magazines or books are lying about, how the couch is positioned and what's in *their* refrigerator crisper drawer? I'm someone who slows down the car in order to peek into windows at night. I mean if the drapes aren't closed—I'm looking! Oh right, and you don't?

Living in the country has introduced me to so many marvels that I had to weave them into my story. Like the smells, the fresh sunshiny stuff I inhale while hanging laundry out on the line. Taking the time to give it a good sniff, well you see so many other things too. Tall majestic white pines with their carpet of squishy needles and the way their branches whisper in the wind. Or the incredible night sky strewn with stars that really *do* burn bright, sounds of crows or owls—the gurgle of our spring on the way to the pond—and frogs. There's a certain time of year when the frogs are so loud even the crickets can't compete. Oh, and dragonflies, they come in amazing colors, watching them swoop and float out over the pond is pure magic.

Time—a lot of what I've come to love about living here in Northwestern Wisconsin is the way time is no longer this huge monster standing right next to me tapping his foot—arms crossed. There's something about being away from all the diversions out there that's forced me to rethink what's important. I'd much rather dangle my feet in the pond, ski off into the woods, or make homemade pizzas with friends than go shopping.

I grew up in Eau Claire, Wisconsin. Like so many places, it's seen a phenomenal amount of growth. There are two rivers that meander through parts of it and a great university, which brings some diversity to this otherwise conservative town. Unfortunately, I did encounter some prejudice because I didn't fit the mold, so that's why I didn't want Eve to be perfect. But you do, I hope, eventually fall in love with her. That's another human trait that I'm drawn to, how so many not-so-perfect people become beautiful when you open yourself and get to know what's inside them. That's the good stuff—what's inside.

As for Ruby, she's what I would call a combo "character." I had a brilliant friend I met in college, her name was Karin (pronounced "ka rin") and I found her fascinating. She had a great British accent, wicked, sarcastic sense of humor and a head of fiery-red curls. Stupid cancer took her away too soon, so I found a way to bring parts of her to life again. The other elements of Ruby are from my mom. She's on the short side, a snappy dresser and has an independent spirit I forever find surprising.

While chatting with my clients, the idea of Eve having a daughter was often met with a similar true-life story. Once or twice it actually *was* their life (I've been sworn to secrecy, so don't ask). There are a surprising number of women out there who either personally know someone or knew *of* someone who experienced the very same situation. I wanted to present this in a light that wasn't full of judgment, but hope. The hope being that one day Eve actually *meets* her daughter and a friendship is born. It's no accident that the initials of Moon Over Madeline Island spell MOMI. Well, okay, maybe it *was* an accident, but isn't that really a clever tie-in?

Now that you've read Eve and Ruby's tale, aren't you curious as to what happens next? I mean, leaving the girls out there on the dock with all that hope of finding Amy, doesn't it make you wonder? Hope so, because then you'll go out and pick up the second installment of the story when it's ready—besides, we need to fix our roof, and tractors don't come cheap!

By the way, if you'd like to drop me a line or see some photos of our life here on the farm, check out my website: www.jaygilbertson.com.

See you soon,

Jay